THERE IS NOTHING YOU CAN DO WITHOUT US KNOWING ABOUT IT

2024

THERE IS NOTHING YOU CAN DO WITHOUT US KNOWING ABOUT IT

2024

A STORY BY

HOWARD ASHER

Uncommon Sense Press

(^_‘)

Los Angeles

Published by Uncommon Sense Press

Library of Congress Control Number: Pending

Publisher's Cataloging-In-Publication

Names: Asher, Howard, author.

Title: 2024 / Howard Asher.

Description: Los Angeles : Uncommon Sense Press, [2021] | Includes appendix and references.

Identifiers: ISBN: 978-1-7330020-4-2 (hardcover) | 978-1-7330020-3-5 (paperback) | 978-1-7330020-5-9 (eBook) | LCCN: 2019-XXXXXX

Subjects: LCSH: United States--Politics and government--2017- | United States--Politics and government -21st century. | Free Speech--Free Thought | Dystopia | Totalitarian | United States--Politics and government --History. | Political culture--United States--Psychological aspects. | Politics and culture-- United States--Psychological aspects. | Social structure--United States. | Popular culture-- United States--Psychological aspects. | Right and left (Political science)--United States-- Psychological aspects. | Woke-ism--United States--History--21st century. | Polarization (Social sciences)--Political aspects--United States. | Political participation-- Moral and ethical aspects--United States. | Truthfulness and falsehood--Political aspects-- United States. | Opposition (Political science)--United States--Psychological aspects. | Communication in politics--Psychological aspects. | Corporate power--Political aspects--United States. | Branding (Marketing)--United States.

Classification: LCC: E912 .A84 2019 | DDC: 973.933--dc23

Book Design: Creative Publishing Book Design

This story is dedicated to you, dear reader

I wrote it for you

PREFACE

by

Dr. Howard Asher

THERE'S A DANGEROUS TENDENCY FOR US HUMANS to be too ridiculous and too stupid for our own good. As a psychotherapist, author, and observer I've been tackling this confounding subject my whole career – most of my life. Everything we should care about rides on whether we can overcome this self-destructive tendency.

Today we face what every generation of every society and culture has faced – collapse into dystopia. That's what Confucius, Buddha, Socrates, Plato, Aristotle, Muhammed, Aquinas, Locke, Lincoln, Orwell, Rand, Bradbury, and William Gibson the author of *Neuromancer* – upon which the movie *The Matrix* is based – among many others have all addressed in some way. This story – *2024* – takes on this generation's very possible collapse into dystopia.

We have always lived simultaneously on the brink of prosperity and destruction. It's a tenuous "perch" all human cohorts throughout every age occupy. Governance is the social mechanism by which we manage ourselves as a society that steers us to prosperity or destruction… and everything in between. Good governance for everybody should be the goal. But too often bad governance is what we get. Bad governance is bad enough. But tearing down a culture, a society – that often fails, yet enjoys successes never before achieved – a society that has been the most free and successful in history yet aspires to be better for all its citizens and beyond, is a horrible thing.

We humans live an ironic contradiction. We either *cooperate* or *war*. It's only these two states in which we interact. Whether it's a civilized discussion on differing opinions or a bad marital verbal fight, whether it's a business contractual agreement or legal battle over a business dispute, whether it's an international treaty or a military confrontation, *cooperation* or *war* are the only two ways humans engage one another.

Because war is war it should be avoided by any means possible to preserve the well-being of the involved parties. But there is a point when war or the threat of war, despite a high unaffordable cost, does more for the wellness of those parties than a higher unaffordable cost for insensible cooperation. This unavoidably dangerous balance depends on both the will to *cooperate* and the will to *war*.

To survive our worst natures so we can thrive in our better natures we must transcend to wisdom. With wisdom we can, in any given situation, discern the tipping point between choosing *cooperation* or *war*.

Clearly, transcending to wisdom has confounded our existence with one another since the beginning of us. While so much of human history has brought magnificent achievements, still endless atrocities causing incalculable grief, distress, and moral depravity have darkened our existence.

We live in an amoral universe. Subjugation, persecution, slavery, and genocide have been constant foul companions to human activity. The gravitational pull toward this darkness is just as strong as it has ever been. But at the same time, if we understand what feeds our worst nature, we can overcome this pull toward darkness and steer our existence into living in the light.

The story you are about to read shows a way to live in the light and enjoy the blessings life can bring. It's about freedom. It not only illustrates what freedom is, it shows that our all-encompassing responsibility – our burden – is to achieve and maintain that freedom. Freedom engages the "big" questions of life. Those big questions cannot just be left to an amorphous collective. Such questions are up to you – or they mean nothing.

You're about to meet Harry Archer. So, take a deep breath and settle in as you begin this story. Read, think, and enjoy… where enjoyment can be had.

Best to you in all good things,

Dr. Howard Asher
Los Angeles, California, March 2021

— WARNING —

To tell this story crimes against the state will be committed.
Words and ideas forbidden by the state
are used to tell this story.

* * *

Under the authority of the state regime,
it is a crime for you to possess this book.
Under the authority of the state regime,
it is a crime for you to read this book.

Read on at your own risk.

ONE

IT'S A BRIGHT COLD DAY IN APRIL. HARRY ARCHER'S state-issued cell phone rattles its irritating buzzing noise, signaling the routine text of the day to all PODs. This daily text informs PODs about the word to be eliminated from the language – forbidden to be used. Today the word to be *vanished* is "strong." From this moment forward, the word never existed.

Harry is standing outside of a bookstore. He is looking at the books displayed in the window. The popular book he authored was once displayed in this very window. It has since been banned by the *Party Regime*, not available to the general public. None of the books now displayed interest him. It strikes him how different it was a few years ago, before the *Party Regime* and its *Great Awakening*. In those days there were always available a variety of relevant, interesting books by good authors. The books available now are not worth reading and are mostly about *Awaken* doctrine, filled with platitudes and banality that are insulting to even a child's intellect.

The government under the *Party Regime* delivers daily texts to the public, identifying words declared offensive. The texts are part of the "public service" called the *Think Right Program*. Getting a text every day at noon always creates tension in Harry. In the moments before receiving the text he's not thinking the word he now is not allowed to think. But after he gets the text, he not only thinks the word, he can't get it out of his mind. As per the text, for thinking this word, Harry is by law a criminal of the state. He can't but wonder if upon receiving the daily text all PODs go through the same uneasy thinking process that he does. To avoid exposing his thought crime, Harry's smart enough not to discuss the word with anyone.

Every day when he sees the new banned word in the state-delivered text message, Harry takes pause at the insanity of this "unthink" drill as well as feeling grave concern for his *fellow* citizens – whom the *Party Regime* call PODs – a term Harry refuses to use unless to ridicule the term's existence. He is struck by the willingness of people to be molded by the state to seamlessly adapt to its requirements. Since the ascension to power of the *Party Regime*, Harry is always in a state of unease and tension inwardly. Outwardly, he is calm and measured. He's good at not betraying thoughts and feelings deemed criminal by the state. With mental "gymnastics" and willpower he momentarily calms the agitation in his mind over today's text until he realizes he just used a word in his head that was forbidden a few months ago – "fellow" … it's a gender reference – not allowed. He thinks to himself – *what was I thinking?!*

It was during the world pandemic of 2020 when facemasks were mandated. After the new president – his party calls him *The Big Guy* – was inaugurated in 2021, he – *The Big Guy* – as the figurehead of the *Party Regime*, issued an edict mandating, all people must wear facemasks all the time forever. This was the beginning of the *Party Regime* in power.

Harry didn't like that at all! But although there is a state mandate to wear facemasks all the time, much less than half the people wear them. For some reason, the state does not uniformly enforce the mandate at this time. Perhaps the state recognizes that even with its power it shouldn't push those who don't want to wear a mask too far and create unrest. Although Harry doesn't wear a facemask, he appreciates the utility of a mask to hide "criminal" thoughts. For now though, he'll hide his "criminal" thoughts by pretending he doesn't have them.

Harry doesn't have a complacent mind. He is driven to think. He deconstructs ideas. If he comes up with anything he thinks is worth saying, he says it. Harry says a lot of things. But ironically, though he says a lot, most of what he thinks he keeps to himself. So much of what he thinks doesn't play well to the "unprepared." Harry doesn't like rattling others, though at times he does rattle others; he doesn't like controversy, though he might weigh in on controversies; he doesn't like making enemies, so he makes no person an enemy – though he is the enemy of many ideas. And though an enemy of many ideas, Harry thinks the worst of the ideas he fights against still have a right to be expressed.

Like flipping a visual focus switch in his head from viewing the displayed books through the storefront window Harry's dark eyes see his six-foot slender frame reflected in the window. He is wearing his usual khaki pants and short sleeved polo shirt. His wardrobe consists of three colors of polo shirts – black, navy blue, and charcoal gray. Today his shirt is navy blue. He wears his shirts casually, not tucked in. When he dresses in slacks and a dress shirt, he tucks it. He owns three suits; he wears a suit infrequently. Today it is cold, so he has on a dark brown tweed sport coat. He mostly wears buck shoes. When Harry was younger, he wore his thick dark brown hair long. Now in his mid-forties he wears his beginning-to-thin, starting-to-gray hair short. He usually shaves clean, but on weekends he doesn't. His wife Penelope dislikes the stubble – "It makes you look old, and besides, it scratches," she tells him.

Harry doesn't wear a wristwatch because he always has his state-issued cell phone in his hand or right pants pocket. In his other pocket he keeps six plastic cards including two credit cards, his driver's license for ID purposes (he sold his and Penelope's cars when the *Party Regime* took over), a roadside emergency card, a health care insurance card, and a debit card bound by a rubber band. He also keeps a leather pouch in his right pocket. The design of the pouch is distinctive with a fold over flap. It holds four keys and a tiny penknife. The penknife was a Valentine gift from Penelope many years ago. The pouch gets a lot of positive comments when Harry happens to take it out of his pocket when others are around.

Harry has a firm grip on reality. A part of that grip is how he magnifies and extends reality to what reality means. His thoughts and feelings are a clarification of what is real. He has a place in his mind he calls *Harry's Cynical Clarifications*. In it he stores information and analytics in an "intellectual algorithmic" system that operates automatically giving him continuous mental engagement. Which means he overrides words from the outside world with the true words and meanings he says to himself. Hence, there's a lot of word traffic in Harry's head. He manages it well, avoiding any "word traffic jams" or "word collisions."

The activity in *Harry's Cynical Clarifications* has been on overdrive for some time. In the outside world, language is now butchered to force absurdities and lies into common acceptance. The routine elimination of words is one such measure in the corruption administered by the *Think Right Program*. By current government standards Harry doesn't "think right." Harry thinks stuff like the *Think Right Program* is stupid, demeaning, and dangerous.

* * *

Harry pulls himself away from the bookstore's front window. On this day, as it is on all days, Harry is in a hurry. Today he has to conduct a Zoom meeting, and as always, the state will be involved. To carry out the tasks of any day, he has to put his tension/thinking out of his mind to the extent he can. Though he focuses well, he can never achieve the full focus he craves, because he can never fully put aside his tension/thinking ever since the takeover of the state by the *Party Regime*. Yet, despite the tension in his head Harry always plows through the things he needs to do, day after day.

Harry is a civil engineer. He works in the firm he started with Penelope many years ago. He calls her "Penelope" or "Penny" or "Pen," depending on the mood and moment. She calls him "Hare" in private and "Harry" in public. They have a nineteen-year-old daughter Daisy and a fourteen-year-old son Billy. Harry and Penelope established their business as sole proprietors and currently employ a staff of five.

Thirty-two months ago, the *Party Regime* took over all assets of Harry and Penelope's business. The firm is now state-owned and completely regulated by the *Ministry of Resources*. While Penelope's MBA certifies her expertise and is invaluable to the firm's operations and its excellent reputation built over the years, it's meaningless to the *Party Regime*. As far as the state is concerned her responsibilities extend no further than to manage email accountability to the state. Such accountability is tedious and inconsequential to any real engineering or business interest the firm has; but it's a strict requirement of the state.

II

A good marriage, Harry believes, is based on luck and a good sense of humor. In Penelope he scored on both counts. He has a running gag with Penelope where he asks her how *he* scores with her? She always answers, "I haven't made up my mind yet."

Harry and Penelope were high school sweethearts. One of Harry's classes was working in Miss Garcia's guidance counseling office as her assistant. Miss Garcia was a well-respected school figure beloved by teachers and students alike. In her late sixties she had a reputation for her skills in education/career planning and her devotion to the students. Harry was aware she had helped more than a few students where it was nothing short of life saving. Although married she went by "Miss" Garcia as a show of respect… and affection. "Miss Garcia" was inscribed on the nameplate to the door of her office and the plaque on her desk.

Something else also struck Harry about Miss Garcia – her relationship with her husband. Harry first met Mr. Garcia when he came by the school to drop off Miss Garcia's sack lunch. She had forgotten it because she dashed out the door that morning.

What Harry particularly noticed about the couple was the way they laughed together. To Harry it looked like their laughter bonded and sweetened their marriage. He saw the care Mr. Garcia showed her and the tenderness with which Miss Garcia looked at him. Harry thought they were lucky to have each other and hoped one day he, too, would find his special partner in life.

Harry first saw Penelope when he was a senior in high school. It was at a Friday night school dance after a football game. Harry played defensive back on the team. He spotted her from across the room. She was simply the prettiest girl he had ever seen. So, at first sight for Harry it was purely visual and a total fantasy. He knew a lot of students, but he had never noticed Penelope before. He asked his friend Jeff Miller if he knew her, and Jeff did. "Penelope Ahern... she's a junior..."

The Monday after the dance Harry went into action. Working for Miss Garcia, he had access to records including student schedules and control of administrative procedures that allowed him to summon students out of their classes to the guidance counseling office. That period Penelope was in Mr. Clark's English Literature class. Harry had a summons for Penelope sent there. Eighteen minutes later Penelope showed up at the office counter and was escorted by another student worker into Miss Garcia's office where Harry was sitting behind Miss Garcia's desk.

Penelope was wearing a collared pale green sweater with a narrow leather brown belt over jeans. She had on black and green saddle shoes. Harry thought she was prettier than he remembered. She was medium height and slim. She had straight light auburn hair pulled back with a hair clip that spread a little wider than the width of her slender neck and fell a few inches below her shoulders. Her hazel eyes sparkled warmly. She had a beautiful natural smile, and when she spoke, "Did Miss Garcia want to see me?" her voice was sweet and mellow.

Harry was stunned that he pulled this off. Or had he? Somehow, he didn't think it would get this far. So, he hadn't thought it through. "Ahh, yeah, yeah. Ahh, hi. Ahh, thanks for coming to the office. Ahh, Miss Garcia isn't here now. But she wanted me to talk with you about your plans after you graduate."

"She wanted *you* to talk with me?" Penelope was starting to think something was off. Harry started to think Penelope could see through him. And he thought even the "fly on the wall" could definitely see something was off.

At his young age Harry had already developed a philosophy on life: *The more something is valued the more you should reach for it. Better to reach for what you want and have your heart broken for not getting it, than to not reach at all.*

Harry cleared his throat and said, "I think you're pretty and I want to see if we could..."

Harry was interrupted by the voice of a female student worker from the next room, "Jeez, Harry, you really got guts or you're really stupid."

Penelope quickly took in the situation, stared hard at Harry, and said softly, "I pick stupid."

Harry responded, "Yes! That's it! I'm stupid! But I'm the smartest stupid a person could be. Penelope, would you come to the Christmas Prom with me?"

Penelope mocked Harry, "*I'm the smartest stupid a person could be?* What does that even mean? And sure, I'm not doing anything that evening. I'll go to the prom with you. If Miss Garcia doesn't have you expelled for being *the smartest stupid a person could be.*"

Right then, Harry fell in love.

Twenty-seven years later, college and graduate degrees completed, an engineering firm founded, fifteen major civil building projects successfully constructed, while being the parents of two kids – now teenagers, Harry and Penelope find themselves living in a world that is against everything they care about. The world is a regime that demands they have no dreams, let alone the ambition to make them come true – as they have always lived to do. The *Party Regime* take over and the *Great Awakening* changed everything for the worse. Now, Harry and Penelope are living lives that are not their own… but they do not accept this insanity for themselves or their kids. They'll do something. But what?

* * *

Harry has everything set up for the Zoom presentation today which he's conducting from the state-issued apartment where he resides with his family. Penelope is at the office. He is in the middle of a project the firm has been contracted to do and there are problems.

Harry sits at his state-issued laptop and keys in the routing code required for the state to approve and oversee the Zoom conference. After he gets past technical loading delays that take 90 seconds an image of participants for the meeting emerges on the laptop's screen. There are four compartment windows. One window is Harry. Two windows are representatives from *All Source*, Harry's – the firm's – client. The remaining window is the compliance officer from the *Ministry of Correctness*. The compliance officer makes for a creepy presence.

In the background wall of each window is the disturbing official poster portrait of former president Bennet Oberton looking slightly up to his left in deep reflection. At the bottom of the portrait are the words:

The Hope and Change Reich

Bennet Oberton was President of the nation from 2009 to 2017. He was and is a popular and beloved figure who transcended his presidency. Oberton is now the inspirational head of the ***Hope and Change Reich*** – the foundational principles of the current and forever *Party Regime*.

In the foreground of each window on the Zoom screen on the lower left side are the words:

You are your group!

Harry begins the meeting with the standard protocol required by the *Party Regime*. He addresses the officer from the ministry. In his head he says, "Comrade Officer, we are graced and honored by your presence to oversee this meeting." He actually says, "Welcome everyone. Thanks for being here." The officer is motionless and speaks not a word. Harry knows the routine: these officers never make gestures or speak.

After the ritual pause Harry continues in his head, "With your permission, Comrade Officer, we will proceed." He actually says, "Okay, let's get started." Harry then addresses the reps from *All Source* and asks, "How do you want to deal with this problem?"

Harry doesn't care what either rep says about anything. Whatever is going to happen on the project is already in the hands of a system of disinterested bureaucrats. The Zoom meeting is just formality. The less said by Harry and everybody the better.

After seventeen minutes the meeting reaches its conclusion. Harry slips into his head to say as if it was a required valediction, *"To the cause of those who watch us."* He also imagines the two reps repeat, *"To the cause of those who watch us."* He further imagines he and the reps simultaneously give a *Party Regime* salute by fisting their left hand and crossing their left arm over their chest, touching their fist to their right shoulder. In reality there is no valediction, there is no salute. Harry actually says. "Thanks for your time, guys. Talk to you later." But as is customary, the officer remains motionless and silent. As Harry signs off his eyes are cast downward, avoiding visual contact with anyone present at the Zoom meeting. He hits the exit key and the desktop screen wallpaper displays the words:

There is nothing you can do
without us knowing about it!

As always after every meeting, Harry is quietly drained and embarrassed. He goes to the bathroom, throws up, and takes a shower.

III

When Harry and Penelope's firm was taken over by the *Party Regime* it was required that the Archer family move from their comfortable single-family home in the suburbs which was assiduously retro designed and reconstructed by Harry to the state-issued apartment where they now reside. As part of their interest in Harry and Penelope's firm the *Party Regime* wants complete surveillance of Harry and his family's life. Harry thinks it's overkill because complete surveillance of all PODs already exists. Harry and Penelope worked hard to secure a mortgage and enjoy home ownership. It gave them a sense of control, accomplishment, responsibility, independence, and security. Since everything in their business and property was confiscated, and private cars had to be equipped with surveillance and tracking devices, the couple decided to get rid of their two cars and use public transportation. Ironically, public transportation is slightly more private than personal cars.

In the state-issued apartment where the Archers now live, nobody speaks. Soft eye contact, head-nods, and hand gestures are the modes of communication. To Harry and Penelope, touching one another's hands is a source of great comfort and intimacy. They can hold hands, touch only the tips of their pinky fingers, "finger dance" in the other's palm, and so much more. The world of Harry and Penelope's hands are a "middle finger" to the *Party Regime* and its *Great Awakening*.

Outside the Archers' apartment is a place Harry and Penelope go where they reasonably think they are not seen or heard by the *Party Regime*. It's at the end of a green belt pathway that runs along the side of their apartment building. The end of the pathway leads into a park with a lake and ducks. It's not only a place they can talk, this particular park is still pleasant and appealing, in contrast to the many township communities that have deteriorated under the control of the *Party Regime* and its *Great Awakening*. They go to a particular small grassy area hidden by shrubbery. To avoid suspicion, they usually don't go there together. This time, Penelope is waiting for Harry at their "secret" place, as they call it. When Harry arrives Penelope whispers, "How did the Zoom meeting go?"

Harry almost forgets himself by not keeping to a whisper. "Why do you ask? It went the way it always goes. It's shit. The worst part of it is the *goon's* frozen silence." Harry sarcastically adds, "If the 'it'– you can't say 'he'– just talked it wouldn't be so bad." He pauses, "Who am I kidding? It's horrible no matter what."

Penelope looks up at Harry, gently places her right hand on his cheek and sweetly kisses his other cheek. They stand motionless for a moment, then pull back their heads, gaze into each other's eyes, smile at one another. Each barely suppresses a laugh.

* * *

Back at the apartment, Harry has time to take a nap before this evening's *Freedom Lecture* – the live broadcasts are required listening by the *Party Regime*. As a young child with what used to be called hyperactive now called attention deficit disorder – ADD – Harry detested naps. But as an adult, particularly in these days of the *Great Awakening*, Harry has come to cherish his naps. He really thinks of them as *conscious napping* or *conscious sleeping*.

Naps and sleep give Harry mental refuge to be himself intellectually. He values the moments before he nods off to think whatever comes to mind. Mostly he thinks of a world that is different than this one. He thinks how to mentally have it "his" way in a "their" way world. "Their" being the *Party Regime*. Harry doesn't mind if he doesn't completely fall asleep. And if he does fall asleep, somehow the things he thinks about stay with him in a dreamlike state.

The times when Harry lies down to sleep or wakes up from a nap or night's sleep are Harry's most quietly reflective moments of the daily cycle. The thought Harry has as he lies down to rest now is about the PODs (written as an acronym, spoken as a one-syllable word) who have been implanted with the *Thought & Locator* chip.

"POD" is the term the *Party Regime* uses to refer to a citizen. The term "POD" is to remind citizens of their humble place in society; the word "citizen" may cause a person to feel "too" entitled. Harry feels the word "citizen" is destined one day to be on the word-elimination list – *vanished.* But so far, the word "citizen" is still acceptable to think and speak.

POD stands for *Person of Destiny*. Harry thinks the term *Person of Destiny* is meant to sound good. But the term doesn't really mean anything. Plus, the *Party Regime* never uses the three-word term. The *Party Regime* says POD as a one-syllable word. So does everybody. Harry thinks it's likely no one even remembers what POD stands for, particularly when you put the "s" on it to make it plural. In Harry's head he sometimes switches POD with the word "comrade."

Harry thinks POD is a disgusting thing to call a person, just as PODs is to call people as a whole. He thinks calling a person a POD or the citizenry PODs is demeaning – as it is intended to be. The term is mostly accepted by people with a confusing mix of affection, disdain, and resignation. Harry thinks it's remarkable the public, although some cynically, is accepting of the term. Harry knows the cruel oligarchy considers itself the elite privileged class, "above" the PODs. These elites are called *regents*. In Harry's head when addressed, a *regent* is called *comrade regent*.

With regard to the *Thought & Locator* chip, only five percent of the PODs have been implanted. The chip is propagandized "to improve your virtue in accordance with the principles of the ***Hope and Change Reich***." Harry has not yet been implanted with the chip. But long before the *Party Regime* announced the chip implant program, he was obsessively worried the *Party Regime* would think to do something like it.

IV

From his nap in a snap moment Harry's awake consciousness returns. He knows who he is, he knows where he is, he knows the state of all things. Harry's thoughts are an endless continuation from his consciousness while awake to his *conscious sleeping* to his consciousness while awake, and so on. He feels an urgency mixed with a slow disengaged depression mixed with anger. This has been Harry's default mood since the *Great Awakening*. "This" *Great Awakening*, this depravity of social order as Harry thinks of it, was made official by the *Party Regime* in *Proclamation PR-1*.

It's an hour before this evening's *Freedom Lecture*. Billy is home from school. In these times of the *Great Awakening*, Harry is cynical of the word "home." Not "home," he thinks, but "POD cage" – is the more apt term. Daisy lives away at the local *Young Adults' Learning Institution* – YALI. The *YALI Transition* is a *Party Regime* state program that has taken control of all public and private colleges and universities and renamed them YALIs.

Primary and secondary schools are still called schools. They, like everything, are run exclusively by the state. Another term for schools has been picking up over the last two years – they are regularly referred to as "POD training camps."

* * *

The restructuring of education and schools at all levels by the *Party Regime* is a sharp disturbing contrast to Harry's formal education which had been rich, enlightening, uplifting, and encouraging of individual integrity. Harry knows true collective responsibility and consciousness for the greater good of community springs from individual integrity not from state coercion. With its indoctrination education, the *Party Regime* schooling system decimated the disciplines of history, math, science, literature, art, and religious studies. Years ago, before the *Great Awakening* Harry wrote in a *Letter to the Editor* piece: *It only takes one generation through corrupt education to wipe out the worthy achievements of humankind and throw our species into an intractable dark age.*

With public works building projects, all educational disciplines intersect: history, math, science, literature, art, and religion or transcendent[1] beliefs… as well as politics, economics, sociology, and psychology. Because good building construction requires this intersection of disciplines, Harry developed a genuine interest and commitment to set a course for himself to be a life-long student of the full spectrum of life.

Harry's serious self-directed education started when he was twelve and read a book called *Building the World* published in 1925. The author Skylar High was a world traveler and journalist. The book highlighted the marvels of human ingenuity throughout history in adapting to the challenges of survival while reaching for functional and aesthetic excellence in architecture. Thrilled and intrigued, Harry wanted to know how early civilizations had designed and built such structures as the Inca Road system. He read everything he could get his hands on about the earliest cities man built. It led him to civil engineering. He has been to all parts of the world, both professionally and as a tourist. It has been his life's ambition to see the structures built thousands of years ago in places like

[1] Transcendent – This is a reach for deep ultimate meaning in life and beyond. Our everyday lives routinely overlook this aspect of human concern. Yet the power of transcendence is well purposed for application and relevance in everyday life. Goodness is cultivated by transcendence.

Peru, Sardinia, Petra, Cambodia, Turkey, and more. What tools had they used to construct such amazingly perfect walls? How were building materials transported? How was labor procurement accomplished? Harry wonders, if the *Party Regime* stays in power, will he ever again see an ancient structure?

The now oh-so vilified classics were also a core part of Harry's education. The ethos[2] of ancient Jerusalem and Athens set a foundation for Western civilization which conceived and instituted the idea of universal moral standards and governance of civil society as a republic and a democracy. Objectivity as a world view, individual initiative, capitalism, private property rights, and accountability are also tenets derived and cultivated in Western civilization. The legacies of Abraham, Moses, Socrates, Homer, Plato, Aristotle, Jesus, Hypatia, Aquinas, da Vinci, Shakespeare, Galileo, Swift, Bach, Mozart, Beethoven, Stowe, Freud, Curie, Einstein, Frankl, Frank, Angelou, King and so many others representing the fruit of Western civilization are now eliminated, canceled – *vanished* – by the educational system of the *Party Regime*. The values of Western civilization are considered a scourge by the *Party Regime*.

Harry laments the *vanishment* of Western civilization in education by the *Party Regime*. He and Penelope make sure to teach Daisy and Billy the classics in philosophy, science, art, and literature. But teaching is just an opening. Discussions about the subjects taught are how Daisy and Billy are

---

[2] Ethos – The characteristic essence of a culture, era, or community.

encouraged to think for themselves with greater depth of understanding. The kids love it, and their enrichment is gratifying to their parents.

* * *

It's Friday late afternoon. Daisy is home for the weekend from her YALI. For a busy family it's a good time to catch up with one another. Harry and Daisy are on a walk to the "secret place." Since she was sixteen Daisy has worn light makeup, as she does now. The top of Daisy's head of dark brown straight hair tied back in a short ponytail comes up to Harry's shoulders. She's wearing her usual jeans and black low top sneakers. Like her peers, she wears T-shirts that have either art images or slogans of social causes printed on them. In the last few years Daisy has been careful not to wear T-shirts with messages the *Party Regime* would disapprove of. Today she has on her *Save the Whales* T-shirt. Harry is wearing the usual, khakis and polo shirt – black. He's got on his blue canvas sneakers.

"Dad?" Asks Daisy.

"Yeah?" Responds Harry.

"You know *The Inferno* by Dante Alighieri?"

"Mm-hmm, yeah, sure."

"Well, I've been thinking about the Nine Circles of Hell in *Dante's Inferno*.

"That's a pleasant subject. What makes you think about that? Or I mean what do you think about that?

"No, your first question is fine. I think about it because it's Hell. And I think we ought to understand what the hell Hell is. Particularly if you're living in it. To your second question, here's what I think about *The Inferno* 'al dente' style. Or should I say, 'al Dante' style?"

Harry chuckles. He likes wordplay. Particularly with his kids as they can be quick and crafty with it.

Daisy continues stoically. "Okay, there's the first circle of *Limbo*. Then you have *Lust, Gluttony, Greed*… hmm, what's the next one?"

Harry pipes in, "I think that would be *Anger*." Then he quips, "Ya know, Daze, I'm kind of partial to *Gluttony*. I'm a glutton for *Gluttony*. I love me some *Gluttony*."

"Dad, enough… Yeah, right, *Anger*. But let me do this on my own. I know them all. Ahh… *Anger*, then *Heresy*, *Violence*, *Fraud*, and *Treachery*. Okay, that's the nine." Daisy is using her fingers to track the count. Then says, "But there's another circle Dante doesn't mention."

"What's that, Daze?"

"*Complacency*. Too many people are complacent. They allow dumb ideas to go unchallenged. *Party Regime* or not, there is no excuse for such complacency! We are now living in the *Complacency* circle of hell. If you fight against the stupid ideas that too many stupid people think are good ideas, those stupid people think you're *Don Quixote* tilting at windmills."

It is insightful things like this that come out of Daisy's head… and Billy's head… that give Harry pride in his kids. It makes him feel he and Penelope are on the right track with their kids. Despite the dire state of society under the *Party*

Regime it is a great comfort to Harry that his kids are sensible, critical thinkers as well as responsible, kind people.

* * *

Like *Don Quixote* the way Daisy spoke about, Harry has another "middle finger" to the *Party Regime*. In anticipation of what was likely to come with the *Party Regime's* ascension to power, and long before that day, Harry had stashed away his fifteen-year-old, renovated HP Compaq 6820s laptop computer. His trusted/hacker computer guy took it off the grid, encrypted it to conceal its detection by the *Party Regime*. It is carefully hidden.

With a rechargeable battery Harry is able to boot his forbidden laptop. Here he documents the rise of the *Party Regime* and regularly updates the progression (or "the progressive/regressive movement") of the *Great Awakening*.

Right now, the laptop and the documents contained in it are a secret. Harry's intention is that someday they won't be a secret. Hopefully, Harry will see that day. But in any case, the documents are intended for posterity.

The document file devoted to Harry's journaling on the state of the world is called:

Apocalypse or Armageddon

It opens with a preamble:

Too many fail to see and hear.
That does not stop me from showing and telling.
I will show and tell.
Maybe this time enough will see and hear.

What you will read herein is an account of the historical, economic, political, psychological, and spiritual perversions of human functioning and cruelty that define the *Party Regime*. There are different sections in the file document. This section focuses on language and words.

Because language and words are changeable, this document contains a glossary. The glossary defines words and terms I use. It explains the meaning and context of words and terms used in society. It emphasizes the fate of everything rests on language. Language and its distortion are the cause and result of human destruction.

But language can also be the salvation from corruption and ultimate destruction. Language got us into this mess. Language can get us out of this mess.

Thus, is offered this glossary. Be wise in its use.

Glossary
of
The Great Awakening

There are six entries from the glossary Harry thinks give a quick picture of the destructive elements of the *Party Regime's* control:

Harry identifies the *Freedom Lectures*. The regularity, repetition, and strategic content are right out of the handbook for mass brainwashing. It's chilling to Harry.

The glossary entry:

***Freedom Lecture**(s)* – Well, the *Freedom Lectures* are definitely lectures – more like unhinged rants – but have

> nothing to do with freedom – more like anti-freedom. The purpose of the *Freedom Lectures* is to keep PODs enslaved. The *Freedom Lectures* are broadcast every evening on all communication devices. Listening is mandatory for all PODs. This tells you all you need to know about the fraud times a million in the *Party Regime*. In the *Party Regime*, words mean the opposite of what they're supposed to mean. It works! "Freedom" in the *Party Regime* is slavery.

♦

Harry considers names, labels, and branding the most powerfully efficient influence in societal and cultural messaging. He understands labeling an era in society with a brand name identifies an encapsulated impression for people to have, whether or not the brand accurately describes the product – the era. In this case the name of this era – the *Great Awakening* – proclaimed and branded by the *Party Regime* not only enhances the brainwash, it also gives the brainwash a "home" and a sense of importance and legitimacy. Harry knows we live in eras that can be named by influencers identifying something far different than our experience or reality. He thinks at its worst, as in this case, the name *Great Awakening* for this era is not just a name… it's a prison.

The glossary entry:

> ***Great Awakening*** – The name of the era proclaimed by the *Party Regime* to brand the *Party Regime's* purpose

> and contribution to humanity. It's an exaltation of a noble aspiration and cause that in reality is a cruel fraud. Its fraudulence works the same as the previous term *Freedom Lecture*. The words mean the opposite of what they're supposed to mean. In this term *Great* is actually horrific and *Awakening* is actually willful blind ignorance. The term is another example of the cruel corruption of and by the *Party Regime*.

Harry understands the engine of societal administration is bureaucracy. Bureaucracy is inherently rife with arbitrariness and corruption. The ministries are the arms of authority. Harry identifies a few of the ministries established under the authority of the *Party Regime*.

The glossary entries:

> ***Ministry of Compliance*** – Ministries are established in governments to show the power, force, and commitment to enforced compliance to mandated rules. That's what ministries are to public perception. In their operation they are vast bureaucracies. Bureaucracies are the cruelest form of enforcement, as they dehumanize governance – the opposite of what good governance does, which is to respect the humanity of all persons. A ministry in the hands of the *Party Regime* is hell on earth. Add to that the ministry's target – in this case *compliance* – you get hell on hell.

In the case of compliance, the *Party Regime* exacts its standards by way of totalitarian authority according to *Awaken* doctrine. What could possibly go wrong?

Ministry of Correctness – Just like the previous term *Ministry of Compliance*, the description and perspective on government ministries is the same for this term. The target of this ministry is *correctness.*

In the case of correctness, who makes that decision? To the *Party Regime*, the question itself is a blasphemous crime. The *politically correct* movement preceded the *Party Regime* by demonizing normal speech. *Political correctness* impugned innocent speech, wrongly attributing hostile motives to innocent speech. This movement empowered the establishment and founding of the *Party Regime*.

Ministry of Diversity – Just like the previous term *Ministry of Compliance*, the description and perspective on government ministries is the same for this term. The target of this ministry is *diversity*.

This ministry enforces quotas on race, gender, gender identification, sexual orientation, age, national origin, spoken language, disability, height, weight, hairstyle, tattoos, body piercings, mental stability/instability, feelings, and stuff that's impossible to imagine. Under the *Party Regime* and the

Awaken doctrine, the irony is there is no diversity for what matters – *diversity of thought*. Go figure.

♦

For Harry how a person or people are referred to tells you everything.

The glossary entry:

POD or **PODs** – Stands for *Person of Destiny*. Its common use is to say it as a one-syllable word. "POD" is used to replace the word citizen. The *Party Regime* considers citizen a higher station in society than "regular" people should be thought of. The term "POD" – or "PODs" for colloquial plural reference to the people – is intended to diminish a person and the people in general. The sound of the term "POD" is disrespectful and dehumanizing. Dehumanization of people is a continuous function of the *Party Regime*. The credo ***You are your group!*** is part of the propagandic indoctrination of the *Party Regime*. Along these lines, "pod people" is the colloquial term for a species of plantlike aliens in the 1955 novel and 1956 movie both titled *Invasion of the Body Snatchers*. The novel and movie reference is a cultural identifier reinforcing "pod person" as being undesirable. The novel and movie are also a look at dystopia via foreign invasion from either other earth nations or outer space.

♦

* * *

Harry's one-word be-all for approaching life is *wisdom.* He drops that word, or a form of it, often. If pressed he is happy to explain what *wisdom* is. He also thinks the word *wisdom* has a self-evident quality. He feels the word *wisdom* can't be evoked too much. Harry ends the glossary section with the reminder:

To repeat: Be wise.

* * *

Also housed in his forbidden laptop is a section where Harry discusses the ill effects of *Awaken* doctrine, the takeover by the *Party Regime*, and the ethos of the *Great Awakening.* He describes how robust the area used to be where his firm's office is located. Once the art center of town and the city at large, since the *Party Regime* took over control, all galleries are closed, the buildings now owned by the *Party Regime.* Most buildings are unoccupied as struggling artists and entrepreneurs in other fields are unable to pay the rent. Businesses across the board closed due to government shutdowns as a response to the world pandemic. Under the *Party Regime* mandated shutdowns continued well past the pandemic's conclusion.

With Harry and Penelope's support a group of sculptors, painters, and other creative types got together and are now renting the first floor of the three-story building where Harry and Penelope's firm occupies the second floor. To make that happen, Penelope had to negotiate – beg – with the *Ministry of Resources*; she contracted an engineering project for the ministry *pro bono.* The contract was a bribe to the ministry. For Harry and Penelope, it was worth it. The first-floor large open space provides areas for studios as well as a large gallery. The only gallery within a hundred miles. Open to the public, the space is well-trafficked and good for other businesses in the community.

On his illegal laptop Harry describes the empty storefronts along a once well-cared for street that was lined with potted trees and annual flowers in beautiful large ceramic containers. Without the businesses, the quality of community life deteriorated to something resembling a ghost town. The trees and annual flowers died long ago for lack of civil government interest and therefore lack of maintenance. The dead potted trees and ceramic containers of dead flowers collect additional debris as if they were trash receptacles. There is no waste management pick-up, so the trash debris in and around the pots and containers continues to grow like a cancer. Under the *Party Regime* this kind of community deterioration is typical throughout the nation. Harry describes his despair and anger over an issue he considers the most serious we have as a community of people – homelessness.

Homelessness didn't start with the *Party Regime*, but the *Party Regime* made it worse. Mindfully, Harry targeted the issue of homelessness when he was in his early twenties. Besides it being a societal travesty and oppression to its victims – which is all of us – he considers homelessness an indicator and result of a broken community system no matter how well other parts of that community and society function. *Homelessness is a Humanitarian Disaster Reflecting a Political and Moral Failure* headlines Harry's remarks on the subject.

With a group of financiers, builders, developers, and concerned citizens, Harry and Penelope co-founded a for-profit enterprise to address homelessness and the associated issues accompanying the problem. Such issues include mental illness, substance addiction, and spousal abuse. The group founded *The REACH Initiative*. REACH is an acronym graphically represented:

The

R*espect*
E*ducation*
A*rt*
C*ommerce*
H*ome*

Initiative

The name, the acronym, and each word in the graphic representation is meaningful to the purpose of *The REACH Initiative*. Reach means reach. It's an important positive action word. The words in the acronym are critical:

Respect – There is no human dignity realized without mutual *respect*.

Education – There is no knowledge without *education*.

Art – There is no connection to feeling and meaning without *art*.

Commerce – There is no access to essential and desired goods and services without *commerce*.

Home – There is no soul in life without a *home*.

The word "initiative" is yet another purposeful designation. It's not a company, foundation, or firm. It's an *initiative* – another proactive positive action word. It means to act to get things done.

Since its inception *The REACH Initiative* has been an unqualified success. With *respect* for all people as the guiding principle *The REACH Initiative* creates enhancement programs in educational and training resources available to anyone. *The REACH Initiative* makes possible for people to have a home. No one should go homeless! It taps into artistic expression disseminating enrichment for the enlightenment and enjoyment of and by the general public. It creates platforms for necessary and desired jobs providing access to goods and services for all people.

The for-profit model of *The REACH Initiative* is the key to its success. There is no reliance on government resources. There is no bureaucracy. There *is* accountability to shareholders and the communities where it operates.

Across the board for all ethnic, gender, and racial groups, in communities where *The REACH Initiative* exists mental health metrics improve, domestic violence is decreased, substance addiction goes down, suicide declines, prosperity increases, and those who were homeless no longer are without the dignity and comfort a home provides. When *the Party Regime* came to power *The REACH Initiative* was shut down as *the Party Regime* determined it to be a racist enterprise, harming global climate, committing financial fraud in business practices, committing tax fraud, and causing voter suppression.

Since the shutdown of *The REACH Initiative* homelessness and all its ills returned in greater numbers and has since been more problematic than ever. The worldwide pandemic hit the homeless particularly hard and caused greater viral spread into all parts of all communities at large throughout the nation. The *Party Regime* could not have designed a worse destruction than with its disinterest and ineptitude regarding homelessness.

For Harry it's just another example of: If there is anything good, the *Party Regime* will ruin it. Those are his closing words in this section housed in his forbidden laptop.

V

From the beginning, Harry knew however necessary auto-updates might be for operating systems and apps, they present a potential for surveillance abuse. Algorithms had long been manipulating our thoughts. Harry anticipated all this would be too easy for a totalitarian regime to abuse. Everything with a chip in it had opened the door to complete surveillance of everybody. The public got used to clicking "I agree."

Harry was not surprised the day the *Party Regime* ordered the confiscation of all older electronic devices and put all newer ones through a general update, meaning all information and communication devices are now controlled by the state. Harry thinks to himself sarcastically – you mean *anti*-communication devices. State-ordered updates are continuously done in the background. All information and communication devices are now controlled by the state. Clicking "I agree" is no longer optional. Harry dodges this intrusion by the state. As part of taking his forbidden laptop off the grid his trusted/hacker computer guy also disabled the auto-update system, making his illegal laptop more illegal.

The intrusion into people's lives is an outgrowth of data-based marketing in a consumer economy business model. It works well in a free market economy. But if there is a totalitarian takeover, databased marketing can be – will be – perverted to exploit and control the populous. Harry said to Penelope, "This is an example of a good thing turning bad as a result of the combination of authoritarian governance and the gravitational pull corporations have to dominate everything in society."

Penelope responded, "Wow, you said that in one breath, Hare."

"Yeah, but it took me three breaths to think of it before I said it. Thinking requires more oxygen than talking," replied Harry.

* * *

The Big Tech Three occupy the top level of domination. They have been running the show for years. The public only knows what *The Big Tech Three* tells them.

Ironically, the bigger the structural and institutional threat/problem the more Harry's attitude is not to sweat it. It's not that he doesn't care. It's because he cares so much. But he has an innate mechanism that keeps him from getting overwhelmed by bad stuff. So, despite the abuses perpetuated by corporate and government institutions and their intrusions into people's lives Harry remains calm. Even though he is aware the bad use of technology will destroy the soul of humanity, he knows the danger of technology has always been present since the discovery of fire… and long before. It's part of human existence. It isn't the technology that is the problem; it's people's use of technology that causes problems. *The Big Tech Three* are not the micro processing chips. *The Big Tech Three* are the oligarchs who monopolistically own and run the micro processing chips.

The delicate polarity balance of Harry's *don't worry/be afraid, be very afraid* perspective defines his attitude about how to take the world writ large and what matters to him at any given time. He detests hysteria but respects the instincts and insights to detect *a gathering storm.*

Harry marvels at the infinite possibilities technologies bring to the world. He considers human enterprise the core of human existence. And he thinks the core of human enterprise is landscaping and technology innovation. That's it… that's what humans do… they pull weeds, reshape foliage and vegetation for all sorts of reasons in public and private places, and they make things do things – technology. But the blessings of technology come with a curse if humans go off the rails. And going off the rails, according to Harry, is what humans do so well.

* * *

This morning Harry is to meet with an official at the local office of the *Ministry of Correctness*. When it comes to humans going off the rails, this ministry's only purpose, as all ministries under the *Party Regime*, is to go off the rails. So, Harry's delicate balance is weighing fully on *be afraid, be very afraid.*

Harry arrives at the Ministry's office on time. He doesn't know why they want to see him. He doesn't know the official he is to meet. To be respectful and safe Harry is dressed in business attire. He's wearing gray slacks, a white shirt, a charcoal gray tie, a dark brown sport coat, and dark brown Oxford shoes. The receptionist tells him to have a seat while he waits for the ministry officer.

Harry takes a seat. He stares at a fifty-inch monitor mounted on the opposite wall. What plays on the monitor is a *Party Regime* propaganda loop Harry and all PODs have seen routinely. Part of the content of the loop includes a full-face image of Jim Biddle with his fixed stare at the viewer. It is remarkable how no matter from what angle Harry looks at Biddle, Biddle's eyes land on Harry. In his live public persona Biddle usually has a pleasant disingenuous smile, but this image of him has no smile. Biddle is tight-lipped. He is serious and stern. He is creepy. The words "*The Big Guy*" appear on the upper left of the image. Across the bottom of the image reads:

"***There is nothing you can do***
without us knowing about it!"

Even though Harry and everybody know every element of the loop, sitting with nothing to do, Harry watches the loop over and over again. He thinks the brainwashing could be so much better if the content were more intelligent and the production quality better.

Harry waits for an hour until finally a door opens and a woman about thirty years old motions to him to follow her. Harry follows the woman down a hallway; when she reaches the destination office, she turns to face Harry; she extends her left arm to signal Harry to enter the office.

Harry walks into a small office where a man who looks fifty-something is sitting behind a desk. The nameplate on the desk says "Robert Burke." Harry likes seeing and hearing names, as over the last three years it has become rare to use a person's name. After the *Party Regime* forced language to be restrictive and awkward – as per no gender references – people now refer to a stranger as "friend." Using a warm, positive, human term like "friend" is one of the few things Harry likes about the current resourcefulness of the general public. The public does it naturally and so far, the *Party Regime* has been silent on the matter – sort of like tacet approval.

On an internet writers' forum, long before the *Party Regime* shut the platform down, Harry wrote an article entitled *Mr, Ms, Mrs, Miss*. The article addressed what Harry called the *devolution of evolution*. His point was that too often, in an attempt to *evolve*, we actually *devolve*. He noted that removing *Mrs* and *Miss* from the traditional social courtesy titles of *Mr, Ms, Mrs,*

Miss is an example of removing the texture of life so nothing can be distinguished or appreciated. It's like listening to a song with one note. Harry warned in the article that the next move toward devolution would be to remove the male/female designation when addressing someone. Harry wrote that he ... *respected the intention for social courtesy titles to reflect the common dignity we should show one another. But unnecessarily stripping social titles of "offences" where none exist numbs our senses to the point of making someone a homogeneous thing, not a multidimensional person.*

Harry's article turned out prophetic. The *Party Regime* has declared gender reference an affront to *Awaken* doctrine. But traditions can be stubborn and unnatural to extinguish. People, including hardcore *Awaken* and older members of the *Party Regime*, regularly say *Mr* and *Ms*. At this time, despite the disapproval of gender references, the state does not vigorously prohibit the common usage of *Mr* and *Ms*. Moreover, Harry purposely and defiantly uses these courtesy titles. That is, he uses them unless the person he addresses prefers he not... which has never happened.

"Come in and have a seat, friend, Mr. Archer," the man says warmly. Harry detects the slightest hint of an Irish accent. He sits in the chair opposite the desk the man is sitting at. Harry appreciates hearing his own name spoken in a formal and respectful tone. Although the man is sitting behind a desk Harry can see this is a big guy – not fat, but with a large build; he estimates he's at least three inches taller than himself. What is particularly distinguishing is his wavy red/orange hair with white streaks. He has blue eyes that are framed by dark tortoiseshell glasses. His full close-cropped beard is the same color as his hair, with the same white streaks. He is wearing a light-yellow dress shirt with no tie.

"Thank you, Mr. Burke. I assume you're Mr. Burke," he says, pointing to the nameplate on the desk to indicate his reasonable presumption.

"Well, when people say 'Mr. Burke,' I think they're talking about my father. But yes, that's me. You can call me Bob."

Harry is struck by Burke's – Bob's – good humor and friendliness. The pleasantries exhibited by Bob momentarily create a sense of ease in Harry. "Thanks, Bob. Please call me Harry," he says casually.

Harry's sense of dread returns when he sees on the wall behind Bob a poster with the three-slogan credo of the *Party Regime:*

DEATH IS LIFE
OPPRESSION IS LIBERTY
WEAKNESS IS STRENGTH

Harry waits apprehensively for Bob to speak.

Which Bob promptly does. "Harry, you were asked to come here so we can try and help you."

Harry thinks not "asked," *summoned to come here*, "Help me?" he asks.

"Yes."

Harry thinks this conversation is going to be interesting. But not in a way he likes. He knows he is already in enough trouble.

He doesn't want to add to it by saying the wrong thing. Which could be anything. He sticks to his *wait for Bob to speak* strategy.

Bob holds up a book. It's *I Built It, The Personal Empowerment of Following Your Dream*. It's the book no longer in bookstores that Harry wrote in 2019, the book banned by the *Party Regime*. Harry and Bob stare at each other. Then Bob chuckles and says, "Hey, it's a very good read, Harry. I really enjoyed it!"

Harry's response sounds a little like a question. "Thank you?"

"No, Harry, thank *you*. It's really insightful and inspirational!" Bob pauses, then continues, "The problem though is in these times your book may not be understood in the right light."

Harry says nothing.

"The thing is, Harry, this book can be used against the *Party Regime*. That means the book is subversive and not in line with the way things are."

Harry thinks: I couldn't agree more; all this mutual agreeing can't mean anything good… after all, Bob wants to "help" me, before exclaiming, "Well, I don't want to be subversive."

Bob chuckles a small chuckle and says, "Don't bullshit me, Harry. It's okay. Just thinking these days makes everyone subversive. At least those who do think."

Harry isn't sure what he's hearing. He hears Bob's words, but does he understand their meaning? He's uncertain where this is going. Still in *be afraid, be very afraid* mode, he keeps thinking this could be a trick – better not say anything that will get me into more trouble.

Bob continues. "Look Harry, what's done is done. And we smart people can't stop being smart. We all have to survive. And the first thing I learned about survival is it requires adaptation. So, what you and I are talking about is you adapting to the demands of the times."

Harry listens and says nothing.

Bob goes on. "Harry, we've been watching you for some time. We think you could be an asset for the *Party Regime*."

Harry gives no indication he is repulsed by the idea. Though, during the *Great Awakening* he'd gotten good at guarding his thoughts and not showing his feelings while not wearing a mask, he has no illusion he is fooling Bob. He always assumes the *Regime* is on to him. Still, he thinks it best in this moment to act reserved and cooperative.

"How can I be an asset?" he asks.

Bob answers, "You write well. Our messaging needs improvement."

"But you just told me my writings are subversive. You don't want to message subversion."

"Well, think about it, Harry. The best person to write convincing messaging is someone who understands the weakness of the *Regime* and its messaging challenges."

Harry had already decided to cooperate with Bob's "proposal," because it isn't an offer, it's a command from the

Party Regime. Knowing now what Bob wants, Harry wants to show he is reflective and agreeable because he has no choice in the matter. Playing it as if he has a choice he says, "Yeah, Bob. That makes sense."

Saying Bob's name gives Harry a sense he has control of the situation, of which he has none. Sounding like he's a dedicated member of the *Party Regime*, he says, "Okay, I'll do my part."

The two men know full well they are playing each other. Harry knows a part of survival these days is being useful to the *Party Regime*. And as dangerous as it is, Harry is somewhat comforted by seeing Bob as an intellectual ally while knowing Bob would crush him without hesitation if the *Party Regime* says *Harry "must go."* Curious, he asks Bob, "What did you do before having this job at the ministry?"

Bob answers, "I was in *waste management*."

VI

Back at the apartment, Harry is still mentally unpacking his meeting with Bob. He's not sure what to make of what happened. He's not sure if this is a bad thing or a good thing. He's beginning to think it's bad or good depending on how he handles it. Harry's thinking he might be able to pull something off. But what?

Harry's mind wanders for a while. He thinks he might now have access to… he isn't sure. Then he has an idea to look at two public speeches: One is not readily available to the public anymore – Danny Tripp's farewell speech as outgoing president. Tripp has been barred from all social media platforms and most of the record of his term as president has been purged from the public record by the *Party Regime*. Moreover, it is now treasonous to view or read unapproved material about Tripp. The other speech Harry wants to review is Jim Biddle's inaugural speech, which is readily available to the public. Indeed, the *Party Regime* requires it be viewed.

Harry calls Bob Burke's cell phone. Harry is correct. Bob informs him now that he is working with the ministry, he can get material that would otherwise not just be unavailable to him, but illegal.

"Thanks, that will help," he tells Bob.

"No problem, Harry. Glad to see you jumped right in."

Harry feels like a *Mission Impossible* operative. The *Mission Impossible* theme song is stuck in his head:

♪ ♫ De de dé dé
De de dé dé
De de dé dé
De de dé dé ♪ ♫
♪ ♫ Da da daaaa
Da da daaaa
Da da daaaa
Da dat! ♪ ♫ …

He is both excited and terrified.

* * *

Courtesy of Bob, in two-and-a-half hours Harry receives the videos and transcripts of both speeches. This is his starting point to break down what is happening to the nation. He is working under the guise of being loyal to the *Party Regime* while trying to bring down everything the *Party Regime* stands for and does. In his mind he is now a double agent! He wonders though, is he *James Bond* or *Maxwell Smart?*

Harry reviews the two speeches. They illustrate the stark differences between the outgoing president Danny Tripp and the incoming president Jim Biddle – *The Big Guy*. To the critically observant the speeches are rich with meaning. Their respective juxtapositions with each other are indicative of how freedom and oppression are set against each other with freedom hanging in the balance.

Harry's review and analysis of the speeches reveal a definitive doorway to exposing the problem with governance driven by *style over substance*. This inspires Harry to write his first article for a *Party Regime* publication. It has a wide readership. Although Harry is writing the article, authorship will be attributed to *Staff Writer*.

The trick is to write the article in "plain sight" of the *Party Regime* with the *Party Regime* believing the article suits their purposes. The article is Harry's calculation to get people to think in a direction away from *Awaken* doctrine and *Party Regime* authority. With the watchful *Party Regime* it's a risky "high wire" act.

Harry thinks he must be a fool for conceiving such a thing. But he can't help himself.

Harry thinks the two speeches from Tripp and Biddle are both remarkable for being solid, intelligent, and well-delivered. There is nothing crazy or extreme in either speech. There are, however, distinct message differences between them. The differences highlight the underlying differences in values and vision for society.

A core part of the Tripp speech lists accomplishments achieved in his administration. Harry thinks listing accomplishments can be frustrating if you're trying to make a point. Because viewed through a politically partisan orthodox prism one person's accomplishments are another person's disasters.

Harry is thinking about this paradox as he sits at his drafting table at the office. He gets up and goes to Penelope's office. He stands at the door to her office; she is sitting at her desk.

"Hey, Penny, let's get a coffee."

"Okay, just hold a moment. I'm finishing up this email."

They walk to the Starbucks on the corner. Harry gets his usual *House Blend* with cream. Penelope doesn't drink coffee. She gets a bottle of citrus flavored water. Beverages in hand they walk out of Starbucks and stroll past the neglected ceramic containers of dead trees and accumulated debris. When focused on a project or subject Harry and Penelope got used to ignoring the deterioration of the district.

"So, Penny, I wanted to process something related to this first article I'm writing for 'you know who… or what.' It's important I hit the right 'note' with this article as it will make or break what I'm really trying to accomplish."

"Yeah sure, Hare. What are you thinking?"

"Okay. There is any number of things I have to make clear in the article without setting a trap for myself… for us."

"I know. You're good at strategy and tactics."

"Well, I like your confidence in me, but this is different. This is new territory. So, let me tell you what I'm thinking. Tripp's farewell speech lists his accomplishments. Now, things can be called accomplishments that people would agree *are* accomplishments and achievements while others would say are failures."

"Yeah, that's true."

"Yeah, well, it doesn't stop there. Further distortion occurs when there is agreement across partisan party lines about accomplishments, but disagreements ensue about the importance of the accomplishments, and however important, who really deserves credit for the accomplishments."

"You're talking politics, Harry. It's politics."

"Yeah, exactly. It's politics. And it's toxic. Politics is a meat grinder, with ideas going into the 'grinder' one way and coming out another mangled way. That's what Biddle did in his speech. His central message was 'unity.' Which means: think what the *Party Regime* wants you to think and we'll have 'unity.' We'll all be 'united.' We'll be 'one.' That's not all. The message goes further. If you don't think what the *Party Regime* wants you to think, you're a racist. Jeez, Pen, that's not promoting unity. There is nothing darker and divisively destructive than this steady, relentless message of racism from the *Party Regime*. Because of his mental decline I'm sure *'The Big Guy'* doesn't know what he's saying. He is just a mouthpiece for the *Party Regime*."

"Harry, it all comes down to a person hears what they want to hear. Included with that, if you like the person, you like what they say. If you hate the person, you hate what they say."

"Hmm, you just reminded me, Penny, of a social psychology study where people were questioned about definitive statements on public policy. When they were told the statements were made by a popular, well-regarded person, people approved the statements resoundingly. But if people were told the statements were made by someone widely considered despicable, they emphatically disapproved the very same statements."

Harry goes on, "In the same way, the impression a speech makes depends on your politics, or even more impactful, your emotions and projections. Like you said, a person hears what they want to hear. If you despise the person giving the speech you won't like the speech even if what it conveys aligns with your values and thoughts."

Penelope nods in agreement then slowly shakes her head in momentary discouragement. "Biases are hard wired. Confirmation bias affects all of us."

"You couldn't be more correct. That's why to avoid falling into such a self-induced trap, I impose a thought exercise on myself. I block out the source of any given idea or message and evaluate the meaning. This way, I don't prejudice my response.

"That's not easy to do, Harry."

"Yeah, it's a difficult exercise. It challenges my intellectual integrity. But that's the point. The demise of everything good is due to the demise of *intellectual integrity!* So, I better begin with myself."

Harry goes on, "Now the protocol of this exercise has two parts. I just told you the first part. The second part totally does rely on the source of the information and messages. In context, the source is all important. The integrity challenge is to not lazily apply only the "source" rationale as default righteousness. It's hard not to fall into this trap of flawed thinking and feeling. And yes, not only can thoughts be flawed, so can feelings. To stay clear of such flaws I always question the source as well as the content."

Penelope stops walking. Reacting to her, Harry stops too – one pace ahead of her. He pivots to face her. Penelope says, "Ya know, Harry, it's a good self-regulatory exercise, I wish everyone did it. Here's to good thought exercises." She raises her bottle of citrus flavored water in a toasting gesture. Harry returns the action by lifting his cup of coffee and taping the cup to her bottle, completing the toast.

* * *

Harry titles his article *A Tale of Two Speeches*. To underscore the way speeches impact society, Harry wrote in his article:

> Elected leaders, those seeking elected office, and those gaining prominence in the culture establish bona fides – whether false or authentic – by way of their

spoken and/or written public commentary. Speeches such as commencements, eulogies, church sermons, State of the Union addresses, farewell addresses, and inaugurations are opportunities for the speech giver to do something rare and profound – to connect the abstraction of living in society to living a private life. A speech should seek to close the gap on the alienation we all have with ourselves and others.

Public speeches on the occasions of a grand platform should be aspirational and inspirational. The trick is to inspire aspiration by word and delivery that resonates with the audience. Danny Tripp's farewell speech and Jim Biddle's inaugural speech resonated with their respective supporters – inspiring aspirations.

The wisdom and sincerity of a speech giver are left to the judgment of the public – individually. But the noise and pressure of the collective can contaminate and confuse an individual's thinking causing them to misinterpret the speech. That's why there needs to be integrity in your thinking.

* * *

Harry is embarking on a dangerous mission he is only able to define for now as a quest for sanity. As per this quest, one of Harry's points of reference is the meaning of the two speeches in the context of the two men, in the context of the culture war, in the context of the "uncivil" war as Biddle put it in his speech, in the context of… Harry isn't sure. He is relieved his article is approved and well received by the *Party Regime* and the public! But he doesn't know if he fooled the *Party Regime* or they fooled him.

VII

Harry goes to work at the *Ministry of Correctness.* He writes articles and copy for various publications and projects. He is surprised how easy it is to fit in and do the work he wants to do. He does not compromise his values in what he writes.

Although the *Ministry's* purpose for Harry's work is repulsive to him, he is determined to snooker and undermine the *Ministry* and the *Party Regime.* Writing articles fully committed to his principles, he cleverly and skillfully writes in a manner like-minded people can detect and comprehend "under the nose" of the *Party Regime.*

Samuel Clemens, using the pen name Mark Twain, wrote this way in his 1884 book *The Adventures of Huckleberry Finn.* His novel sailed "under the radar" of a racist subculture and mindset to reach its real audience of critical free thinkers. Harry is striving to do the same in his articles. He is currently writing about the *Awaken.* Appearing to support the *Awaken* despite his rejection of their ideology, he writes, "The *Awaken* are enlightened by no better cause than to ensure, as the 'pledge' says, *liberty and justice for all.*"

Since the start of his "tour of duty" with the *Ministry of Correctness* when immersed in a writing project Harry likes bouncing his ideas off Penelope. She has a "dry" sensibility he loves and respects. Tonight, they are out for one of their sunset walks, a time and place they feel free from being watched and heard. Stopping their progress for a moment, Harry says, "Ya know, Pen, when you break down what being 'awaken' should plainly mean, it's *liberty and justice for all.* But the *Awaken* movement means something different – such as *racism is forever, and society is guilty and must pay forever.* These are distinctly two different messages. The *liberty and justice for all* message is not controversial to any normal person. The *racism is forever, and society is guilty and must pay forever* message victimizes and destroys."

Penelope engages his point, adding, "That's because the *Awaken* don't respect people. After all, to them people are PODs. To them PODs will believe the last thing you say to them. To them – the *Awaken* – the contradictory messages they deliver never matter because it's only the last thing that is said that counts even if it differs from what was said before. You should write about that, Hare. But don't fall into the trap of chasing down your opponent – your enemy – with logic. Make sure you're writing to your reader who actually cares about logic and rationality."

"Yeah, Penny, that's good. I'm going to put that into the article. You want co-authorship?" Harry's playing with Penelope since they both know his articles are published as authored by staff writer.

"Get real, Hare. We both know your articles are published as authored by *Staff Writer*. So, leave me out of it. I'll stick to coaching from the 'sidelines.' One gladiator in a death match is enough for this family."

"Okay, *Coach*. But I have other things I want to run by you. Remember in school at the beginning of the day and at school assemblies they all started with reciting *The Pledge of Allegiance?* I suppose like all kids I just went along with it as an expected part of the day. We all took the 'pledge' for granted mostly because we were kids. But there was another more subtle and profound reason we took it for granted. And that's because of the success of this nation; life was good in this nation. The goodness of this nation is what we took for granted!

"Of course, it wasn't perfect by a long shot. We all knew there were poor people, racism, corruption, depraved people loose in society, and injustices of every kind. But there was a foundational sense that we lived in a society that was 'free' in a way no other society ever had, throughout history."

"… and the practice of freedom is how freedom is perpetuated," Penelope interjects.

"… and the practice of freedom begins with *free thought* and *free speech*," adds Harry. He continues, "Somehow, as kids we knew that. Through lots of things including the ritual reciting of *The Pledge of Allegiance* we knew about this nation's idealism of freedom. For goodness sake… really, *for goodness sake*, the 'pledge' ends with *liberty and justice for all!* Under the *Awaken* doctrine and the authority of the *Party Regime*, we don't have that today."

"Yeah, Harry, that's what it has come down to. You lose good things when you take them for granted. It's kind of a 'catch-22.' You build something for its benefits and enjoyment. And because you enjoy it, and it feels like it will never go away, you start taking it for granted. You forget it's valuable, so you don't take care of it. It's human nature: you build then destroy by ignoring what it took to build it in the first place. *The most insidious kind of destruction is assuming good things exist without caring for them.* We're basically always fighting our human nature to be lazy and inattentive about things that matter."

Harry takes Penelope's hand as they turn back toward the apartment. "You sure you don't want to co-author with me, Pen?" Harry asks with more playfulness as a compliment to Penelope's insights.

"I'm sure, Harry. That's *my* human nature."

"Well, the unfortunate point is the 'pledge' has fallen out of fashion and favor with the *Awaken*, even though the 'pledge' is what the *Awaken* 'say' they are about – *liberty and justice for all.* I can see how making a pledge could sound fascistic. But *The Pledge of Allegiance* is neither fascist nor mandatory. No one gives up anything essential to their self-interest by making this pledge. And if a person doesn't want to make this *pledge* out loud, or in their heart for that matter, they are free to abstain. That's their business. No big deal."

"I'm with you, Harry."

"There's something else I've been thinking about, Penny."

"What's that, dear?" Penelope doesn't say "dear" often. She's saying it now to inflect her sense that Harry is about to raise an issue he wants her to take seriously. By her inflection she's signaling Harry that she knows him all too well and knows what he wants and needs.

Harry goes on, "Basically, all this is about *shaping public opinion*. Sometimes I get uneasy with that. On the one hand, it sounds like determining for others what they should think. On the other hand, opinions are shaped from somewhere. So, it's not so much about being shaped as it is about the source of the shaping. It's also about what is being appealed to in the shaping – fear and ignorance or integrity and sound reason." Harry pauses as he dives deeper into reflection – almost talking to himself. "Hmm… the balance of opinion tilting toward sensibility rests on the influences – shaping – energized by *unalienable rights*. This is the perspective from where informed opinion has the best chance of being good opinion. That's the opinion I'd like to shape."

"Harry, stop it. You just went full circle from bad motivations for shaping opinions to good motivations and the reason your work is necessary and good. I know thinking is your 'thing.' It's the 'thing' you do. You are so *Descartes. You think, therefore you are!* But don't overthink *you* and the world. As you always say, 'There's a *sweet spot* for everything.' Well, Hare, there's a *sweet spot* for thinking too! Find your *sweet spot*."

"Penny, I found my *sweet spot* a long time ago when I met you. You're my *sweet spot*."

* * *

After jotting down notes the *Party Regime* would find acceptable on his state-issued laptop, Harry retrieves his other laptop – his secret, illegal laptop – and adds notations to other notations he keeps on this forbidden device. He refers to these notations when he writes articles, weaving these observations and principles into his writings in ways that make the point but seemingly don't violate *Party Regime* doctrine.

The notations on his secret laptop are Harry's descriptions of the layers and power structures in societal and cultural institutions. The idea of a book begins to take shape from the notes Harry makes. He continues to work on it as a book project using the working title *The Age of Insanity*. The book project is a sharp look at the current societal condition. It identifies and explains dynamic institutional, interactional social structures as they intersect with psychological drivers. These dynamics mixed with individual and collective emotional impulses gave way to widespread irrationality, delusion, and insanity throughout society embedding into government administration, bureaucracies, public service messaging, and societal institutions. Harry sees the spread of this insanity having a stranglehold on humanity and it's not going away unless enough people see and understand what's happening. Seeing and understanding what's happening is the first step toward the cure to this insanity.

Harry knows well publication of *The Age of Insanity* as he is writing it would be a crime under the *Party Regime*. But he continues to write it with the intent to get it published and distributed even if it can only be dispersed in illegal "underground markets." For now, though, Harry is focused on his forbidden journaling, note-taking, and book writing. He can think about book distribution later. Being careful is also high on his priorities. But at some point – which he figures is already past – Harry thinks it's less about being careful and more about gamesmanship. What a "high wire" act he muses as he closes his Compaq 6820s laptop and hides it away.

* * *

In his articles, Harry is always mindful of the reader as a person with whom he is talking, as if they are in his presence. He assumes they are sensible and that his words speak to their sensibility.

Harry thinks the key is to connect with the individual, not the crowd. The *Party Regime* message to the crowd is designed to minimize and dehumanize the individual. To the *Party Regime* one's relevance in existence is their identification not as a person but as a member of a group.

The *Awaken/Party Regime* doctrines glorify diversity, not of ideas but immutable differences to get individuals to see themselves as a "group thing" not a person. The *Party Regime* always virtue messages its prioritization for inclusion and respect of different groups in which a person might identify – racial, gender, national origin, creed, etc. Harry believes having respect for all people of such groups is obvious. But he took note when the *Party Regime* slogan ***Celebrate Diversity*** gradually went away and was replaced with the updated slogan ***You are your group!*** As disturbing as the newer slogan is, Harry appreciates the slogan's honesty of what the *Party Regime* really means. He thinks the *Party Regime* is so full of self-righteousness it doesn't even try to hide its real intentions anymore. Harry thinks of it like "mission creep" when short term military objectives expand gradually to long term or permanent status. In the same way the *Party Regime* carries out totalitarian "mission creep" to take over at any time whatever they decide they want and impose it on everyone.

Group affiliation means nothing without strong development as a person. In psychological terms Harry understands this to be *healthy ego strength.* Harry embeds words and phrases into his messages that connect with his readers' own best independent thinking, immunizing them from the *Party Regime* message.

VIII

Harry was born on January 15, 1979. He grew up in a suburb of Los Angeles, California called Reseda. From Reseda's small town in a big city atmosphere... and from television, movies, radio, music, books, newspapers, journal periodicals, fortune cookies, graffiti, bumper stickers, cereal boxes, the internet, billboards, art, sports, parents, grandparents, friends, girlfriend/wife, children, school, libraries, museums, teachers, coaches, mentors, bosses, clients, celebrities, strangers, religion, priests, rabbis, Buddha, atheists, and imagination Harry learned about the world.

It was from a community near Reseda where Harry and Penelope built their life and home, they were forced by the *Party Regime* to move to their state-controlled apartment in another nearby suburban community. It's hard to pinpoint the exact start of the "decline," as Harry calls it, but he began to call it the "decline" when Daisy was nine and playing on her youth league soccer team. The soccer league decided to follow the new national decree for youth sports to not keep score. There would be no winners or losers. Even Daisy said, "That sucks! What's the point then?!"

Next, the school curriculum ceased to focus on subject discipline. Grading was eliminated for content mastery and a grading system for behavior and attitude was initiated. A student could fail in math and still pass with no letter grade and be subject to a letter grade from "A" to "F" for "POD conformity."

Harry and Penelope were regular attendees at Public School Board Meetings. Only Penelope was allowed to address the Board – on one occasion. She spoke for two minutes on the value of interdisciplinary subject integration – a topic the Board members clearly knew nothing about, didn't care about, and didn't understand. After she spoke the Board member running the meeting thanked Penelope for her comments. The next day Penelope received an email from the school district scolding her for taking up valuable time at a School Board Meeting. The email ended with the words: *Schools serve the community not individual families!*

The biggest blow to the Archers came when an official from the *Ministry of Resources* came to Harry and Penelope's office to advise them about the "*Restructuring*" program. Not only was control of their business without recompense transferred to the state via the *Party Regime*, the Archers would be moved out of their home. It was bad enough to lose control of the business, but it was never made clear why their home was confiscated. Harry did learn that the son of a *Party Regime* official is now living in the house that was once their home.

Even with the government assaults on his family and his livelihood, Harry maintains an optimistic core. But it's not easy. He's not surprised to see everything good collapse under the *Party Regime*. He isn't even surprised the collapse occurred just as the world was turning into an era of great prosperity for more people of all backgrounds, ethnicities, and races. But like a red giant star it imploded, leaving a black hole where nothing can leave its gravitational pull into the dystopian void.

Harry is frustrated and tired. He wonders: How many times in history can this implosion of human worth bent on destruction happen? This is a rhetorical question he asks himself; he has a cynical answer as if he lived throughout all human history – like a man (yes, a man) of all ages. When frustrated and tired, Harry's optimism fades as he lapses into the despair expressed in this question. But his answer to the question is his way to turn back his frustration, reenergize back to action, and regain his optimism. His answer is: The question is irrelevant. Harry understands the challenge of survival is never ending. He figures when challenged with survival, you either respond with "do what it takes to survive," or you perish. In other words – *deal with it.*

Deal with it! always snaps him back to action and his optimism returns.

To *deal with it,* Harry believes you have to understand the "it." For Harry the "it" is always connected to the grand questions of life and cosmic relevance. His interest in these grand questions put him on a never-ending course to understand and articulate what he understands. It's why beyond becoming a civil engineer, he became a writer.

Early in life Harry developed a keen sense of historical context. While other kids his age were uninterested in history – thinking what does history have to do with today? – Harry always understood there is no "today" without yesterday – history. His understanding of the last half of the twentieth century informed and enlightened his worldview. He understood the post-World War II era ushered in a wave of prosperity complimenting the pent-up desire to reset an ethos of innocence and idealism that defined the Fifties in this nation. Harry was intrigued that despite the idyllic optimism of the Fifties there were dark elements lurking in the "landscape" of our ethos. The "communist scare" created a "boogie man" during that time, warning that prosperity and idealism can't be taken for granted. But as often happens, as Harry understands, our collective anxieties are fueled by hysteria. Hysteria itself is a "boogie man" that can be and will be used for political purposes.

Harry well understands the Kennedy assassination marked the beginning of the next era. The war in Viet Nam, the protest rallies against the war, the riots in the streets associated with racial injustice, the women's rights movement, and the cultural upheavals related to generational divisions defined the turbulent times of the Sixties and into the Seventies.

Popular music is the soundtrack of our times. Harry knows this "soundtrack" is a powerfully evocative stimulant for condensed ideas, ideologies, and sentiments. When he was growing up among the wide range of music his parents listened to and to which he was exposed included late Sixties and early Seventies protest music by Bob Dylan, Joan Baez, Pete Seeger, Richie Havens, and many others. They also listened to classic Motown music. Marvin Gaye was among these artists. When the world heard him ask by soulfully singing *What's going on?* it took its place in the soundtrack of that era. But it transcended its time becoming an anthem for all times, appealing to society to understand its troubles and fix them. Harry's parents exposed him to this song and its meaning in a troubled society – a troubled world. He thought the song posed the right question to maintain the reflection and action it takes to keep building a good society. The song haunted him back then as it does now!

Harry carries the words – the question – *What's going on?* in his head. He thinks *What's going on?* is as basic as it gets. "It's a good way to look at the grand questions of life," he told Penelope when she came upon him singing the words to himself. Knowing Harry's ongoing interest/obsession about the state of things in human existence and his talent for writing she told him to write an article and submit it for publication. He did just that. It appeared in a civil engineer trade journal. He titled it *What's Going On?* It was an unusual kind of article for that trade journal. But the editor was impressed with its relevance and insights; it was published for its reach and importance. The reader response was overwhelming approval. From there it hit the internet and found a cross-over audience; and in the "old age of information" before the *Party Regime* took over, Harry's article went viral.

The article had touched a nerve. Harry observed that people in society often if not always "lead lives of quiet desperation," as Henry David Thoreau had put it. One of the consequences of this "quiet desperation" is the not so quiet life-stopping "headlock" people get into with others or with society in general or with themselves for that matter. As such Harry thinks pausing to earnestly ask *What's going on?* is critical to getting our bearings and making better decisions for our lives. The article was for all times and for all "seasons." It was a grand perspective on who we are and why we are. The article provoked a lot to think about.

Because the article received so much interest Harry was interviewed and on panel discussions on TV, radio, podcasts, and internet live streams. He wrote more articles for various publications. Harry's articles and "discussion tour" resonated with a growing number of people. His writings and public discussions in media also brought harsh criticism and ridicule from a large influential political class adverse to his ideas.

This political class was to become the driver for the *Party Regime*. Harry doesn't mind challenges to his ideas. But he knows the *Awaken* and *Party Regime* have no interest in challenging ideas. They are only interested in eliminating any voice in slightest contradiction of *Awaken* and *Party Regime* doctrine. Their defense of their doctrine is to extinguish any discussion of ideas by labeling them "unsafe," "misinformation," or "dangerous." To this political class ideas outside their doctrine are blaspheme and deserve no forum.

What's Going On? was the article that brought Harry wide public recognition for his ideas. He sometimes cynically thinks it was the article that started all his troubles. The article begins with a preamble:

> As a civil engineer I have a duty to build with integrity on a foundation of integrity. Civil engineering is the ever-present awareness that what you build will affect everybody. The harm done to all of us in the false name of virtue is a rot on integrity and our individual souls. 2+2=4 no matter who you are or what group you declare you belong to. For the bridge to hold, for the engineer who builds it, and for the public who uses it, 2+2=4.
>
> The light of wisdom is our only way out of this rot. This article is written to be that kind of light. I hope you will read it. I hope it will speak to what matters to you.

* * *

The article and media activity that followed put Harry on a trajectory that adds to his obsession with the great questions of life. He calls this his *What's going on?* obsession. Fueled by this obsession he wrote *I Built It.* As Bob Burke would tell him a few years later, the book's publication attracted even more interest in Harry and his ideas.

Harry was conscientious about his civil engineering business but couldn't help spreading himself thin with his writing and interest in civil society and the wellness of the individual in civil society. He had always felt the goals and challenges of civil engineering were metaphorical to all of life's issues – like a building and a marriage. As a person "plugged into" a *What's going on?* tract of concern, Harry undertakes perpetual development in interdisciplinary expertise. It is as if he was becoming a sociologist, anthropologist, historian, political scientist, theologist, economist, philosopher, and psychologist – all in one.

* * *

Harry was invited to be a guest on a popular podcast to talk about his articles. He felt trepidation about stepping out too far with his persona and ideas. It was risky. But he reasoned it was an opportunity to further define and clarify his appeal to sensibility. He knew it would draw a lot of attention. After all that was the point of his writing.

"So welcome dear listeners to the *Eric Blair Show*. Today our guest is Harry Archer. Harry is… Harry, how would you describe yourself?"

"Gee, Eric, I was looking forward to hearing you introduce me. I was curious to hear how you would 'package' me to your listeners."

"You're right, Harry, sorry about that. Listeners, my guest today is Harry Archer, Harry is a world-class wise-ass!"

"Thank you, Eric, that's much better. That's a perfect description. And much appreciated."

"Harry, really though, you've been making a splash since you wrote that article *What's Going On?* and there's your book *I Built It.* Give the listeners an overview."

Harry was thrown a bit. He didn't expect Eric to mention his banned book. Although before it was banned it was a top seller. A lot of the public already knew about it. He thought it's like a genie that can't be put back in the bottle. No matter the *Party Regime's* lust for book burning, Harry's book is still out there "subverting the way."

"Yeah, Eric… yeah… ya know I don't mean to come off goofy, but I have a tendency when starting to explain big ideas to fumble my words before I zero in and sharpen my explanation to a *single unifying theory.* I like core principles that are descriptive and applicable to all things."

"What the hell does that mean, Harry?"

"Right… let me try that again. Let's start with the *What's going on?* thing. It's the 'light bulb' that goes off in your head when you *get it.* Eric, how often do you see people around you *get it?*"

"Never!"

"Right! If there was a button you could push that would have people *get it*, would you push that button?"

"I would push it and never let up on it!"

"Right… that's the point of caring about and asking *What's going on?* So, we can *get it!* Let me say more. We're all frustrated and alienated. We are distressed by dysfunction, disease, and failure. If your car has a mechanical breakdown you have to figure out what's causing the breakdown. If you have a physiological problem, you have to find out what's causing it. If your business is failing, you need to identify the causes of the failure. It's pretty basic. Dysfunction, disease, and failure of things vital to us such as your car for transportation, your physical wellness, your mental wellness, your business stability, and so much more, requires good diagnostics. You need to know *what's going on*."

"Well, yeah, Harry, that's obvious. But why don't we do what's so obvious?"

"Good question, Eric. If it's obvious that good diagnostics will lead to solving all the problems that matter, why aren't good diagnostics used by everybody?"

"Is there a 'thought' echo in here? That's what I'm asking."

"Echo or not it's still a good question. The answer is because not everybody wants to solve the problems. There are groups or sectors or political interests that depend on problems for their existence. For their cause they will even make up fake problems."

"Yeah, that's ridiculously true."

"You see that, don't you? Understanding that, is understanding *what's going on* as I just said as an answer not a question. That's part of *what's going on.* Not everyone wants to solve vital problems. Those factions that rant they want to solve non-problems – fake problems – are making more problems, making the whole mess worse.

"Harry, what was that *single unifying theory* thing you mentioned? What's that about?"

"For me, Eric, it's my 'go to' when the world is squeezing me on all sides. There's lots of *single unifying theories.* Gravity is one – physical or metaphorical – 'gravity happens.' Another one is *The Golden Rule* – treat people the way you want to be treated. Can you imagine, Eric, if the world problems, community problems, personal problems were more often met with sound *single unifying theories?"*

"Fewer problems… better life for more people?"

"You think?"

"Yes, I *do* think."

"Well, you're right, Eric. But I have a disclaimer."

"Uh-oh."

"The troublesome/tricky part of the 'question' of *What's going on?* is the 'answer' to *What's going on?* The answer is subject to both rational, well value-based formulations as well as irrational, ill valued-based formulations. Which puts us right back where we started – *tribalistic dysfunction.*"

"Wow, Harry, that's a great term. I never heard it before. Who came up with that?"

"I just now made it up.

"So, you just reduced things… hey, like a *single unifying theory*, to *tribalistic dysfunction*."

"Eric, you're getting good at this. The disclaimer about *single unifying theories* as related to *What's going on?* really means what's *really* going on? And that's where people retreat to their 'tribes.' What's touted as real in one tribe is fake in another tribe. To be sure all tribes are subject to influences that are real and fake. Going the fake way is the result of any or all of the following: naiveté, ignorance, corruption, prejudice, projection, stupidity, poor judgment, poor values, and other weaknesses."

"Sounds hopeless."

"In some ways, it is. But there's a way to get to the 'real' answer to what's *really* going on. It's not enough to declare *What's going on* as an answer. Given all the influencers – good and bad – to which we are all subject, puts us at variable risk for good or bad results."

"Harry, I'm waiting to hear the way to get to reality."

"You have to wade through all of it – the bad and the good, the good and the bad. That only comes from *free thought* and *free speech*. Any restriction of either, anywhere in society, is the beginning of the end. I'm not talking about obscenity standards. That's a different thing. But even with obscenity that can be a slippery slope to include political ideas you don't like."

"So, the way to what's real, and hopefully betterment, is *free thought* and *free speech*."

"Yep, *free thought* and *free speech*."

"Okay, folks. I hope what Harry said got through to you. That's why I had him on. He says things in a way you don't often hear to make the best sense of the world around you. We kidded around a little bit, but that doesn't take away how serious Harry's message is. We're going to have him back. So, just remember, always ask *What's going on?* See you tomorrow!"

* * *

After other public appearances and publications, Harry gains a cult following. This creates some benefits and drawbacks. On the one hand his writings and speaking appearances are touching a nerve. He is resonating with people frustrated with the incompetence, stupidity, and character persecutions happening in society and culture – hijacked and appropriated by the "false god of politics," as Harry puts it. On the other hand, the voices and activities of "wackos" who identify – rightly or wrongly – with the perspectives Harry espouses, muddy the messaging "waters" he is navigating through with their over-the-top noise.

The way Harry deals with this "fly in the ointment" is to do nothing about it. He doesn't worry about it. After all, he is consistent in supporting the "wackos'" *free thought* and *free speech* as he does for everyone.

There is, however, a new disquieting effect taking hold. With all this attention, exposure, and activity Harry now regularly experiences twinges of fear he hadn't known before. He feels paranoia about the dark forces of political enemies who stop at nothing to destroy those in opposition. And opposition is any person or group that isn't pro *Party Regime*. When he gets bouts of fear Harry forces himself to shake it off.

TWO

IT'S THE MIDDLE OF THE MORNING. HARRY IS IN BOB Burke's office, sitting across from Bob, who is sitting behind his desk. Harry is dressed in his usual casual wear – khakis and a black polo shirt. Bob's wearing what he always wears – dress shirt, slacks, no tie.

"The *Ministry* likes your work," Bob says with an air of satisfaction and self-credit.

"Thank you?" Harry's facial expression betrays some cynicism.

"Ha… always suspicious."

"Not suspicious. Just careful."

Bob is in the mood to banter. "Same thing." In an attempt to be reassuring, Bob says, "You don't have to be careful with me, Harry. I know you're a good guy. And I mean it. The *Ministry* likes your work… and I like it too. We're lucky to have you."

"That's what concerns me. The obvious irony of it."

"Look… isn't that what life's about? Exploiting each other so long as each gets what they want out of the deal."

"Bob, are you getting what you want out of the 'deal?'" Harry does a one-handed air quote with his right hand, punctuating the word "deal."

"Gosh, Harry, I didn't know you cared about me."

Harry is anxious that the rest of the conversation might get seriously serious. But as usual he does not betray his anxiousness with any kind of facial expression or body language. Harry's thoughts are mixed with two competing impulses: 1) to bond with Bob out of some sense that good sense could be shared with anybody if you just handle it well; and 2) don't trust anybody, particularly someone who appears approachable. "Bob… I do care about you," he says.

"Harry, you're making me feel like Claude Rains when Bogart says, 'Louis, I think this is the beginning of a beautiful friendship.' You know, it's the last line in *Casablanca*, as Rains and Bogart walk off together on the wet tarmac in the night fog. Like lovers."

"Yeah, Rains and Bogart." Harry pauses, then says, "You know in *Casablanca* they had a 'respectful-but-don't-cross-me' kind of relationship – which was tested throughout the movie. That last scene finds them on the same side of the 'cause.'" Harry is beginning to feel at ease and bolder through this *Casablanca* referential/analogous/vehicle discussion. He feels he can both hide and still be transparent with this device.

"Harry, I always thought we are on the same side."

Harry snaps back to anxiousness. He is mentally exhausted. He can't keep ping-ponging his thoughts and feelings. He thinks it's too late to stay in protection mode, but who am I kidding? I'm already out. The *Party Regime* knows me. And Bob is right. I'm just being exploited. Harry thinks this isn't "hide and seek." This is a "chess match." All my moves are out in the open. Everyone can see what I'm doing. Everyone knows I'm playing to win. But can they see how many steps ahead I can see? Can I see how many steps ahead my opponent – the *Party Regime* – can see? Harry wonders: Can I "play chess" well enough to win the match?

Harry makes his next "chess" move. "We are on the same side, Bob. That's always been my position. That's what I write about."

II

On the bus back to his apartment, Harry reflects on the game of chess. He is prone to bumping into a subject or idea that intrigues him, then thoughtfully exploring it for meaning and connections not typically made. Or very typically made but underappreciated.

From now on chess is a part of Harry's intellectual quarry.

The game has been around for centuries. But Harry doesn't know where it originated. When he gets home, he goes on the internet to find out.

The internet was the "Wild West" before the *Party Regime* took power. To be sure the "old internet" was rife with misinformation, vulgarity, and cruelty. Too much of the old internet was not a place for children, the weak of heart, or the weak of mind. Despite the disreputable and reprehensible content throughout the "old internet," it was still an invaluable source of readily available credible information invaluable to any legitimate research. The internet is a miraculous achievement hard to get your mind around. Ironically, the internet makes available the infinite wealth of information and knowledge or restricts information and knowledge out of relevance and existence. So, under the power of the *Party Regime* with *the Big Tech Three* pulling the strings, the internet created profound restrictions. Now vastly disproportionate to the universe of information – only a minute amount of all the information is allowed. *Awakenpedia.state* is the state approved general information website. For research and information, it is mostly useless and completely propagandistic. But on some topics, Harry can tease through it to get what he needs. Right now, the topic of chess is his mission.

The game of chess is a representational exercise in the elements necessary to defeat an opponent. On the chessboard neither player has an advantage at the start of the game. The only advantage a player may have is their wits. To win the game, a player needs to think about the board, the pieces, the variety and limitations of moves, offense, defense, and potential moves in advance of any current board positions. The game is multidimensional. Mathematics, psychology, timing, and patience are key components in playing to win.

Although a simplified representation, the game is also metaphorical of life's challenges. Chess is an affirmation that our greatest asset in survival and surviving well is the best use of our intellect. Foresight, an appreciation of consequences, calculating risks, cost/reward analysis are some of the intellectual muscles developed and used in playing chess that also have value in life.

Harry learns that according to *Awakenpedia*, the origins of chess are a bit uncertain but there is reason to credit India, Persia, Central Asia, and China with its beginning in the early Seventh Century. The oldest known chess rulebook was written in Arabic around 840 AD.

Harry is genuinely interested in learning more about the place in culture and history chess occupies. But he becomes dismayed as he reads further into the internet article. As restrictive as the website is, he doesn't expect *Awakenpedia's* fact alterations on this topic. The chess pieces called king and queen throughout history are changed: "king" is now called "ruler," "queen" is called "vice ruler." A notation reference provides a vague explanation. The notation reads: Male and female references are considered insensitive and inappropriate. *In compliance with approved societal standards the names of chess pieces have no gender identification.*

Harry feels the way Charlton Heston's character astronaut George Taylor felt at the end of *Planet of the Apes*. Taylor comes upon the half-buried Statue of Liberty and realizes he was on Earth all the time, that humans self-destructed. He falls to his knees and yells his outrage, "You finally really did it. You maniacs! You blew it up! Damn you! Goddamn you all to hell!" Harry wonders if the Statue of Liberty in the movie also symbolizes the destruction of freedom as part of the apocalypse on Earth eons ago. Harry sees this is happening today.

Harry reads the notation again: *In compliance with approved societal standards the names of chess pieces have no gender identification.* Now his response is visceral as he thinks – You just couldn't leave chess alone. You had to do it… You finally really did it. You maniacs! You blew it up! Damn you! Goddamn you all to hell!

Harry's cell phone vibrates on the table next to his state-issued laptop. The screen shows it's Daisy. He taps the phone icon talk circle on the touch screen. His mood switches from a distraught *damn you, goddamn you all to hell,* to a cheerful, "Hey, Daze!"

"Hi, Dad. How you doin'?"

"Never better."

Harry is painfully aware that otherwise welcomed – or at worst tolerated – relationships are breaking apart in the cultural/political tension-filled climate of the times. He calls this phenomenon which is reflected in and perpetuated by politics and the political wars for power: *the crisis of the unbridgeable divide that severs human relationships.* He thinks it's tragic, disturbing, dangerous, and wholly unnecessary.

Harry is given to reflect on the best of something and/or the worst of something. He often thinks the worst thing about the *Party Regime* take over establishing a totalitarian state demarking the era of the *Great Awakening* is that it was a factor in creating *the crisis of the unbridgeable divide that severs human relationships* which it continuously nourishes. That the *Party Regime* calls for *unity* while promoting this crisis is definitionally impossible and absurd.

Harry laments the loss of relationships that would otherwise be intact if it weren't for politics and political differences. But the ironic thing to Harry is, it isn't the politics where the divide rests. It's the projecting of values onto another person without fairly understanding the person that causes the divide. It's notable to Harry the phenomenon of this crisis mirrors the ill effects of censoring *free thought* and *free speech* in society. The "unbridgeable divide" happens when people refuse to talk with those they disagree with. And in their refusal to listen, hear, and try to understand a person they think they disagree with; they *vanish* that person. Again, for Harry the ills to society and likewise interpersonal relationships come down to cutting off *free thought* and *free speech*.

* * *

Harry sits at his unapproved laptop and uses an unapproved email account to email his friend Tom Bright. Tom is passionate about his brand of politics, which like most of Harry's friends differs from Harry's.

Despite their political differences, Harry and his sphere of friends somehow manage respectful discussions. Underlying the discussions are the to-date useless attempts by each other to change minds. Harry never "pushes" a point. Rather, he tries to find the inside track to any given issue where no controversy exists. He's not always successful in getting a stipulation of no controversy. But he does pull it off a fair amount, often getting a "you have a good point, Harry."

Tom regularly texts and emails Harry newspaper and magazine articles as well as internet videos that are approved by the *Party Regime*. Harry doesn't mind getting Tom's texts and emails. Given the present state of society, the current power structure, and the extreme political climate, he is more than aware of the differences he has with his friends. Tom's texts and emails keep him in touch with their ongoing divide. It also never ceases to provide more insights. It helps Harry stay up on *what's going on*.

Harry emails Tom:

Hey Tom,

Hope you and the family are well. Since I've been working for the *Party Regime* (I know, go figure) I was thinking about the slogan – the credo:

DEATH IS LIFE

OPPRESSION IS LIBERTY

WEAKNESS IS STRENGTH

It's about as crazy making as it gets. Which it's intended to be – make you insensible and crazy. Then normalize the insensible by recalibrating reality. By intimidation and repetition of disempowering, dehumanizing principles, you get a new breed – a new generation – of PODs to serve the *Party Regime*. It's like that old movie *Crazy Making* where the sinister husband wants to make his wife go crazy by rearranging the furniture in their living room and telling her nothing is changed when she notices and tells him the furniture's been moved around.

I know everybody who talks politics these days uses the term "*crazy making*" that originated from that old movie to trash their political opponents. I just like referencing the "furniture thing." I know it's a cruel thing to do to the wife. But if the wife had a shred of what the psychologists call *ego strength*, she would have told the husband, "I know what you're doing. Knock it off! And oh, you can get rid of that ugly sofa your mother got us. I never liked it!"

Which gets me to the people – the PODs. If they would tap into any amount of *ego strength*, they would tell the *Awaken* and the *Party Regime*, "Knock it off! Stop treating people like soulless objects! And oh, you can get rid of that stupid credo you mother-effers came up with. We don't like it!"

* * *

After finishing the email, Harry rereads it. He whispers to himself, "Too risky." He deletes it.

IV

"Stupidity." That's Harry's answer to his good friend Rick Morrow when Rick asks Harry what he has against the *Awaken.* Rick does consulting work for the *Department of Transportation.* The *Party Regime* renamed the *Transportation Department* the *Ministry of Movement.* Harry calls it the "Ministry of Stoppage." But he doesn't say that to Rick.

It's Saturday morning. Harry didn't shave; he's showing the stubble that Penelope dislikes. He's in his usual casual clothes – actually more casual than usual, he's wearing the same clothes he wore the day before. Rick's in old jeans and a ragged T-shirt. He didn't shave either. They make for a slobbish pair hanging out in Rick's garage.

"Rick, it's not hard to understand my thinking about the *Awaken.* They're stupid. Their ideas are stupid. Their causes are stupid. Anyone who buys into what they stand for, they're stupid too. And they're not just stupid, they're destructive."

Rick responds, "Whatever you call them – the *Awaken,* 'the virtuous'... the whatever – to me it's just them making noise." He glares at the Rolex he wears on his right wrist.

"Say that to the guy who loses his job because of *Awaken* 'noise,'" replies Harry. "The guy about who the *Awaken* 'police' dig something up on – like something he posted on social media when he was thirteen. After apologizing – usually for something he shouldn't have to apologize for – he gets fired anyway. He gets fired from a job where he's done really well for the company, or for the institution, for whatever." Harry goes on to ask Rick a rhetorical question: "Which is more powerful – culture or government?" Harry doesn't wait for Rick to answer. "Culture… culture drives society. The *Awaken* are smart enough to know that… that culture drives everything. With their hold on culture, the *Awaken* are smart enough to drive stupid ideas."

"Go on."

"Tensions in society are not really political. Politics are just the tools of cultural causes. The cause could be good or horrible. Slavery as an example of horrible was a part of the culture as it has been throughout history and in all cultures. This nation had a war over it, which had never happened over the issue of slavery, other than periodic slave rebellions. What was it about this nation that our ancestors went to war over slavery? In the most real sense, the conflict over slavery was a *culture war*. Just like today. What we're going through is a *culture war*, Rick"

Rick checks his watch again.

"You have to be somewhere, Rick?"

"No, I'm fine. Go on."

"You sure?"

"Yeah, go on."

"Okay, well, what I'm getting at, Rick, is the *Awaken* have been waging war on the culture and the culture doesn't know it… well, not enough people in the culture know it who are willing to get into the war and fight back. It's like my daughter Daisy told me not long ago – too many people are complacent… too complacent for our own good. It's a serious problem threatening our very existence. The *Awaken* are already having the effect where it's like the frog in a pot of water that's slowly being heated. The frog doesn't notice the water's getting hotter. By the time the water reaches boiling it's too late for the frog. He's – it's a boy frog – he's cooked."

"Hmm."

"We're all frogs in a pot of water being slowly heated. We're about to be cooked and too many of us don't feel it, or should I say see it. The weapon *against* the culture so *Awaken* can *be* the culture is stupidity. Yep… stupidity is both the vulnerability and the weapon. If the *Awaken* can exploit our stupidity and functionalize it as the default collective mindset, we're cooked. A good example is the *Party Regime's* establishment of the *Ministry of Diversity*… Sheer stupidity."

Harry continues, "The *Awaken* – that's how we lost *Mr. Potato Head!*"

Rick's attention is suddenly gripped. Harry mentioning *"Mr. Potato Head"* touches a nerve with him, "Harry, you're right. I heard about *them* getting rid of *Mr. Potato Head.* I grew up with him. *He's* Great! Ya' know, I always like talkin' with you, Harry. You're a good 'dot-connector.' Until you said it, I didn't see the connection between the *Awaken* and *vanishing Mr. Potato Head.* I love *Mr. Potato Head. He's got a friend in me.* If anyone tries to take him away, they gotta answer to me."

"Good to know, Rick, where you draw your line – *Mr. Potato Head*... Just make sure you draw your line in a place where it's not too late and you get cooked."

* * *

After his talk with Rick, Harry continues thinking about stupidity. He thinks most everything – not everything, but most everything – government does is stupid.

Then Harry thinks about how the founders of the nation understood this about government. It's why the founding documents are basically restrictions on government. It's remarkable to Harry how people fail to grasp that the benefits and power of decisions rest with people as individuals, not with government as an institution. He reaffirms the wisdom of the nation's founding principles in his mind – the government isn't in charge of your religion! The government isn't in charge of your thinking or your philosophy or your values! The logic is clear to Harry – that's because inevitably the government is stupid on those matters and all other matters. The founding principle of the nation is based on the individual's unalienable rights – the only thing the government is charged to protect. Harry knows anything else the government ventures into is bound to get stupid quickly, that no matter what party is in power, stupidity will reign. But he also knows it still matters what party prevails in an election cycle. He always worries the wrong party for unalienable rights will devastate the reach of humanity while that ill-suited party holds power – as is the case with the *Party Regime*. Less is more. A constrained government is a less stupid government Harry says to himself.

V

Harry calls the ideas and subjects rattling around in his head "his little troublemakers." Having "little troublemakers" in your head would otherwise be an indication of hallucinatory mental disturbance. But for Harry this isn't mental disturbance. It's an amusing and creative way to perpetually sort things out. He likes to personify things, even ideas and thoughts. It's not enough for Harry to just think to himself that he holds ideas and thoughts in his head like anyone else. By personifying them it helps him confront the soundness of his thinking. By calling them "troublemakers" it helps him to respect there will be trouble if his thinking isn't sound.

He treats his little troublemakers the way enablers treat alcoholics and drug addicts. He gives them free rein to roam in his head and do what they want. Harry does, though, have one requirement of his little troublemakers. He requires them to explain themselves persuasively, as if to make a case for their existence to someone who doesn't believe in them. His little troublemakers well know Harry sits in judgment of them, that he loves them conditionally. If they want to take up space in his head, they have to earn it. Harry is reasonable though. He does have many little troublemakers – probably most – that are a perpetual work in progress. So, as long as a little troublemaker works hard at their craft, they are welcome in Harry's head.

Of course, Harry has contempt for the idea of "thought police," which the *Think Right Program* was established to be. When he pushes his contempt for the *Think Right Program* aside, Harry is amused with the absurdity of it. He has a hard time imagining what the "police" can enforce in his head. To try and enforce what is in his head or anybody's head is like trying to herd cats. If the "police" encounter any of his little troublemakers, they might qualify for hazard pay.

Sometimes, to relieve the tension of a particularly noisy little troublemaker, Harry lets it play outside of his head and mingle with another person. Today, Harry is letting "truth" come out and play with Bob Burke.

It's a bright warm day. Bob is taking a break from the office and asked Harry to join him. They are outside, taking a walk in the city plaza near the ministry office. Both have on sunglasses. Bob's wearing a tan baseball cap.

Harry asks Bob, "Do you believe in truth?"

"What kind of question is that?"

"You find the question odd?"

"I find that you and I are asking each other questions that we're not answering."

"Well, that's because we're both trying to get our bearings on a straight-forward/not-so-straight forward thing – truth."

"Help us get our bearings, Harry. Say more."

"Well, with the way things are… you know, the whole thing, a person who is naturally curious about… this thing…"

Bob cuts Harry off. "This thing? Could you be more vague?"

Harry shoots back, "Really, you think I'm vague?"

Now it's like a ping pong rally as Bob slams back, "Again with the questions."

"Look, Bob, if you hold your breath long enough, you're going to have to gasp for air at some point. It's the same with truth. If you believe in truth and you're cut off from it long enough, you reach a point where you gasp for truth. Like air, you need it, or you die."

"Yeah?"

"So, do you believe in truth?" Not hearing an answer, Harry then asks, "Bob, are you in jeopardy of dying due to truth deprivation?"

"If you put it that way, I'm not sure. What's truth?"

"Ah… you are in jeopardy. You're not being truthful by pretending not to know what truth is."

"So… how do you know what's true?"

"Now that's a different question using an adjective form of the noun 'truth.'"

Bob's sunglasses conceal his eyes rolling but not his lips tightening. He's impatient but interested as he says, "Go on."

"Okay… the way you know what's *truth* is, you start with believing in *Truth*. You believe *Truth* has a rarified value in human interaction and worldly understanding. You then factor in something of equal value to *Truth*. And that is – *that which matters*. You need to know, or want to know, what matters. And the way you know what matters is through *wisdom*."

Bob halts his walk and Harry stops with him. They each stand looking at the other's sunglasses through their own sunglasses. Confirming Harry's verbal treatise on Truth, Bob asks, "That's it? You believe in *Truth,* and you factor in *what matters* which you understand from *wisdom.*"

Harry responds, "That's it."

They start walking again. Then Bob says, "You know you're right. *Your* description of *Truth* doesn't come at you like a mandated doctrine of self-serving dogma. It's more like an appeal to the value of *Truth* if you have the wisdom to recognize it. But you left off at *wisdom.*"

"Glad you noticed, friend." Harry says "friend" without a thought before he says it. But he thinks about it after it comes out of his mouth. He thinks whether or not it's prudent/dangerous to say the word "friend." He craves the warmth friendship gives to be himself. He craves the discussion he's having with Bob, whether or not he is being foolish to have the discussion at all.

Nevertheless, Harry continues. "Wisdom is truly the key. And it's hard enough for an individual to be wise let alone the collective of a community, a nation, or the collective of all humankind to be wise. So, Bob, if you think of a person and parable about wisdom who comes to mind?"

"King Solomon?"

"Good job, my man!" Harry has a bounce in his speech now. He went from "friend" to "my man." He feels at ease, slightly joyful, and free. "Yes, good old King Solomon," he says. "We know his wisdom from the story where he sits in judgment of a child custody matter. It's a great story, rich with profound meaning. But the back story about Solomon's values identifies why he's *wise*. Solomon asks God for wisdom. And because it's a good ask, with no corruption or self-interest, God gives wisdom to Solomon. But I think he's wise by virtue of his value of it – wisdom. Which in a spiritual way is the same as God granting wisdom to Solomon.

"Getting back to the story of Solomon and his decision regarding a dispute between two women over a baby. Each woman claims to be the baby's rightful mother. There are variations of the story. But I'll tell it this way: Tragically, one of the women, while sleeping side by side with her infant child, accidentally rolls over onto the child, smothering the infant to death. In the mother's grief she steals a healthy baby from another mother. Of course, this is a terrible trauma and horrible situation that finds its way to King Solomon's court. Solomon hears each woman emotionally plead her case of being the true mother of the baby. Whoever Solomon is inclined to believe, his decision is to cut the baby in half! If you think about it, it's barbaric but brilliant. A half baby… I should say a *dead* half baby to each woman is useless, ridiculous, and murderously immoral. But Solomon is wise enough to understand sometimes we need to be confronted with the consequences of atrocity to appreciate what matters. With great anguish, one woman speaks out that the other woman is the true mother. 'Please, lord… please don't kill the child!'

Solomon then knows the woman begging to spare the baby's life no matter if she can no longer be the mother in the child's life, is the true mother. Solomon orders the baby returned to this woman – the rightful mother."

Bob is staring down at his shoes. Then he looks up at Harry and says, "Of course, I know the story. But the way you told it still had me transfixed. I was relieved to hear the outcome and I'm comforted by the moral it teaches."

Harry boldly changes the mood, pointing to the so-called elephant in the room to say out loud but in an intense whisper, "Yeah, this bullshit that's going on… this war on thought… this war on wisdom is going to get us all killed!"

"What can we do about it?" Bob asks sheepishly, with a sense of resignation.

In a steady slow point-by-point rhythm and confident tone, Harry answers, "Bob… we're doing it. We're doing it now. We're talking. Now that we're talking out loud, let's have some *Truth* in it. Let's focus on what matters. And let's not forget wisdom."

* * *

After being with Bob, Harry comes back to the apartment. He sees Penelope in the kitchen, her back to him, unaware of his presence. The Alexa device in the living room is playing a cover of Neil Young's *Harvest Moon*, performed by The Brothers Comatose & AJ Lee: ♪ ♫ ♩… The lyrics speak of the special love that two people have for each other.

Penelope is swaying back and forth lost in the romance of the song. Harry walks quietly toward her and gently puts the palm of his hand on her waist. Smiling, Penelope turns into her husband's embrace. They are slow dancing in the middle of the kitchen, in the middle of a workday, to the song *Harvest Moon*. To them all that matters is each other. The world can go… The music plays on hypnotically: ♪ ♫ ♩… The lyrics are sweet and mellow…

As they move to the music Harry and Penelope are in a trance. Abruptly and harshly the words "***There is nothing you can do without us knowing about it!***" replace the song. As occurs every thirty minutes on state-controlled broadcasts for all content, there is a two-minute public service message selected among the usual credos from the *Party Regime*. At this moment, the soft music is interrupted by the stern male voice saying over and over:

There is nothing you can do without us knowing about it!
There is nothing you can do without us knowing about it!
There is nothing you can do without us knowing about it!
There is nothing you can do without us knowing about it!
There is nothing you can do without us knowing about it!
There is nothing you can do without us knowing about it!
***There is nothing you can do without us knowing about it!*…**

As the spoken message "barks" and drones on, Harry and Penelope continue dancing at the same rhythm and pace in each other's arms. They are together with each other, free of any worldly distraction. All they hear is the sweet music of:

♪ ♫ *The love they have for each other* ♪ ♫

VI

The movement of the *Party Regime* existed long before former President Danny Tripp became a political figure. But his election to the Presidency caused alarmed disbelief by the *Party Regime*. It ignited their resolve to make its move as the singular power controlling governance, education, media, and thought. Its control was to be absolute. Any challenge to its righteousness and authority was an act of societal and moral blaspheme. Anyone violating or suspected of violating the authority and rules of the *Party Regime* would be *vanished.*

Despite the absolute authority of the *Party Regime,* it does not control technology – *The Big Tech Three*. If anything, *the Big Tech Three* control the *Party Regime*. But for their respective interests, the *Party Regime* and *the Big Tech Three* have a symbiotic relationship. Each does the other's bidding.

The election of Danny Tripp presented a onetime historical opportunity for the *Party Regime* to mobilize every political, bureaucratic, oligarchic, media-dominant, academic-institutional resource to counter the Tripp doctrine – *Let's Be Great Today* – and defeat Tripp's re-election to the presidency. The *Party Regime,* with every social influencer under its control, challenged, ridiculed, and condemned everything said and done by Tripp, the Tripp administration, and his supporters. Things the Tripp administration did that were objectively good and positive were particularly savaged by the *Party Regime* because it happened under Tripp's leadership. Tripp had to be denied credit for any successes.

Tripp's popularity grew despite – and in some ways because of – the relentless negative campaign against Tripp. The more popular he became the more intense the political attacks were. To the point Tripp was impeached not once but twice.

With Jim Biddle replacing Danny Tripp as president, the *Party Regime* went into overdrive to "fundamentally transform this nation," as Bennet Oberton had said was the objective when he campaigned for the presidency in 2008.

The *Party Regime*, by way of single party control of the legislative branch, put forward the *Reimagined Election Act*. Under the guise of rectifying unjust voter suppression, the *Reimagined Election Act* allows the *Party Regime* to control election outcomes, making their control of governance permanent unless enough people organize a revolt against it. Given the state of disinformation, public complacency, and support for the *Party Regime*, a revolt of that sort is a longshot. The tyrannical governance and control by the *Party Regime* are, however, causing more people to take notice that life under the doctrines of the *Party Regime* is not what people bargained for, particularly as quality-of-life declines.

Together, the *Party Regime* and the *Awaken* make voter suppression a "hot button" issue behind the "curtain" of bureaucracy. To be sure, real suppression of voters has an ugly history of racism and racist politics. The Ku Klux Klan and other racial supremacist groups and sympathizers actively, viciously, and murderously prevented minority groups, particularly of African descent, from voting let alone living normally, un-harassed and un-persecuted in the community.

Harry's friend Chuck Stephens is a history professor of whom Harry often asks all sorts of questions. Chuck's expertise is in medieval Asian history. But Professor Chuck is nonetheless well-equipped in his knowledge of Western civilization. He currently teaches at a YALI in another state. Chuck is a smart guy who doesn't like the YALI system. He doesn't like being an unemployed professor either. So, Chuck does what he can in a bad system to survive teaching his students as best he can. He's careful but teaches in a way that gives his students a chance at understanding *what's going on.*

Harry remembers having a conversation with Chuck about the origins of voting in the history of the world – the kind of voting where common citizen-types of people voted. While voting can be traced to ancient Athens and may have existed long before on a small scale in one form or another in known and unknown tribes, Chuck made it clear that citizen voting – voting by the people – is a rare and restricted event throughout history.

Harry goes to make notes on his illegal laptop. Waiting for the aged device to boot up he reflects on the constitutional founding of this nation. Voting was established as the great revolutionary equalizer not equally allowed to the people of the nation. Harry thinks – just when you have a breakthrough idea for suffrage in self-governance it's not a breakthrough for everybody. Some privileged structure – just or unjust – plays a part in voting rights and practices. Harry reflects: good ideas – such as voting – are not perfect ideas. Whether or not voting administration and practices are rightly carried out, voting – one person/one vote had remained among the most sacred of foundational principles in this Republic. Voting therefore is both a reinforcement for democracy if voter integrity is maintained as well as a vulnerable target for corruption if voter integrity fails.

Chuck had explained, "For political advantage and what I call 'power-gain voting,' political opponents – enemies – go into mortal combat over the vote. That is, political opponents are in an endless fight about voting law and voting procedures." The laptop ready, Harry starts writing notes:

> The endless fight over voting laws and procedures is where the term *voter suppression* is repurposed for today's political/culture war waged by the *Awaken* – to paint their political opponents as *racists*. If the stench of *racism* sticks to their opponents and those who side with their opponents, their opponents and supporters lose.
>
> Motor voter; same day registration/voting; early voting; voting with no ID required; month-long voting; failing to clear voter rolls of deceased or those who moved out of a voting district; voting rights extended to convicted felons serving time in prison; ballot harvesting; lack of bipartisan oversight at polling precincts and counting centers; mail-in voting; how counting machines are calibrated; conduct at polling precincts; lowering the voting minimum age; and lack of bipartisan oversight to prevent any imaginable fraud are all continuous moving

targets in the voting rights lexicon in which political warriors engage. If any of these things are questioned or challenged as a problem to voter integrity, the *Awaken*, backed by the *Party Regime*, charges the question or challenge as racist and *voter suppression*, which are meant to be synonymous.

Harry pauses his writing. He thinks it's interesting that as far as he is aware mental illness issues such as psychosis never come up as a voting rights issue. He thinks having good sensibilities[3] unaffected by mental illness problems, including the delusions that occur with otherwise mentally stable people, is essential to personal decision making as well as decisions made affecting the public, such as voting in civil elections. He isn't sure how this issue should be dealt with. So far, the issue seems to be ignored.

Harry continues writing:

Other than mental illness issues, all the other pieces of voter accommodations are the battle grounds for the fights where the outcomes will determine the integrity of voting results. Failure of voter integrity is a form of anarchy. If a totalitarian regime assumes power where the general electorate has no confidence in the electoral legitimacy of that regime, the decline of democracy in

[3] Sensibilities – The way you think and how you are affected by complex matters. The way you think is an aggregate of logic, perspective, values, emotions, awareness, and relevance.

that regime is inevitable. But democracy doesn't matter when the totalitarian regime makes a run to destroy the Republic. The stakes are always high *every* election cycle. About elections, in the words of Joseph Stalin: ***"It is enough that the people know there was an election. The people who cast the votes decide nothing. The people who count the votes decide everything."***

* * *

The political climate during the Tripp administration and now continuing through the Biddle administration is on fire. There has been no bridge, or as Biddle calls it, "unity," to make the nation cohesive enough – to bridge the differences – to put out the flames of destruction. As Harry sees it, the thoughts, the speech, and the people – the pool of brain trust – to build the bridge are being *vanished* by the *Awaken,* the *Party Regime,* and *the Big Tech Three*, which Harry calls *the Trinity*. His use of the word "trinity" is purposeful, as it is associated with religious meaning. Such meaning underscores the "faithful" adherence people can have to an ideological infrastructure which includes political parties.

Harry came to understand the downside of political parties the way George Washington disfavored them when he read a few histories on the first president's life and times. *The ultimate purpose of a party is power*. This presents an intractable conundrum. Power and authority must be had to govern a society. But power as its own end, which is what parties fight for, is blind to what matters and what is good in the governing of a society.

As such, parties are essentially religions. Political parties are religions the whole of the citizenry doesn't buy into. It's the reason there is no state religion in this constitutional Republic. Parties, however, can easily go off the rails and impose themselves on the Republic as the state religion. This is what *the Trinity* has done. This is what Harry not only stands against but works against.

A *vanish culture* to eliminate voices against *the Trinity's* "religion" has been inflicted on society and culture by *the Trinity* itself. They are now the power. To round out their "theology," *the Trinity* adopted Danny Tripp as their "devil," their "Antichrist." Tripp serves an essential role to personify the evil from whom *the Trinity* protects humanity. Danny Tripp is a businessman with vast real estate holdings. Not of his choosing, Tripp also holds a huge amount of real estate in the heads of *the Trinity* "bosses" and their adherents. They are incapable of moving on without keeping Tripp in their sights for complete humiliation and character annihilation. Tripp and anyone supporting him or anything about him must be stamped out – *vanished.*

One of Tripp's talents is messaging. This is evident as he brings his doctrine and signature slogan together. *Let's Be Great Today* messages on so many levels. Harry is amused by the "coded" meaning in one level: Tripp is constantly and wrongly accused by his political enemies as being homophobic and against people who identify on specific parts of the "gender and lifestyle spectrum." He refutes the charge by supporting lesbians, bisexuals, gays, and transgenders as all people who have a right to the greatness of *life, liberty, and the pursuit of happiness*. The initials of *Let's Be Great Today* also stand for Lesbian, Bisexual, Gay, and Transgender – LGBT.

In his messaging, Tripp often playfully "winks" at a public smart enough to see what he cares about. It amuses Harry to think of Tripp as a "chess player" – *queen takes knight.*

VII

Harry had a history teacher in high school tell him, "Harry, *if you don't know history you won't get the jokes.*" Whatever advancements in all things of human life – community governance, sustainability, religion, philosophy, art, entertainment, scientific discovery, and everything else – is wholly reliant on all history and all culture. All of it – the good and the bad… the great and the horrible. This is how Harry thinks about history and culture, and why he considers no other topic more important than history. Historical and cultural markers are essential to provide perspective for the present and good prospects for the future. On a panel discussion Harry said, "*Eliminating the past stagnates the present and dooms the future.*"

So, every time a piece of history, a piece of culture, a piece of us is condemned and banished to a mythical purgatorial state of never having happened, Harry feels another cut of the thousand cuts that may accumulate that will kill not so much of his body but his soul. Banning literature, books, movies, and such is a soul killer of the only species with a human soul.

"Book burners" have existed throughout history. The *Awaken* are the current incarnation of "book burners." The autoimmune[4] psychopathology of rabid *awakenness* threatens the human in humanity. Those who are not rabid but go-along unaware of the destruction caused by *Awaken* doctrine tacitly fortify the hard-core, rabid adherence to *Awaken* doctrine. This allowed the *Party Regime* to take and keep power. It is the goal of the *Party Regime* to use the *Awaken* doctrine to bury forever the country's history and culture.

* * *

Harry reads a list of books, some movie adaptions, and other literature that are banned, prohibited, or restricted by the *Party Regime*. Published materials and content considered inappropriate, seditious, heresy, or any manner of undesirable were confiscated from libraries, public schools, and other institutions private and public.

The list from which Harry is reading identifies banned material. The list itself is prohibited and illegal. He obtained it from Bob Burke. It reads:

Gone with the Wind by Margaret Michell
To Kill a Mockingbird by Harper Lee
The Adventures of Huckleberry Finn by Mark Twain
The Adventures of Tom Sawyer by Mark Twain

[4] Autoimmune – As the word is used in this context, it refers to both its meaning in physiology and an analogous description of how we turn destructive forces against ourselves. In this regard, autoimmune means self-destruction.

Dr. Suess series by Theodore Suess Geisel
The Iliad and The Odyssey by Homer
Of Mice and Men by John Steinbeck
The Grapes of Wrath by John Steinbeck
1984 by George Orwell
Animal Farm by George Orwell
Peter Pan by James Matthew Barrie
Atlas Shrugged by Ayn Rand
The Fountain Head by Ayn Rand
Hunger Games by Suzanne Collins
Ulysses by James Joyce
Ben-Hur: A Tale of the Christ by Lew Wallace
In Cold Blood by Truman Capote
Martian Chronicles by Ray Bradbury
Fahrenheit 451 by Ray Badbury
The Jungle by Upton Sinclair
The Lord of the Rings by J. R. R. Tolkien
All the King's Men by Robert Penn Warren
The Call of the Wild by Jack London
A Farewell to Arms by Ernest Hemingway
Death in the Afternoon by Ernest Hemingway
For Whom the Bell Tolls by Ernest Hemingway
Neuromancer by William Gibson
The Matrix – the film written and directed by Lana Wachowski and Lilly Wachowski
A Tale of Two Cities by Charles Dickens

A Christmas Carol by Charles Dickens
The Greatest Gift by Philip Van Doren Stern
It's a Wonderful Life – the film produced and directed by Frank Capra
Slaughterhouse Five by Kurt Vonnegut
Goosebumps series by R. L. Stine
The Kite Runner by Khaled Hosseini
Fifty Shades of Grey by E. L. James
Brave New World by Aldous Huxley
The Three Little Pigs by James Halliwell-Phillipps
Little Red Riding Hood by Charles Perrault
The Handmaid's Tale by Margaret Atwood
Harry Potter series by J. K. Rowling
Pinocchio by Carlo Collodi
Bambi by Felix Salten
Uncle Tom's Cabin by Harriet Beecher Stowe
The Catcher in the Rye by J. D. Salinger
The Color Purple by Alice Walker
The Holy Bible Believers believe these scriptures are the inspired words of God. The first five books – the Old Testament – the Torah – believers believe to be written by Moses.
The Holy Quran Orally revealed by the prophet Mohammed, believed by Muslims to be the word of God – *Allah*.
The Tipitaka Buddhist scriptures, authorship attributed to Harivarman.

The Vedas Hindu scriptures compiled by Vyasa.
Anne Frank: Diary of a Young Girl by Anne Frank
A Clockwork Orange by Anthony Burgess
I Know Why the Caged Bird Sings by Mya Angelou
Irreversible Damage by Abigail Shrier
Marlon Bundo's A Day in the Life of the Vice President by Charlotte Pence
A Day in the Life of Marlon Bundo by Jill Twiss
The complete works of William Shakespeare by William Shakespeare
On the Origin of Species by Charles Darwin
The Great Gatsby by F. Scott Fitzgerald
When Harry Became Sally by Ryan T. Anderson
One Flew Over the Cuckoo's Nest by Ken Kesey
Lord of the Flies by William Golding
Lolita by Vladimir Nabokov
Remembering Nygel by David Jacob
Zen Your Work by Karlyn Borysenko
Actively Unwoke by Karlyn Borysenko
Building the World by Skylar High
What's Going On? an article by Harry Archer
I Built It, The Personal Empowerment of Following Your Dream by Harry Archer
A Loose Grip by Howard Asher

Harry notes the list includes a spectrum of viewpoints from different ideologies, philosophies, political perspectives, and other contexts. He thinks banning intellectual material is a "slippery slope." It starts with one thing and eventually consumes everything for no good reason.

Notably, the *Party Regime* did not include *Mein Kampf* on its banned list. Harry believes it should never be banned. *Mein Kampf* is history. Harry is reminded of the saying "Those who don't know history are doomed to repeat it."

Harry reads the list again, slowly, pausing on each title. When done, he stares into space for a moment then casts his eyes on the list without focusing on any title. He knows more books will be added to the list. He doesn't cry, but inwardly mourns the loss of humanity's soul. He takes a deep breath. With a sense of resolve and self-anointed empowerment he says out loud, "Not while I'm alive."

He considers his next move.

He whispers to himself, "*Push Harry the h-pawn with tempo.*"[5]

* * *

It's noon. In midtown at the Federal Building Harry is attending a *Party Regime Reimagine Rally*. These *Reimagine Rallies* take place whenever new policies, regulations, and edicts have been enacted. The purpose of the rallies is to indoctrinate and work people into a frenzied mob acceptance of the "new

---

[5] *Push Harry the h-pawn with tempo* – In chess tournaments **the pawn of the h-file, or** *h-pawn,* is affectionately called *Harry* (^ _‘). *Push* means moving a pawn forward. *With tempo* means a move **is made** that openly threatens a valuable piece **so that** the opponent is **forced to react in defense**.

order" and the edicts that go with it. The rallies are like evangelist meetings, designed to trigger boisterous crowd enthusiasm through social pressure and intimidation. Mainstream factions of the media supporting the *Party Regime* record the events to broadcast and replay for news and propaganda. Today's rally is to promote the elimination of both Mother's Day and Father's Day. The *Party Regime* has declared these days a violation of "gender referencing" as well as inappropriate regard for the significance of parents. The *Party Regime's* goal – the destruction of the nuclear family. After all, Harry thinks rhetorically as he watches the speakers line up to address the crowd and incite them to become a mob, what's the first thing an insidious cult does with its new members? Separate them from their family.

Harry drifts back and forth in his thinking: from *he can't believe what is happening* to *of course this is happening*. Despite being unbelievable, Harry understands it's happening because the *Party Regime's* "reimagining projects" rely on the tacit consent of the people – Daisy's Tenth Circle of Hell, *Complacency*, comes to his mind. The people allow the *Party Regime* to turn the world upside down, which brainwashes people to think a "bizarro" world is normal. It's like an autoimmune disease of the masses. The people's natural immunity to fight off lethal absurdity is confused. Sensibility is killed off, leaving absurdity to finish the job of killing the host organism – the soul of the people.

Harry is at the rally because he's preparing an article that will include his commentary about this event and *Reimagine*

Rallies in general. While the rallies always have a sizable number of raucous supporters for whatever the *Party Regime* is selling, there are also many who show up at these events voicing opposition to the destructive nonsense promoted by these events. Among the many placards Harry sees in the crowd is one in support of eliminating Mother's and Father's Days. It reads:

Birth Parents & Non-Birth Parents
Are Functions, Not People

In contrast among the protest placards opposing the *vanishing* of Mother's Day and Father's Day is one that reads:

What's next? Apple pie?

These rallies have always been occasioned by pockets of violence – sometimes large sometimes small. It's obvious the violence comes from thugs organized by the *Party Regime* to choreograph disruption to turn the event into a riot and blame it on the peaceful protestors or any persons present who are neutral or even in support of the rally – whoever's convenient. These physical attacks are to make an example of those against *Party Regime* authority. The *Party Regime* is skilled at this kind of thing, it comes right out of their "playbook." Harry's attendance at this rally presents risks to himself in the forms of reprisals against him as well as being physically harmed.

There are several speakers saying ridiculous things: "It's time we shed the shackles of arbitrary family lineage!"

"Honoring a father and mother for no other reason than being parents is an outdated idea!" "Gender identification is not only a fallacy, it's an offense to the natural force of fluidity in all things!" The speakers are cheered when they punctuate a line that sounds like soaring oratory even though it's senseless and often incomprehensible. The speeches are angry and frenzied, igniting hysterical passions in the crowd. It doesn't take long for the crowd to take on the mindless emotions of a mob moved by blind hate.

The relatively small clusters of opposition to the rally's message and the rally itself wave their signs and chant into the raucous pro-rally crowd: *"What's next?! What's next?! What's next?!..."*

The high level of emotional speeches, cheers, and boisterousness would be all there is to the rally except for the formulaic additive of organized thugs planted by the *Party Regime*. One group of thugs calling themselves *Anti-Haters* is all about hate. They are the most violent hateful group that terrorize for the *Party Regime*, whose existence the *Party Regime* denies. Within thirty minutes, the *Anti-Haters*, dressed in red including red face covers that extend over their heads in ninja style start the anticipated pushing, turning-to-slugging, turning-to-kicking, turning-to-clubbing. The violence of this manner tends to be in a few contained but high attention-gaining pockets that the media flock to catch on camera. From this point, the trajectory of the event is predetermined. The violent disruption is allowed to continue with no police intervention. There is vandalism of property and looting of businesses in the area. More than a few injuries require paramedic assistance and ambulance rides to local hospitals.

Harry observes the event from a distance. Disgusted, he decides he's seen enough, he starts to walk away. A woman and man – yes, a woman and man, Harry doesn't have a switch allowing him to turn off his gender detector even at an "anti-gender reference" rally – both dressed in black suits and wearing horn-rimmed sunglasses, come up to him.

The woman speaks, "Where are you going?"

Harry responds, "Huh?"

The woman repeats with more hostile inflection, "Where are you going!?"

Harry just looks at the two. His eyes move from the woman to the man and back to the woman.

The man speaks with feigned concern for Harry's welfare, "You should be careful, Harry."

The woman and man walk away.

Struck that the man said his name, Harry stands motionless staring straight ahead, seeing nothing. He isn't conscious of the crowd or event. All outside noise is silent to him. He imagines he hears an unfamiliar ominous voice in his head whisper creepily, "*Check,* Harreee…"

VIII

Steve Reed is a contractor Harry's firm does business with. Steve is coming to Harry's office to work out some tricky construction details on a public works power plant. Steve has always been reliable, coming through for Harry on some difficult projects. He is a good "go-to" guy. But Steve is a talk-your-head-off know-it-all who never stays on subject. So, Harry never knows what subject he's going to end up on when the discussion starts. Since any call or meeting with Steve takes a lot of time, Harry clears his schedule so he can have time for his "Steve talk."

Penelope is at the front counter when Steve walks into the office wearing a gray industrial jumpsuit. He is coming from a jobsite. Ever the flirt, Steve says to Penelope, "Hey, Penny, when you leaving Harry to come away with me?"

Unflapped and without missing a beat she "volleys" back, "Nice try, Steve, but I'm sticking with a sure thing. Besides, you're lucky to have Carol (Steve's wife), so behave yourself!

"Carol's the best! I am lucky. I'm just trying to make sure 'Harry Boy' appreciates you, Penny." Whenever Steve comes to the office, they repeat this well-worn scripted vignette.

Harry walks into the front office and joins Steve and Penelope to deliver his lines, "Steve, to know Penny is to appreciate her. Now, let's you and I get to work."

Steve looks at Penelope and gives her a wink. With the ritual greeting performance completed, Steve says, "I'm going to the draftsman's room and change out of these coveralls." He's carrying a small duffle bag with his change of clothes.

"Okay, Steve, I'll be there in a minute."

Not yet finished with "flirt theater" as Steve walks to the draftsman's room he says, "It's, Penny, I want. Not you, Harry."

Harry goes over some purchase orders with Penelope then says, “This is going to take a while. I’ll see you later at the apartment.”

“I’ll have something you can heat up for dinner when you get home.” They peck each other on the lips.

Harry walks into the draftsman’s room as Steve’s finishing his outfit change. He’s buckling the belt on his cargo pants, adjusting his T-shirt, and slipping his feet into canvas slip ons.

“Hey, Harry, it’s been a while. How you doin’?”

“I’m good… I mean, okay… Ah, you know… What are you going to do?” Jeez – Harry thinks – what a stupid response to a *How you doin’* question.

“Jeez, Harry, what an uptight response to *How you doin’*.”

At least we’re on the same page, Harry thinks. “Ah, yeah. Sorry, Steve. I just have a lot going on.”

“Hey, pal, unload. What’s going on? I’ll tell you what to do.”

Ugh great, Harry thinks, now I’ve opened the door to Steve’s brand of fixing things that don’t need fixing. I may not have allowed enough time for our meeting. “Well, it’s nothing,” he says. Then he thinks of something he figures will piss off Steve. Steve likes being pissed off. What Harry will bring up also pisses off Harry. So, this could take up some good “Steve talk” time. “Yeah, Steve, I saw another stupid article about 2+2=5. Made me wonder if the state regime would like us to use that kind of ‘new math’ to build the project you and I are working on.”

"2+2=5? What do you mean?"

"Well, the reason I sounded uptight… thought I sounded stupid… I've been distracted so much by the corruption and destruction of societal institutions adopting insensible standards and passing it off as acceptable. If 2+2=5, *we're screwed… forever.*" This isn't exactly why Harry sounded uptight/stupid. But the "2+2=5 thing" is just the kind of subject Steve will "cut up" and be critical of.

"Oh, that. Didn't you write about that once?"

"Yeah, I did. What do *you* think is up with that?" To Harry this is a rhetorical question. He knows it's a demagogic challenge by the *Awaken* to "Western culture persecution" of the racially disenfranchised. He just wants to hear Steve go off on it.

Steve does go off on it. "Yeah, it's ridiculous! It's the way malcontents want to tear down standards." He continues sarcastically, "The 'wicked establishment' arbitrarily decided 2+2=4. And because the establishment is 'wicked,' we the 'oppressed'… the 'malcontents' don't have to take this '2+2=4 shit' anymore. So, 2+2 can be 5. Up is down, in is out, death is life, oppression is liberty, weakness is strength!"

Wow, Harry thinks, Steve rightly punctuated his point by mentioning the stupid *Party Regime* credo. "Right on!" Harry whisper-shouts, while sarcastically adding a raised fist, "Down with the man! Ah, I mean person! I mean thing!"

Steve and Harry laugh until Steve breaks in soberly, "Yeah, Harry, you're right. *We're screwed… forever.*"

A moment passes as the mood turns serious. Harry reflects, "You know, Steve, it does get to me that people can jump on a 'mob train' fueled by a slogan. A mob is made up of people who chant a slogan to identify with something that feels important, and it empowers them. The slogan sounds good to the point it becomes righteous. So, any challenge to the mob is a challenge to righteousness. Everything turns backwards – what 'destruction mobs' do is now called good and the efforts to prevent 'destruction mobs' are called bad. Everything is ass-backwards.

"When you say 2+2=5, you're not just saying it's another way to see things, as the mob falsely and disingenuously claims. It's an 'FU' to an imaginary ruling class. The mob thinks the 'house' of this ruling class is 2+2=4. So, the mob wants to burn down the house. They want to burn the house down by saying it doesn't equal 4. It equals 5, or whatever they want to say it equals."

"Gosh, Harry, for a guy who fumbled with a simple *How you doin'* a few minutes ago, you broke down a complicated social/cultural homeostatic disruption into a concise explanation of social psychology. You not only broke it down. You nailed it! That's exactly what's happening."

"Well, I'm not done," says Harry. "It's bad enough 'mob ideology' – 'mobology' – infects the mob. But to make things worse, organized *Awaken* 'religiosity' aligns with the false cause of the mob, pretending to abhor violence and destruction while silently rooting for the mob to create unrest, chaos, and damage through violence and destruction. The *Awaken* stake their claim on stupid ideas, which in a free society they're free to do. But they don't want society to be free to have ideas different from their *Awaken* doctrine."

"Yep," Steve says, shaking his head slowly.

Just then Penelope comes into the room holding a plastic bag. Harry is surprised and says, "I thought you went home."

"I *was* going home. But I thought you boys could do with some Chinese take-out." She puts the bag on an adjacent table.

"That's great Penny!" Steve says appreciatively. "Boy, Harry, you sure did score by getting her!"

"I know, I always tell her that. But she's still figuring out if she got a good deal with me."

Penelope winks at Harry which Steve notices and says, "Harry, I don't think you have to worry about that."

Penelope asks, "What were you boys talking about?"

"Oh," Harry answers. "We're just discussing advanced mathematics."

"Ha," Steve reacts. "Yeah, very sophisticated and advanced mathematics – a deep dive into 2+2."

"Okay, fellas," says Penelope. "I'm sure mathematics are in good hands – brains – with you guys. I'm going to go. Enjoy your food."

Penelope walks over to Harry. They peck each other on the lips again.

When Steve and Harry finish eating the food Penelope brought. Harry says, "My favorite part of eating Chinese is the fortune cookie at the end. But since fortune cookies are now banned by the *Party Regime*, no more fortune cookies. I miss them."

"Yeah, why did they ban 'um?" Steve asks.

"The reason is BS. The *Regime* said it had to do with fortune cookies being *witchcraft*."

"You know, Harry, they may as well call it *witchcraft* since that's how they treat anyone who opposes them or thinks opposes them. We are all living in one big '*Awaken* witch trial.'"

"Yeah, Steve. And I don't even know if you're allowed to say 'Chinese' anymore."

For the next two and a half hours, Harry and Steve go over details of the building project they are working on. They both keep side-tracking each other with unpredictable subjects like wormholes, frisbee golf, and giraffes. In their side talks they also pondered if a parrot was domesticated in France and later taught English, would the parrot speak English with a French accent?

As usual, Steve has lots of advice for Harry. Harry has a mental "Steve file" where he keeps Steve's advice. All in all, it is a productive meeting. But Harry's take away in the pessimistic swing of his mood is Steve's validating comment, "Yeah, Harry, you're right. *We're screwed... forever.*"

* * *

After Steve leaves the office, Harry reaches into his pocket to get his cell phone to call Penelope. He sees a voice message with text he received an hour ago that he hadn't noticed. As he taps the screen to hear the recording a surge of fear goes through his body. A kindly female voice says: "Greetings from the state. This is a gentle reminder that compliance with the standards directed by the precepts of the *Great Awakening* is mandatory for your own good and the good of your family. *The Big Guy* has detected recent unapproved conduct and speaking by you. We are certain you did not mean to violate the standards and you welcome our intervention to help you be a proper POD – Person of Destiny. We have scheduled your *Thought & Locator* chip implant for next month. Have a *Great Awakening* day. And remember – ***There is nothing you can do without us knowing about it!***"

Harry could feel his skin go cold. He thinks – *I'm screwed... forever!*

IX

Wearing black slacks, light gray dress shirt, no tie, and a brown tweed sport coat, Harry walks into the building that stands on the Southeast corner of the well-known intersection in the high-end business district. Atop the building is a massive sign – *Jacob Publishing.* Harry has a meeting with David Jacob. He is the owner and CEO of the publishing firm that bears his name. The firm's publications command the highest market share of readership considered the best informed and "rational" by Readers Profile Research, Inc. Jacob contacted Harry to engage him to write what may be a farewell article for its flagship publication.

The *Party Regime* has its sights on Jacob, as an enemy of the state. They intend to shut him and his publishing firm down. Bob Burke knows Jacob and suggested he have Harry write an article that would stand as a definitive commentary on human existence – forever branding the publishing firm as a source and demonstration of *freedom's reward to humanity* as Bob pitched it to Jacob.

Navigating two security checkpoints – one in the lobby and one on the seventh floor – Harry makes his way to the lavish penthouse office suite to meet with Jacob. When Harry enters the suite, he is greeted by a tall slender man with short dark gray hair in his fifties wearing casual business attire. "Mr. Archer."

Harry responds, "Mr. Jacob?"

"No, I'm David's assistant… uh… associate… uh, ya know after twenty-six years, I'm not sure what I am. But I'm not David. He'll be here right away. Come sit over here." The man walks through a door into an office and points to a sitting area.

Harry follows the man into the office and sits in one of the chairs where the man pointed. "Thank you, sir, I'll be fine." Harry didn't know why he said he'd be fine.

As if the man heard Harry's thoughts, the man walks out of the office calmly and reassuringly saying, "I know you'll be fine." Harry had the sense he couldn't hide the nuances of his thoughts from this man even if he tried.

While sitting alone Harry sees a fine finished wood plaque on the office desk. It is aesthetically inscribed:

The pen can be sharper than the sword.
But a dull pen is no match for a dull sword.

As Harry stares at the inscription, and as if in a trance loses himself in its meaning, he is abruptly jarred by the sound of his name, "Harry!" It was spoken by another man in his fifties who is just entering the office. Harry looks up at the man. He is just under six feet, medium build, dark complected with dark eyes, curly blackish hair peppered with gray. He is also dressed casually but businessy. "Mr. Jacob?"

"David, to you, Harry. Allen – the guy you just saw – said you were here. I'm eager to talk with you. But first, I'm going to have an iced latte. Do you want one too?"

"Uh, yeah, sure. That would be great. No sugar."

David yells to the reception room outside the office, "Hey, Allen, please get Harry and me two iced lattes. I mean one latte each. I mean – duh – him a latte and me a latte. Both with no sugar. He drinks it the way I drink it. Thanks, Allen."

From the other room Allen's voice shoots back faintly, "Already on it."

David turns to Harry and says, "Allen's great. I don't know what I'd do without him. The success we've had at this firm is because of him."

"Yeah, in the brief moment and few words we spoke I got the sense that Allen is a very intuitive fellow."

"You're right, Harry. Allen is one of those guys who knows things and knows how to do things. In fact, after I spoke with

Bob Burke about you, Allen was the one who said you were the guy to write the article we want."

"So, what did you have in mind for the article?" asks Harry.

"Oh, I'm leaving that up to you. This meeting isn't about objectives or strategy. I just wanted to meet you. After Bob called me, I already knew we were going to collaborate – that is, you do your thing and I – my firm – will do our thing. I didn't know much about you, Harry. Allen and I looked into your background and your public presentations, which of course include your writings. We like your work. Allen and I have a name for guys like you… I mean people like you – women, men, whatever." David slowly shakes his head side-to-side, tightens his lips expressing his self-annoyance at being unnecessarily cautious. "Boy, do you notice how correcting your own 'politically incorrect' faux pas always takes you off topic? Anyway, the name we have for guys like you is 'the emperor has no clothes guys.' Harry, you're the quintessential *the emperor has no clothes guy*."

Harry likes hearing that Allen and David see him that way. He keeps the subject going by adding to David's comments, "It's too bad *the emperor has no clothes guys* are rare."

David reflexively banters a supporting enhancement, "It's too bad we need *the emperor has no clothes guys* at all."

"Yeah, but we do. And I don't know how to say, 'the emperor has no clothes' in a way it will have the effect that enough people will *get it*."

David points his chin slightly upward to his right and tightens his lips again before saying, "Stop being pathetic, Harry. You do know how to say it. You wouldn't be sitting here if you didn't know how to say it... write it."

Harry feels the odd mix of the sting of a virtual hand slap across his face combined with getting a compliment from the wise admirer who gave him the "slap across his face."

David continues, "Harry, I don't waste my time. You're already having an effect. Things are building up. And you're... we're moving forward with the 'emperor has no clothes' thing."

The more David speaks the more Harry feels the weight of the proposed assignment. His insecurities about being worthy to the task kick in. He counters his insecurity with a philosophy he crafted for himself when he was a teenager: *Being up to the task isn't the issue. Being selected to do the task is what matters. So do it.*

Harry takes in a deep breath of confidence and recalibrates his words and strength of presence. "Look, David, I misspoke. I know exactly what to write." He really doesn't. But he is riding a wave of "so do it."

"I know you do, Harry. Dealing with public willful blindness is exhausting. The trick is you don't need to change minds. Just talk to those who already see what you see but don't yet know they agree with you. You find the 'common ground,' you mutually verify it, then go from there to connect a 'dot,' everybody gets enlightened, nobody gets hurt. Preaching to the choir is a good thing. And the 'choir' is much bigger than you think. But you can't take them for granted just because they're in the choir. You have to respect them by articulating the logical foundations that strengthen each person's own sensibilities to stand for reason and against idiocy. Because our battle *is* against idiocy.

"Harry, you've been 'out there doing the job.' You've been 'hung out to dry.' Not maliciously, but the way people get hung out to dry when they're the right person for a thankless job. Is there any way we can help you while you're being 'hung out to dry' and getting 'creamed'?"

Harry is curious. "David, do you mean helping me *not* get 'creamed?' Or do you mean helping me *when* I get 'creamed?'

"Ha… that's a good question."

Allen walks in with three lattes in a cardboard cup carrier – he got one for himself. Having heard the last part of David and Harry's conversation, Allen says, "Speaking of creamed, I've got your lattes here." Amused with himself, he repeats in a Philadelphian mobster accent, "I got ya lattaays right here." He chuckles to himself. David and Harry do not react to or acknowledge Allen's antics. Then he talks like his normal self. "I also got some shortbread biscuits. They're good with iced latte."

Looking at Harry, David makes a "thumbs up" gesture, winks, and says, "See what I mean about Allen? What would I do without him?"

"That was quick," Harry says. "Where did you get the lattes?"

Both David and Allen answered together, but not quite in unison and not quite the same words which sounded like, "we have/the building has a coffee shop/café on the/for our staff/guest/clients."

Harry takes a sip of his latte and says, "That's nice."

Allen sits in the last available chair in the sitting group. Harry says. "Well, fellas, it looks like we are the newest 'Three Amigos' in the world." Allen and David chuckle. Harry then says, "I have some questions."

David says, "Shoot."

"Can the *Party Regime* really shut you down?"

David answers, "As long as I've been in publishing, I've always acted like I could be shut down at any time. The *Party Regime* is just the latest machination – although by far the most formidable and threatening – of the forces against not only publishing but of free speech. It will never end. The threat of shut down never ends."

After a second sip of latte Harry asks another question, "Is publishing the most effective way to reach people?"

Allen answers, "Publishing is an invisible uncertain force that must be present whether or not you know its immediate effectiveness. It does have enormous impact when a piece goes viral. But viral doesn't mean what people think it means. It really means that people are talking – not reading. People don't read… that is, most people don't read. What most people know or think they know… are things in publications they've heard about. And more often what they've heard is from people who haven't read it firsthand or if they did read it, they tell it to others differently than it was written."

"Wow, that's a lot of filter barriers. It seems more likely what you write won't get read or understood by anybody."

This time in perfect unison both Allen and David say, "Riiiight."

"Hmm." Sounding like he's changing the subject, but he's not, Harry says, "I've been thinking about two things that have nothing in common except one important thing – survival.

David asks, "What are those two things?"

Harry answers dryly, "Honey bees and standup comedians."

Allen says, "Ha… my first thought is anything but survival until my next thought is we couldn't survive without either one – honey bees or standup comedians."

"Nice job, Allen," Harry says with satisfaction leaning forward pointing his right index finger downward across his chest. "That's the point. I think the best way to reach the most people with the intended message intact is to present an idea that people don't expect. That way the listener's preconceptions won't contaminate the idea. From there you provoke interest and originality to worldview thinking. You make the idea appealing by pointing to positive outcomes. The idea of a positive outcome amidst dire circumstances is key. Otherwise, you're left with doom. No matter how bad things are, people want – need – to look forward to something good." Harry pauses, then continues. "The article I write is going to be about honey bees and stand-up comedians."

David responds, "Yeah, that should be unexpected enough."

* * *

David and Allen give Harry no instructions on what to write. They had high expectations for the article and are not disappointed. The piece is titled *Culture Drives the Herd* subtitled *Why Honey Bees and Stand-Up Comedians are Essential.* And Harry gets a byline. David and Allen think the article expresses the right words for the time.

The article is one of the widest read articles in the publishing firm's history, causing a lot of positive reader responses. Predictably, in competing publications and the media, the article is viciously attacked as unpatriotic, seditious, and pathological. It is posted and then banned on various well-trafficked media platforms. The attention the article gains effectively causes it to be seen in an increasingly favorable way. Public pressure gets it reposted on platforms that had banned it. It gets even more attention. It goes viral the way Allen described viral.

X

"Mr. Archer, just relax. This won't take long. You'll feel a little pinch in your arm and it will be over," are the words spoken in the female voice of the young medical technician. Harry is on his back on the examining table looking up at the ceiling tiles. He turns his head to the left and sees a framed picture of *The Big Guy* above a placard that reads:

Thought & Locator Chip Implantation Center For Proper Thinking

When the procedure is completed, Harry feels lightheaded. He feels like he's in a trance. His thinking is automatic without any sense of caring what he thinks and how he thinks. He then mumbles but his words are clear, "I love *The Big Guy*."

Harry's eyes spring open! He's fully awake. He's lying in his bed on his side next to Penelope who is sleeping. The room is dark as it's the middle of the night. He's startled and anxious. He knows that was a dream. Or was it? It felt so real.

* * *

The petroleum market as the foremost indicator of the overall economy's health is what Harry pays a lot of attention to. Crude oil prices, refinery costs, oil transportation and distribution, and prices at the gas pump tell the story of the state of money fluidity and access in the commerce related to quality of life throughout the nation.

As a civil engineer, Harry knows well how gasoline prices to the end user affect the economy at large. When gas prices go up, building costs go up; there are delays in delivery of materials and goods; employment numbers decrease. The gasoline market is so sensitive Harry has reason to look at a one-penny increase in gas price as a catastrophe for someone – many someones. He can mathematically demonstrate that with each penny increase in gasoline at least one family loses their home.

The moment Biddle was sworn in as President, gasoline prices went up. Once in office, *The Big Guy* signed a series of executive orders affecting the domestic petroleum market, causing another sharp spike in gasoline prices. Harry knows a catastrophe is in the making. Lives are being affected for the worse at an epidemic scale. Harry thinks ironically – the real epidemic isn't biological, it's the financial collapse of self-reliance.

The popular news outlets fail to cover this story.

The news and media are focused on preferred pronoun practices.

* * *

Harry is now doing research on the petroleum market and the economic dynamics for an article he is writing for the *Party Regime*. In doing his research, he is not able to access internet websites banned by the *Party Regime*. He calls Bob Burke to ask if he could meet him at his office at the *Ministry of Correctness*. Bob says, "Sure, come on over."

Harry is sitting in Bob's office, alone. Bob has been momentarily called away. Harry notices a sticky note on Bob's desk that he reads upside down. It isn't in Bob's handwriting, so he presumes the note is written to Bob. The note says: *We know what you're doing. Your time is up*.

Bob comes back into the office. In one continuous motion he sits in his desk chair, grabs the note, looks at Harry, and lightheartedly asks, "How ya doin', Harry?"

Harry responds, "How are *you* doing?"

"Fine. What's up?"

"I mean it. How are you?"

"Harry, I don't think you came over here to ask how I'm doing. Although I know my well-being is of the utmost importance to you."

"Come on, Bob. I know high stakes word-banter amuses you. And I don't mind a good joust. But something's up."

"You mixed some metaphors – word-banter… joust."

"No, I didn't. 'Word-banter' is maybe redundant because banter is with words. But it's not a metaphor. It stands for what it is – banter. Joust *is* a metaphor. I didn't mix anything."

"Harry, I'm glad we get right to the matter. No distraction or foolery with us."

Harry takes a breath to reset the discussion, then says, "I came over to talk about internet access to banned websites so I can do research, but I'm worried how long we can keep this going until the game's up. I'm worried someone or all of us are going to get hurt."

"You mean killed, Harry."

"Yeah, Bob… killed."

THREE

HE DOES NOT KNOW WHERE HE IS. THIS IS A PART OF the city in which Harry has never been. The wide streets are lined with overgrown Ficus trees and office buildings mostly unoccupied. There are few cars on the road and almost no pedestrians. The officers, wearing black suits and crisp white shirts, are driving Harry in the *Ministry's* black SUV. Harry is more than worried. The SUV comes to a typical five-story office building with no identification other than the address numbers affixed above the street entry doors at the front of the building. They pull into the underground parking garage and stop at the security guard booth. The driver shows the uniformed man in the booth a plastic identification card authorizing entrance. The gate is lifted; the SUV drives in; not a word is spoken.

The SUV drives to the curbside of the building's elevator. The driver remains in the SUV as two officers step out of the vehicle. One of the officers motions to Harry to step out. Harry with the two officers – one on either side of him – stands at the elevator door. The officer on Harry's right takes from his inside coat pocket the same kind of plastic identification/authorization card the SUV driver presented at the security guard booth. He inserts it into the card slot on a panel next to the elevator. The elevator doors open. And as if choreographed, the three men walk in unison into the elevator. Halfway into the elevator, the three pivot to the left until they face the front. Harry almost laughs out loud at the optics of the moment. But maintaining the sobriety of the situation, he restrains himself. He's also having his now familiar surge of fear.

The elevator doors close. Without either officer manually touching the interior control panel, the elevator starts to move upward. In a normal situation, this would be the time when Harry, like most people who want to stay silent and avoid eye contact with strangers in an elevator, would feel self-conscious and awkward. But in this moment and in this situation, Harry is so consumed with the purpose, mystery, and awaiting danger, feeling awkward is not registering in his psyche.

Harry can't help noticing there is no floor indicator above the door. He hadn't noticed from the outside as they drove into the building's garage, but his expertise as a civil engineer "kicks in" as he estimates this to be a five-story building. He judges by the speed and duration of the elevator ride, they have reached the fifth floor when the doors open.

Again, in unison, the three men step out of the elevator. The first thing Harry sees is a large 120-inch monitor screen on the opposite wall about fifteen feet away. The screen is emblazoned with three slogans. All in capital letters:

DEATH IS LIFE
OPPRESSION IS LIBERTY
WEAKNESS IS STRENGTH

Coming from the corridor on Harry's left is the sound of leather-soled shoes clicking on the hard floor at a slow pace. The shoes and pace belong to a man whose stature is on the short and pudgy side, looking about sixty. He has short gray hair that's thin and balding on top. He is clean shaven and smartly groomed. Harry can smell his cologne. The man is wearing a charcoal gray suit, white shirt, and solid purple tie. He walks up to Harry, extends his hand, and cheerfully says, "Ah, Mr. Archer. May I call you Harry? My name is Winston Smith. Please call me Winston."

The officers had picked Harry up off the street as he was walking to his office. So, he didn't dress for the "occasion." He's wearing his usual casual fashion. He shakes Winston's hand in a cordial manner and says, "Yes, certainly, call me Harry." Harry notices the two officers have disappeared. He hadn't heard them walk away. It's weird and creepy. But in these times and circumstances everything is weird and creepy. Harry knows he doesn't have time to indulge his usual quirky curiosity about things he observes and/or thinks about. He returns his attention to Winston.

Winston says, "Harry, come with me so we can talk."

Harry follows Winston down the corridor from where Winston first emerged. They walk side-by-side. Winston offers some small talk, "It's good weather today."

Harry hasn't cared about the weather for at least two years. "Yeah, it's nice."

They come to a door on their right, Winston opens the door, leading to an office suite. "Here we are," Winston says. They walk through a reception area. No other person is present. As far as Harry knows, no other person is in the building.

They go into what Harry figures is Winston's office. It's the kind of office an important person has, with a low panoramic view of the city. There is a desk with a leather chair behind it and two well-upholstered chairs in front of it. Some short distance from the desk is a sitting area with a sofa, coffee table, and two upholstered chairs.

"Let's sit over here." Winston points to the sitting area.

Harry is "playing chess." He understands with "power meetings" where you sit is a chess move. He sits in one of the chairs, forcing Winston to sit in the other chair. Harry reasons sitting on the sofa is the weak position Winston would avoid. To his surprise, Winston sits opposite Harry on the left arm of the sofa. Harry thinks, so much for predicting an opponent's chess move. Let's see how the next move plays.

"You're well-known around here," Winston says. Harry already knows that. But where is "here?" It's terrifying to hear Winston say it. His cheerful demeanor doesn't help; it makes things more terrifying. Harry feels the palms of his hands sweating as he waits to hear more.

"*We* have a plan for you which *we're* very excited about. I hope you'll like it as much as *we* do."

In a different world this pitch would be wonderful music to Harry's ears. He thinks as he listens to Winston – what a cruel cosmic joke on me. Plan? What Plan?

"Harry, how do you win people over?" It's a rhetorical question. Winston answers it. "You win their hearts and minds. The *Party Regime* has currently won the power, but it's losing the hearts and minds of the people."

Harry suddenly feels decisively bold and unguardedly honest, "That's because they don't care about the hearts and minds… of anyone."

"Ahh… I hoped we would talk plainly. You're not disappointing me, Harry."

Winston definitely has Harry's attention.

"Here's what *we* want to do. *We* want to promote you, by name, as the 'every guy' – that everyone can relate to. Instead of your articles and copy being ostensibly written by an unknown party bureaucrat, your name – Harry Archer – better known as just 'Harry'– will be identified openly. You will reflect *the heart and mind…* you will be *the heart and mind* of the *Party Regime!*"

Harry doesn't know if he will be sick, uplifted, disengaged or intrigued. He sits stone-faced, betraying nothing.

"Surprised, aren't you?!" Winston says empathetically and smiling.

"Yeah… yeah."

"*We* – you – are going to have a regular article and media spot – a media presence – called – branded – *Here's What Harry Thinks.*"

Limply – Harry responds, "Yeah… yeah… um… that's great. But what about… what about the… what about the… you know, the thing?"

"Hmm, Harry, right now you don't quite sound like the great communicator you usually are."

"Winston, this is what an 'every guy' sounds like in a situation like this."

"Good man. Now you're talking."

With undramatic boldness, Harry says, "The *Party Regime* and I don't think alike or agree on anything. But they want *me* to be the face of them!?"

Winston explodes with a laugh that if you didn't know him you would think it's the hardest laugh he ever laughed.

Harry waits for Winston's laugh to subside to say, "Glad you see the humor. The basis of humor is irony. And this is more irony than I've ever experienced personally, let alone how this would play out to the world at large. It's a bit much."

"Yep, you're not disappointing me at all," says Winston.

"Let's talk about the 'little' irony."

"Let's."

"Right now, the 'ruling party' is operating on pure power. That *heart and mind* stuff is a fallacy because the moment a thought entertains logic fueled by *heart and mind* 'octane'

– oops, I made a fossil fuel reference – the party is over. Or, I should say the *Party Regime* under the cover of *Awaken* doctrine is the only party allowed. It's a self-perpetuating problem. Isn't it?"

"Of course, it is. That's where you come in, Harry. You have a *way about you* that if you say what you think the way you do it in your writings, like you just did, with your personality, nobody can say the *Party Regime* doesn't allow *free thought* and *free speech*."

"Which they *don't* allow!"

"Exactly!" Winston then lets out a hard short laugh.

"This feels like *Who's on first*… Look, we can go around forever trying to make sense of the senseless. At this point I'm already in deep. You know me. I can't hide. I have nothing to lose but everything I care about. Goodness, help me! I'm in." Harry leans forward, claps his hands in a single clap, and folds his arms across his chest as he leans back in his chair.

Winston says, "Yep, Harry, you don't disappoint."

Harry thinks to himself – *castle kingside*.[6]

II

Harry knows it's a trap. He also knows the "trap" is where the game is played. Chess is about stepping into a trap and turning being-in-the-trap against your opponent. Thinking

---

[6] *Castle king side* – A chess move that rearranges the board dramatically in one move.

about his perilous situation this way gives Harry some comfort. But he can't avoid his insecurity about if he "has game."

With resignation, Harry jumps headlong into his elevated public profile as the *every guy* face of the *Party Regime*. With the resources of the *Ministry of Correctness*, it is seamless. From his media exposure, people recognize him on the street. There are always more than a few who ridicule him with harsh comments and dirty looks. But Harry is surprised. There are many nice passersbys who yell out things like "Hey, Harry!" "Hey, *every guy*!" "Hey, Harry, *what are you thinking?"* Harry thought despite being a fairly agreeable person, now that he's public with his name attached to incendiary subjects, most everyone would dislike or hate him. Rather, it appears most like him or at least like recognizing him. He constantly reminds himself not to be fooled if the "tide" looks like it's going either way – with or against him.

* * *

A soulful blues style cover of The Rolling Stones song *You Can't Always Get What You Want* starting at the chorus sung by a raspy-voiced male accompanied by just a guitar starts the broadcast: ♪ ♫ ♩... The lyrics speak of making the best of life with what you have...

The song fades with guitar strumming as Harry speaks over the fading guitar...

"Hello, good listeners. Thank you for tuning in. I'm Harry Archer and the producers call this show *Here's What Harry Thinks*.

"I not only report what's going on, I break down what it means. It's my ideas that I'm telling you about. But if you find I make a good point then it's your idea too. So, let's get started and see if you and I are good thinkers."

This is Harry's signature opening for his daily broadcast airing on a network of radio markets, podcasts, and internet video live stream platforms.

"Two days ago, something happened that if you watched or read about it on any news outlet you don't know what happened and you won't know what it means. So, now you've come to the right place if understanding the world you live in is important to you.

"I'm going to tell you about what happened in a way that avoids the irrelevant and focuses on the true take-aways. How's that for the best use of your time?

"In an east coast state eight people died from a mass gun shooting. I'm not going to tell the name of the killer because I don't want him – yes, it's a guy – I don't want him memorialized as a media curiosity or take a place in the historical hall of fame for the depraved.

"Now when there's a mass shooting, the 'regular' news which follows the *Awaken* doctrine has a checklist of what the story is about before it knows anything more than what I just told you. I want to repeat that because I want to emphasize the 'regular' news – the news everybody gets is already reporting on it without knowing what happened. That technically makes it *not* news. Nevertheless, that's what everybody calls it – news.

"The news we consume, all of it, is always filtered through politics, ideology, and a philosophical value set. Some conglomerate of information and/or supposition are squeezed through this 'value set' filter to give the desired narrative. The *narrative* is the product and purpose of the news... and media... and tech industries.

"All news outlets do this – the ones you like and the ones you don't like do it. I do it. It's necessary to do it. It's necessary to do it if the events in our collective lives are to be relevant. It's not a corruption to do it. But it is often done corruptively.

"Honesty, good faith, accuracy, logical cohesion, and credibility are how corruption is avoided. These standards are typically not employed by the news/media industry. But you come here to listen to me because I do employ these standards.

"Ultimately, it's you – the consumer – who rightly or wrongly judges the credibility and value of the news and media product. In this judgment, you have a responsibility beyond the officials and leaders of our state. Don't take this responsibility for granted. Don't squander it. Unless you don't mind living a life some 'disinterested-in-your-wants-and-wellbeing' bureaucracy has planned for you.

"So, let's look at what happened with this mass shooting and the product – the narrative – the news fed to you. We'll start with the product/narrative. That's where the news outlet starts – what do we – the news outlet – want the product/narrative to be this time: The product/narrative of this story was: *Racial supremacy with its bigotry and subjugation by racists is the number one issue in civil society. All the bad that happens comes from racism.*

"Now I have a side note: At this time in our society, the product/narrative I just told you – *Racial supremacy with its bigotry and subjugation by racists is the number one issue in civil society. All the bad that happens comes from racism.* – is one of three or four products/narrative that news and media pick from its repertoire of 'virtue' products to feed you… to sell you. That's right, the product/narrative is being sold to you. The question is, are you buying?

"Getting back to the story, now that we know the product/narrative: This guy shot people. Eight died from the shooting. So far… and we may find out something later to support it being racially motivated with supremacy overtones, but so far there's no evidence race played any role in this atrocity. So far, there's evidence to the contrary that this was *not* racially motivated. But the news/media have a product/narrative to sell that won't be obstructed by truth, facts, and context. A product is a product. The news/media have told you the shooting was the result of racial supremacy and bigotry. President Biddle, *The Big Guy*, gave a televised address to the public linking the shooting and the scourge of racism behind racist attacks.

"Racism is a scourge. Which is why it shouldn't be evoked as political rhetoric. The atrocities of madmen – deranged people – are not validations for the claimed and charged failings of political opponents… as the *Awaken* – and Biddle

– would attest. Be aware of this wrongful tactic by any political or advocacy group.

"This story and the media coverage of it is a perfect example of what I'm calling *cross-sectional interest buffet-feeding*. I know – too many words. But each word is necessary in this concept I want to brand here and now. *Cross-sectional* is the spectrum of all the causes supporting a core narrative. *Interest* is the cause *du jour*… of interest. *Buffet-feeding* is a metaphor for the 'pick and choose' way news, media, and activists cobble together a 'Frankenstein monster' of an idea and call it a legitimate point upon which to hold a belief and conviction.

"Anything touched by *Awaken* doctrine undergoes *cross-sectional interest buffet-feeding*. After visiting the 'buffet counter of interests' the 'plate' of the *Awaken* looks much different than the 'plate' of someone with un-*Awaken* sensibilities.

"The story was about mental illness, behavioral addiction, human trafficking, and gun owner controversies. Racial supremacy, bigotry, inter-racial violence, and hate crime motives were nowhere to be found or indicated in this story thus far. But because *Awaken* narrative is hungry for inter-racial discord and hatred, the news and media 'trafficked' *a story* that was different than *the story* – the real story. And too many of the public buy it – the 'trafficked' story.

"The news and media loaded up the 'buffet plate' with additional selections from the 'buffet counter' that included racial blame for the recent virus pandemic. Get it? We went from a mass shooting by a nut case who had behavioral addiction to who's to blame for a virus pandemic.

"With regard to the pandemic, no person or group with influence and standing in society blamed any race of people. Yet the *Awaken*, along with the Biddle administration promoted this 'Frankenstein' idea which the press reported as inter-racial persecution.

"A bad idea – a false premise – a lie – can be propagandized. You plant it in the fertile ground of *common ignorance. Common ignorance* is another term I want to brand with the meaning I'm going to tell you now. Ignorance, meaning not knowing, is often wrongly thought to be a derogatory word. Sometimes it should be derogatory, if the thing not known should be known as an expected course of being adequately informed about immediately relevant things in your life and the world around you. But more often there's nothing derogatory about ignorance. You simply do not know something until you know it. We are all ignorant of an infinite number of things all the time. That's what I'm calling *common ignorance*. It's normal.

"The problem is propagandists take advantage of – rely on – this normal ever-present *common ignorance*. The bad idea – the false premise – the lie – is planted in the rich soil of *common ignorance*. Then it's 'watered' and nourished with repetition until one day it's accepted and becomes unquestioned reality.

"Anyone opposing this *false reality* is thought to be and therefore characterized as a disreputable extremist. Racism and bigotry are disreputable and extremist. So, to the targets of *Awaken* propagandists the 'shoe' of racism and bigotry 'fits' those who are not *Awaken.*

"The buffer to *common ignorance* is critical thinking, respect for wisdom, and wisdom itself. Wisdom involves critical thinking. And critical thinking is something you need to work at. You need to control your impulses and knee-jerk reactions. You need to consider a range of information and understanding presently beyond your reach. It's beyond your reach in the sense you need a ladder to get on the roof of a house. The most reliable 'ladder' is honesty. Honesty is the high regard and practice of integrity. You must be willing to be honest to see clearly. From there, new information and understanding are now reachable. That's where wisdom lives.

"There is still a more insidious effect of *cross-sectional interest buffet-feeding.* It reinforces the propagandists themselves – the adherents to the cause – the *Awaken.* It's red meat. It's oxygen. It's crack cocaine. Bad ideas – false premises – lies – however forceful are still weak because they're bad ideas – false premises – lies. To remain in force, they need constant nourishment to ward off the corrective effects of cognitive dissonance. As a reminder put simply, cognitive dissonance is inconsistent thinking. Here's a tip to know you've entered the 'land' of inconsistent thinking: your rationalizations aren't truthful. Honesty about inconsistent thinking continuously keeps in check your attitude, behavior, and worldview. *Cognitive dissonance is inconvenient to fools.*

"There's yet another thing to point out. The *Awaken* calls out horrible things about un-*Awaken* people and actions to divert attention from the things that are horrible about *Awaken* doctrine, their people, and their actions. The high crime rate, broken families, and despair in communities and regions governed and controlled by *Awaken* officials are examples. The public policy failures engineered by *awakenness* would not continue if the 'soldiers' of the *Awaken* and the news who do their public relations didn't always point away from themselves to point to un-*Awaken* and hysterically cry out – look over there, there's the *boogie man!*

"I'm telling you, folks – 'Junk in/junk out.' It's up to you. It's up to you to *get it.*

"*Okay, that's enough for now.* Think about what I've said here. Behave yourselves… and as always, *best to you in all good things.*"

As Harry says, "Behave yourselves… and as always, *best to you in all good things*" the sound of his signature sign-off for the show – the guitar introduction to the Beatles *Here Comes the Sun* plays softly over his words and builds to the lyrics: ♪ ♫ ♩… The lyrics speak of the bright new day that's coming…

IIII

Later, Harry calls Bob's cell number. It's ringing, but then there's a click sound followed by a recorded female voice in robotic manner saying, "This number has been canceled. Have a *Great Awakening Day*. And remember – ***There is nothing you***

can do without us knowing about it!"Then a disconnection click. In his mind Harry sees the note on Bob's desk: *We know what you're doing. Your time is up.*

Harry stops breathing. After some moments, he takes a deep breath. He knows Bob is dead.

Harry is intensely aware of his despair. He immediately challenges himself to see if he can forget what he now knows – Bob is dead – for at least a brief moment, before realizing it and feeling it again. But for the rest of the day he isn't able to get a momentary respite from the constant mindfulness of Bob's death. Harry goes to sleep with Bob on his mind.

When Harry wakes up the next morning, he realizes he slept well throughout the night –without his usual *conscious sleeping*. What he tried to do the day before – not think about Bob –happened/didn't happen – while he slept. No *conscious sleeping* with thoughts about Bob. And no dreams about Bob. Not even symbolic images about Bob. No Dreams at all. Harry slept like a rock.

But moments after he wakes, as he is aware of his waking consciousness, it all comes rushing back. It's as if yesterday was a bad dream. But it's all too real.

Like every day, there are things to do. Penelope is already at the office doing accounts receivables. Harry is in the kitchen with Billy. Both eating Wheat Chex with milk and bananas. They're wearing sweatpants and T-shirts.

The bananas remind Harry of Bob, because under the *Party Regime* trade agreements with banana growing countries are disrupted, making bananas a rare commodity. One of the oligarchy perks of working with Bob and the *Party Regime* is Harry can now get bananas. Harry had told Bob how he missed having bananas in his Wheat Chex. Bob told Harry he could take care of that. Harry appreciated the offer but said to Bob he didn't have to. Bob insisted. Since then, the Archer household has never been without bananas.

Harry decides not to tell the family about Bob. They don't know him anyway.

The flatscreen in the family room automatically comes on at 7:00 AM and loops a repeating ten-minute message given by *The Big Guy*. State approved flatscreen monitors are in all households – they monitor household activity as well as televise approved content and required broadcasts. *The Big Tech Three* has a guaranteed lock on the flatscreen market with exclusive monopolistic government contracts controlled by the *Party Regime*. The money that flows to *the Big Tech Three* never ends. In all history world financial dominance by the fewest number of people has never been as extreme by a multiple of at least a thousand.

Harry and Billy eat their cereal at the kitchen table in silence. They can hear *The Big Guy* on the monitor drone on about loyalty to the *Party Regime*. He says the word "unity" what seems like every other sentence. These looped messages have a hypnotic effect: Even if you think the messages are nonsense, with constant repetition over a period of time most PODs become intellectual zombies – programmed to think and do what the *Party Regime* tells them to think and do. Not Harry. His resistance to *zombification* is absolute. But for most PODs when scaled throughout the nation this creates an army of intellectual zombies marching in lockstep and bowing to the authority of the *Party Regime* unable to hear other voices, not even their own – they are the "zombie *Awaken*" as Harry calls them.

Not long ago there was a run on the market for earplugs. Shortly thereafter the *Party Regime* banned the sale of earplugs. They became a black-market commodity. Being in possession of earplugs is now a crime. Harry has earplugs.

Since there is no talking in the Archer household, the "secret place" outside the apartment is a welcomed destination for family members to meet and talk with one another. After their cereal, Harry and Billy get dressed for the day and go there. Billy's not in school today because it's a school holiday – not a national holiday – a once-a-month holiday for students as teachers meet for state curriculum/reeducation instruction.

Billy is a lanky kid who's been on a growth spurt the last year that has those who know him saying he's going to be taller than his dad. For now, he's still shorter than Harry by four inches. Billy has dark eyes like his dad. His sandy colored straight hair is a bit shaggy in a way that suggests he doesn't pay attention to how it looks even though he does. He doesn't shave yet, but the beginnings of pubescent facial hair are making their appearance. Billy is dressed in his usual combat camouflage green cargo shorts and T-shirt.

Harry starts with his usual non-interesting question, "How's school?" Long ago, Billy got used to this question and decided to be tolerant of it as just a conversation starter.

"It's okay… if you don't mind being told what to think."

"You know, it's not bad being told what to think if you're also told to think about what you've been told to think and decide if what you've been told to think is good thinking. What do you think about that, Billy?"

Billy is used to his dad picking up the pace with very little to go on and make it something silly and possibly profound. The silly part was guaranteed. The profound part is hit and miss – mostly miss. To keep up the pace with his dad, Billy responds, "I think if I heard that without knowing who said it, I'd know it was you that said it. It sounds just like something you would say. That's what I think."

"That's my Billy. You're a good thinker. Don't let school or anyone keep you from thinking your own best thoughts.

"Pops?"

"Yeah?"

"How are you doing?"

"Oh, me? I'm in my head a lot."

"Who isn't? And you didn't answer my question. How you doing?"

"I'm fine."

"No, you aren't." Billy is perceptive and has good intuitions.

"Well, *I am fine*. What you're picking up is me trying to stay fine. I'm trying to stay fine in a world that's more confused than it needs to be. That's why I'm obsessed with thinking. I have this belief that we can think our way out of the bad stuff to a better… well, to better thinking. If we think better, we'll be better."

Billy playfully but sincerely repeats to his dad what his dad just said to him. "Hey, pops, don't let anyone keep you from thinking your own best thoughts."

"Good advice, Billy." As they walk back to the apartment Harry puts his right arm around his son and gives him a one-arm hug from the side.

IV

Harry walks out of the Starbucks he frequents with his cup of *House Blend* with cream. Two men in dark suits walk up to him. One speaks. "Harry Archer, I'm Detective Tennison and this is Detective Berry. We want to talk to you about Bob Burke." Both men are wearing mirrored aviators.

The grief Harry feels that Bob came to his end at the hands of the *Party Regime* is bad enough. But now with these two guys showing up to "talk" with him, Harry fears he's next. "You mean killed, Harry." was the last thing Bob had said to him at their last meeting! He fears the detective's next words will be something like – *Let's take a ride somewhere so we can talk.*

Detective Tennison says, "Let's take a ride somewhere so we can talk."

Harry looks down at the cup of coffee he just purchased. Then he looks up at Tennison. Tennison says, "Bring the coffee with you."

The three, with Harry in the middle, walk over to – what else? Harry thinks – a black 2024 SUV. Detective Berry remains silent and opens the rear passenger door for Harry. He gets in. Berry closes the door, comes around and gets into the rear passenger seat beside Harry. Tennison drives. On their way to a destination unknown to Harry, he thinks he may never see his family again. He wonders: Will Daisy come up with another Circle of Hell? Will Billy grow taller than him? Will Penelope make up her mind that she scored with him? Twenty minutes later the SUV stops at a 1950s ranch-style house in a suburban area. Harry has not taken a single sip of his coffee.

They all exit the SUV and stand for a moment outside the vehicle. Tennison says, "This is it." Harry thinks, *Don't let this be it.*

Tennison motions Harry to walk in front of Berry and him. They walk to the front door with Harry in the lead. Tennison says, "Go ahead, Harry, open it… go in." Harry is now certain he is done for… just like Joe Pesci in *Goodfellas.* Harry thinks if this gets rough, he can use his now cold coffee as a weapon against his assailants. Then he thinks, *cold coffee with cream? – pathetic – I'm screwed.*

Harry opens the door and walks in. "You're alive!!"

Standing in the middle of the room is Bob Burke. "Well, 'Bogie,' I guess you *do* care about me," Bob says, smiling.

"Oh gosh!" Harry joyfully walks over to Bob and hugs his large frame. Bob hugs back.

"Yes, 'Bogie,' I care for you, too." Bob is still smiling.

With Harry's joy and relief, he now craves the taste of the coffee he's still holding. "Hey, Bob, I have a question. Is there a microwave in the kitchen? I'd like to heat this up." Showing Bob the cup in his hand.

This is Harry's lucky day. First, there *is* a microwave in the kitchen; he's able to heat up his coffee to his satisfaction. And second, Bob is not dead.

Just the way people have been showing up, then disappearing lately in Harry's life, when he returns to the living room Bob is alone while Tennison and Berry are gone.

Harry, with his coffee and Bob, with his bottled water in hand, sit in facing upholstered chairs.

Bob speaks, "It's time, Harry, to fill you in on the big picture. I'm going to show you the little parts that make up this big picture."

"That would be good. I'm all ears."

"Harry, when we first met you asked me what I did before working at the ministry."

Harry wants to show Bob he remembers. "You said *waste management*."

"Yeah, Harry, that's what I do. I do *waste management*. That's what 'this' has all been about – managing the waste product of societal stupidity and destruction which manifested by the *Party Regime*. The *Party Regime* is waste matter. It has to be defeated or we will all be consumed by this garbage… and *become* waste matter ourselves. So, you see? *Waste management*.

"I gave you a hard time once when you were rambling on about 'this thing' as you called it. Of course, if you apply the slightest amount of good reason in considering the landscape of power politics, societal/cultural functioning, and the soul of a single person, you will encounter confounding intellectual frustration, which leads to emotional despair. So, it's understandable and fitting for those who feel frustrated and besieged by societal stupidity but are courageous enough to be sensible, to contemptibly call the ills of what's going on 'this thing' like you did."

Harry feels validated by Bob for whom he is feeling growing respect. He loves hearing the word "stupidity" the way Bob said it. He also liked what Bob said about waste matter.

Bob continues. "*This thing* is as bad as you imagine, Harry. But there are more people aligned against *this thing* than people are aware. I'm an example. You know the term 'deep state?' Of course, you do. It's true there is a *deep state*. I was thought by *deep staters* to be one of them. I acted like one of them. But I'm not."

Bob pauses, lifts the bottled water to his lips but doesn't drink. He lowers the bottle propping it on his knee and says with feeling, "You know the Martin Luther King *I Have a Dream* speech? With that speech, King put the word 'dream' on the aspirational map in a real way. There are two ways you can think about a dream. One is it's a dream, so it isn't possible. The other way is to think nothing's possible until you dream it. The second way is how I look at it. And so do you. And I think... I believe, most people do if they do not allow themselves to be overwhelmed by power-political-virtue intimidation."

Bob now takes a sip of his water. Then he says, "Here's *what's going on* as you are famous for writing and saying, Harry. People working in government and bureaucratic offices and other places throughout the country who want to push back against the *deep state* and the *Awaken* covertly organized the *dream state*. These *dream staters* look like *deep staters* but are *dream staters*." Bob chuckles. "How's that for conspiracy?"

Bob takes another couple of sips of water, "The thing about totalitarian rule, which we are definitely submerged in, is it only takes a few people in key places to terrorize the rest of us. These few people – these 'puppet masters' – are not the problem. What happens in greater society is always in the hands of the public at large... too many of whom are asleep at the wheel. Right now, the *Awaken* have platforms and communication channels that *dream staters* and the like are excluded from. If no action is taken against this totalitarian wave and their tactics we are done for. The *dream staters* are taking action.

"I got caught by *deep staters* for being a *dream stater*. I knew it was just a matter of time. But I prepared for it. I went 'ghost.' And I'm letting you in on it now.

"The thing is, Harry, there's really no true conspiracies anywhere. The things that look like conspiratorial oligarchies are really *individuals* pulling in the same or similar direction, making some headway by virtue of opportunistic 'trade winds' and 'tidal currents.' The strongest trade winds and tidal currents are based in public opinion. Harry, in this moment the two of us are a conspiracy. The moment we physically part company, *we each spring back to being an 'island' – we're on our own.*"

"Harry, you were on our – *dream staters'* – radar for some time. We started you on writing articles that didn't identify you by name on the byline. When you passed that test – and you did with flying colors – our team got you on the *Eric Blair Show*. That was a test market tactic. It was my idea to have Eric mention your banned book. That risk paid off. There's a big black-market demand for your book now. Jacob Publishing can handle printing and distribution. Your appeal in the public is in positive numbers. We can take advantage of that to try and "slay this dragon" called the *Party Regime* and its *Awaken* adherents.

Harry hasn't moved since Bob started talking. He's transfixed with Bob's revelations. He hasn't even taken a drink of his much-desired coffee. He's also thinking if his book is selling on the black market, he should be getting black market royalties. Harry can discuss that with Bob later.

Bob takes another sip of water. "Harry, let's rattle people out of their state-induced trance… coma. Together with other *dream staters* I'm… we're going to set you up. We're going to put you on the 'big stage.' We're going to put *you* in position to bring down the full weight of the government on you. How does that sound?!"

"That's great, Bob… can I go back to thinking you were killed and you're dead?" Harry's voice is full of sarcasm.

"Ha… Harry, it's just the government. It's just the *Party Regime*. It's just President Biddle."

"If it were only Biddle, I would *not* be worried. The government and *Party Regime*… well, those are forms of psychopathology that pose unrelenting danger."

"Psychopathology. Yeah, you're right, Harry! That's why 'our guys' – *dream staters* – have your back."

"Is this where I say 'okay' I'm in?" Harry finally sips his coffee which is now cold again.

"Yes. Except for one thing."

"What?"

"You're already in. Oh, and, Harry, don't worry about that *Thought & Locator chip* BS. We took care of that. Nobody is going to implant you. You're off that roster."

"Bob? You mean it?"

"Yes."

"Bob?! You mean it?!"

"Yes. Yes. I… mean… it!"

Harry believes Bob and sighs.

Bob sips his water as Harry sips his cold *House Blend.*

V

Harry is in Manhattan at a civil engineering conference. It's 9:47 AM. Harry's cell phone vibrates. The screen shows the *YCN* logo and the words "Your Cable News."

Harry answers, "Hello?"

A female's voice says, "Hi. Is this Mr. Archer, Mr. Harry Archer?"

"Who is this?"

"This is Linda Graham. I'm the producer of the *Derrick Lime Show* on *YCN*.

"Yes, it's me."

"Great! You've been getting a lot of press, Mr. Archer."

"Call me Harry."

"Thank you, Harry." She pauses slightly. "We, Derrick, would like to have you on the show."

"You know, Linda, my writings have been exposed to stand for things Derrick is against. Let's just say we don't have the same worldview."

"Of course, we know that. But you recently went public with your regrets about the things you've written. You're interesting, Harry. You're news."

"You mean, you want to use me for a 'perp walk,' a 'confession,' a 'repentant apology.'"

"Harry… that's what I said, you're news."

"Linda, if you want me on the show, I actually think it's a good idea. I would like to say where I was wrong. It could be helpful to the public.

"Great!"

"But I will do it on the condition we do it live in-studio face-to-face, Derrick and me. I will not do it recorded or remotely."

"That's not a problem. We know you're in town. We saw a piece in the paper on you. I respect your condition and I appreciate your willingness to be open with how your ideas evolved. A limousine will pick you up at your hotel later today in time to make this evening's broadcast."

Linda and Harry wrap up the call, exchanging respective contact information, details, and pleasantries.

The call over, Harry feels the dread of doom one has walking into the "lions' den." He takes a deep breath. Courage, he thinks… courage … *pawn takes queen.*

* * *

Harry arrives at the *YCN* studio. He's dressed for TV, wearing his just clean and pressed dark blue suit, powder blue shirt, and solid maroon tie. He is warmly greeted and introduced to Derrick Lime. Lime is gracious, friendly, and quite dapper in his dark wool suit, white shirt, and grayish green tie with matching pocket square.

With a group of production staff standing around the two men, Harry quips, "This should be interesting."

Lime and the group chuckle. Then Lime says to Harry, "Let's save it for the cameras."

Harry responds genially, "I'm with you."

Harry is escorted to a room where he gets a little hair and makeup treatment. The makeup artist, an older man, in a moment when they are alone, leans into Harry's right ear and whispers, "I like what you write." He then stands upright and says, "This should be interesting."

Harry whispers, "Thank you… you took the words right out of my mouth."

Harry is now on the set with Derrick Lime. A crew technician gets him "mic-ed-up," fishing a wire under his coat and clipping the end with the small mic to his coat lapel. He sits in a high stool type chair at a table with a clear plexiglass top. Harry has always wondered how the tabletops on news shows with this same glassy surface always look clean and smudge free on TV. With his hands folded on the glassy surface he's self-conscious the moisture building in his hands will smudge the now clean surface.

Another crew technician comes over to Harry and kindly pulls at Harry's coat and shirt collar, adjusting the apparel for a good on-camera look. In a low voice the technician says to herself, "This should be interesting."

Hearing the comments from the crew, Harry thinks – every now and then it's nice to have unanimous agreement. In a whisper, he mutters to himself, "This is *definitely* going to be interesting."

Harry now hears the opening "newsy" style music introduction to the show. Derrick Lime comes on with his usual opening line which is the name of the show, "*It's Time for Lime*" as the music fades out, "Hello, everybody! We have a lot to talk about." He continues, "Tonight, we have repentant rabble-rouser Harry Archer in studio. You have to have been living under a rock if you haven't heard about him. Harry's made a lot of noise about our current administration and the cultural landscape of which until recently he was hypercritical. He's here to express regret for his subversive writings and grandstanding."

Lime pauses, so Harry takes the cue, responding dryly, "That's not what I'm here to do. My writings are not subversive, and I don't regret what I've written. If I regret anything it's not having more skill to get through to people who share your view of people and the world, Mr. Lime."

"But you recently listed the mistakes you made in your criticism of what you call the *Awaken* movement."

"*I* didn't label it the *Awaken* movement. But it *is* a good label and I regularly use it, as the term is intended to insult the hypocrisy and irony of those who adhere to its viewpoint. Also, there's a big difference between subversion against good things and criticism against bad things."

"I'm confused."

"I agree. You are confused. And too many people are confused. And I can clear that up if you and they have the courage to hear me out."

Lime is about to "pull the plug" on the interview and go to a backup story when he hears the urgent voice of his producer, Linda, in his earpiece, "Keep this going! This is great! The switchboard is lighting up! Viewers are tuning in at a rate we've never seen! It's already trending! Let him talk!"

With clear contempt for Harry's boldness, Lime looks into Harry's eyes. He pauses, then says, "Moments ago, before going on air you said this should be interesting. So, I don't know if it's a question of courage, but for the sake of having an 'interesting' discussion, I would like to hear more."

"Mr. Lime, I appreciate your consideration. So, I can speak to something I know you will agree with. And in this moment, you *are* being *courageous*. And from where I sit, we all need courage."

Lime hears Linda's voice again, giving director instructions, "This is great! Good job! Keep it going. Don't worry about the commercial break – I'll cue you."

Lime feels less contempt. He settles into what is unfolding with his own newly acquired sense of interest. "Harry, from what I know about you, I'm sure we don't see eye-to-eye. But I am confounded by the insensibility, bigotry, hatred, and anti-science of your positions."

"As you should be, if I and those who have a similar world view *are* insensible, bigoted, hateful, anti-science A-holes. Can I say A-holes?"

"You just said it twice. It's cable. Yeah, continue."

From his earpiece Lime hears, "Great!"

Harry goes on. "But, Mr. Lime, what if I and others – half the country of others – who are called those bad things by the likes of the *Awaken*, are none of those bad things? If you persecute people for unsubstantiated evils, you stop the free flow of ideas. Moreover, given there is no good reason to think these people are polluted with evil, they should not be silenced." Harry pauses before saying, "And even if anyone speaks evil or any absurdity in your eyes – or anyone's eyes – silencing them not only goes against a free society, it strengthens bad ideas. Having bad ideas out there for everyone to see with other ideas countering provides the way to discover the best in us."

Lime's interest grows, but he also looks as if he doesn't know what to say. Harry senses a moment to disarm his host, change the tone, and make a connection. "Mr. Lime, what do you know about me?"

"I know what's been reported about your writings. I know you do a radio broadcast."

"Right… so, you know nothing about me. And though I see you in the media – a constant fixture – I know nothing about you, Mr. Lime. You see, when the public discourse plays out on media platforms, when the cultural discourse plays out on media platforms, when political discourse plays out on media platforms, what we get is a verbal food fight between caricature personalities and caricature issues – with the purpose of character assassination instead of intelligent discussion.

"Mr. Lime, in real life you're not a caricature. And neither am I. If I *knew* you, I might think differently of you than the media impression I have of you. And I assure you, if you *knew* me, you would have a different opinion of me than what you think you know from the media. I can tell you this, Mr. Lime, you're conducting a good interview here. You let the interview be about what I have to say whether you like it or not. You haven't made it about you. You're listening and you're respecting your audience by letting them listen. From here on out, we can all think for ourselves what this means. I think we're all better for it. Thanks for having me on your show."

Lime hears in his ear, "Wow, this guy's timing is good. Go to a commercial break."

Lime relaxes. "Well, Harry, that *was* interesting." He takes a sip of whatever is in his network-logoed mug. He clears his voice and says, "I look forward to having you come on the show again."

"Thanks, Mr. Lime. Be happy to."

The show cuts to a break. Lime and Harry look at each other silently with the same calm demeanor. The silence is broken when Linda "bounces" up to the plexiglass table, "I knew that was going to be good!" she enthuses. Turning to Harry she blurts out like a tattletale gossiping about the *YCN* executives, "Nobody but me wanted to book you, Harry. Derrick didn't want you telling your 'filthy' lies."

Derrick pipes in, "That's not what I said."

"Oh, yes you did, Derrick."

Linda and Derrick's remarks sound like good-spirited banter to Harry. He's amused.

"What I said was… ah… um… ya know, you're right… I did say I didn't want to hear Harry's filthy lies."

Harry chimes in, "It's nice to know my 'filthy lies' brought us all together."

They all laugh.

Harry looks down at the tabletop surface where his hands are still resting. He notices some moister residue on the table surface. He looks at where Lime's hands had been resting and notices the same residue. When they leave the table a crew technician swoops in with cloth and glass cleaner to clean the smudges on the tabletop. Seeing this, Harry thinks to himself – hmm, that's how it stays clean.

As Harry leaves the studio, Lime walks with him and says, "I'm glad we met. You're right, Harry. *Knowing a person is different than knowing about a person.*"

Harry responds good-naturedly, "I'm glad we met too. See you soon."

* * *

Since Harry's appearance on the Derrick Lime show viewer ratings for the show went up. To increase ratings and broadcast relevance, Lime and his producers made a decision to get out of their usual *Awaken* echo chamber and book authentic voices from different perspectives. The shows are now lively, interesting, and focused on what matters. From almost no viewers, ratings improved and continue to increase as the show sticks with its new policy of being a platform for different credible views.

Harry now understands Bob Burke is a bigger deal than he first realized. Bob is the guy who gets things done. If ever there is a "chess master" at "mission impossible" operations while playing a stooge at the *Ministry of Correctness* – a disconnected irrelevant bureaucracy – Bob is the guy. He is a leader among leaders on the "dream team" of *dream staters*, as Bob puts it. Winston Smith works with Bob at the same level.

Bob's words to Harry are now etched in his mind. "... we're going to set you up. We're going to put you on the 'big stage.' We're going to put *you* in position to bring down the full weight of the government on you."

Harry doesn't doubt it. Nonetheless, it still amazes him that through his appearance on Derrick Lime and other media exposure, Bob and his team of *dream staters* have orchestrated exactly that – Harry's been set up. The brief surges of fear Harry has come to experience have become more prolonged and more frequent as a congressional hearing approaches. Harry will be addressing the congressional committee on *Thought Subversion* as he stands charged with "activities" against the state.

* * *

It's 1:22 AM. Harry and Penelope are lying in bed. Harry is on his back, staring at the ceiling fan watching it go round in a shadowy, blurry image. Penelope is on her side watching Harry. Her left hand rests on the back of his hand nearest her. She whispers, "Can't sleep."

"You or me?"

Penelope answers, "Both of us."

"I don't like saying it out loud Penny, but I'm scared. I can try and tell myself I'm not, but I am."

"I know what you're going through, Hare. But I'm proud of you. Maybe more proud because you're scared. When you're scared of what you face in the act of doing something good, but you do it anyway – that's courage. And courage is the rarest of virtues. You didn't let your fear stop you from..."

Harry abruptly fake coughs to cover over and cut off the rest of what Penelope is saying. Although unlikely at this hour, he doesn't want to take the risk that audio surveillance by the state is activated. As he moves to get out of bed he reaches for Penelope's arm and gently pulls, prompting her to join him. In less than ten minutes they are walking on the path to their secrete place, both hastily dressed in whatever clothes they had thrown onto the bench at the foot of their bed. The moon is not out. The only illumination is from dim streetlamps along the greenbelt. They walk side-by-side not touching each other or holding hands. As they walk Harry and Penelope continue their "pillow talk" – now without the pillows and possible surveillance.

"Pen, I'm not just scared for me. I'm scared for you and the kids. These *Party Regime* goons play for keeps. In two days, I'm going to be the 'whipping boy' on display for the public at a congressional hearing's version of a 'kangaroo court.'"

"Hmm, 'whipping boy,' 'kangaroo court.' You've got your metaphors mixing it up again."

Harry feels like Penelope and Bob have a thing about mixed metaphors. "Penny, I don't think we can laugh our way out of this."

"We're not laughing our way out of anything. Besides, getting out of challenges, particularly those with everything on the line isn't what laughter is for. You know, Hare, laughter can create either closeness or distance. But it's also for perspective and sweetness."

"Well, I... ah..."

"Sorry, Harry, I'm not done. The stuff that matters in life comes with danger. Thinking is dangerous... particularly in these times. But it's more dangerous not to be allowed to think... again, particularly in these times." Penelope pauses to think then continues, "Harry, I have something *cosmic* for you."

"Cosmic? You sound like me."

"I just know how to speak *Harry*. I started to learn that language when we first met. It's an interesting language."

Penelope reaches for Harry's hand and holds it tight. Smiling, she turns her head to look at him even though it's too dark for him to see her face clearly. "It's just the kind of thing you like, Harry. It's an idea. Here it is: The greatest physical force in the universe is *gravity*. *Gravity* has its way with everything... until humans come along with nothing more than ideas... ideas that counteract *gravity*. That makes an *idea* the most powerful thing in the universe."

"Penny, I didn't see *that* coming. Hmm, an *idea* is more powerful than *gravity*. I mean *gravity* more often than not 'wins the day' – like always. But ideas did lead to catapults, helium balloons, airplanes..."

"And rocket propelled outer space travel."

"Hmm, an *idea* is the only thing that willfully challenges *gravity*."

"That's it, Harry! It doesn't take much for you to take complicated ideas and make them simple to understand. That's your gift. And as long as I've known you, you've been generous with your gift. Harry, you're a builder, a thinker, an idea maker. You can't help it. Your ideas are in a class beyond the goons who want to destroy us on they're way to destroying everything that's good. They're the ones who should be afraid. Not you. But their too stupid to be afraid and see that they are on a path to self-destruction. All their actions against humanity will ultimately be used against them – by them – to demolish their own existence. Like applying judo leverage principles all you need to do, Harry, is help them destroy themselves. You've already been doing it. Something else… like it or not, Hare, you're the kind of person that exposes an important reality about human living: chaos and order in civil life are as much of an ongoing problem as chaos and order are in a singular personal life. People are uncomfortable with that reality. So, you are attacked for being a person who exposes that reality just by being you. I know the attacks are hard, but don't stop being you, Harry.

"As for the kids… we really lucked out with them. Whether we raised them right or they just came out that way or both, they get it. They're smart enough and mature enough to be in this as a family… and be who they are."

"Jeez, Pen, did you take a course in 'pep-talk-ology?' All of the sudden I'm not afraid of the goons anymore. Now I'm afraid of wasting the best pep-talk ever by not living up to its call."

Penelope stops her stride. She turns and firmly pulls Harry against her to face him eye-to-eye. "Harry, I said it to Steve

Reed and I'm saying it to you right now when it matters most: *I'm sticking with a sure thing*. Harry, you're my 'sure thing.'"

They hold each other under the flickering light of a streetlamp.

VI

Wearing a business suit appropriate for the occasion, Harry sits at the "witness" table, which in this case is the "accused and condemned" table, at a nationally televised congressional hearing, described by the press and the *Party Regime* as sedition cleansing. Harry is to be *cleansed.*

The Chair of the committee is a short round-build, round-faced man in his sixties wearing black-framed readers halfway down his nose. His hair is short and appears to be dyed a darker shade than its natural color. He's been in Congress forever. Gaveling the hearing to order, he says, "Mr. Archer, at this hearing you stand charged with aiding and abetting treasonous thoughts through your subversive writings and public appearances. You have spread lies about the current Executive administration and the *Party Regime*. It is particularly heinous of you, as the Executive administration and *Party Regime* are aligned with the best interest of the state.

"Your actions, Mr. Archer, are a flagrant disregard for the good of the state, aimed only to serve your own warped self-interest. Your writings and actions are subversive, are racist, are counter to climate wellness, and are an enemy of decency.

"This hearing has convened to determine if this Congressional committee should recommend that the newly formed *Ministry of Compliance* bring indictments against you. Mr. Archer, there is no more serious matter than the reason we are here now."

For the rest of the day's proceedings, eleven Congressional representatives from the *Party Regime* take their respective turns to bellow scathing narratives about Harry's "contemptible" ideas. "Humanity has no place for so low a creature as you, Mr. Archer," seethes one of the representatives.

Finally, the Chair of the committee gavels the end of the day and calls for a recess; the hearing to continue tomorrow.

* * *

The following day, Harry is back in the "witness chair." As Penelope had insisted, Harry is wearing a new dark gray suit, a new white shirt, a new blue tie with a barely perceptible geometric pattern in it, and new Oxford shoes no one will see. He is breathing slowly, trying to stay and look calm. He's looking up at the raised dais which looks like an elongated judge's courtroom bench behind which the Chair and eleven *Party Regime* representatives are sitting in judgment of Harry. He watches the activity of Congressional staffers behind the committee on cell phones, shuffling papers, and leaning forward to whisper into their bosses' ears. Harry thinks about the insane number of hours, emails, phone calls, pizza deliveries, and alcohol consumed, all on account of him. He feels it's both ridiculous and oddly flattering. The Chair and eleven representatives look serious and determined.

The Chair calls the hearing to order, makes his opening statement, and addresses Harry: "Mr. Archer, this now is your time to address the committee."

"Thank you," Harry says softly. He looks at the Chair. "May I stand?"

There is a pause as the Chair, seated mid-panel, looks to the representatives on his right and then his left. He then looks at Harry and says, "Yes, Mr. Archer. If you'd like."

"Thank you, Chairman." Harry stands up and takes a few steps to a nearby lectern. He deliberately doesn't stand behind the lectern. He stands beside the lectern, his right hand perched on the top of it. Harry looks down at the floor, takes a breath, raises his head with dignity and confidence, looks at the representative at the end of the panel to his left. He makes eye contact, then pans slowly to his right until he has visually engaged each representative.

Standing this way aside the lectern – all of this physical posturing and pacing is a "chess move."

Harry speaks without notes in a warm, balanced voice.

"Life, liberty, and the pursuit of happiness. Or *fear, ignorance, and the corruption of power*. I do not speak to you here to defend myself of any charges brought against me. The charges against me are an indictment against the *Regime* that brought the charges." Slowly turning his body and head smoothly to one side, then back to the other side, Harry is speaking

personally to each representative making eye contact continuously and fluidly.

"My speaking here is an appeal to *our better nature*. Upon which we have cultivated too little to meet the challenges and requirements for a decent society. Another person during a similar time of crisis to humanity called it *the better angels of our nature.* Again, I emphasize we are painfully in short supply of it.

"There is, however, a 'wellspring' of infinite resource where *our better nature* can be continually cultivated, nourished, and harvested. That is *the wellspring of freedom of thought and speech*. Block access to that 'wellspring,' and we are doomed to extinction. And we will deserve such self-destruction for our foolishness.

"Without emersion into this *wellspring* with free thinking and speaking we face the darkness of delusion. Good thinking requires work. That includes sharing our ideas with others to get feedback. Restrictions on either thought or speech will kill this vital process. I'm reminded what John F. Kennedy pointed out, '*Too often we enjoy the comfort of opinion without the discomfort of thought.*' What I present here will not be understood if you remain comfortable. Your discomfort, however, may open your eyes… if not for you on this panel, maybe for those witnessing this."

Harry moves his hand from the lectern bringing his arm to his side. He looks down for a moment then raises his head signifying the start of his next point.

"Much has been said about truth and lies. John Adams weighed in, '*Facts are stubborn things*; and whatever may be our wishes, our inclinations, or the dictates of our passion, they cannot alter the state of facts and evidence.'

"For some reason, apprehending facts as a nation of people is a formidable challenge. *As easy as it can be to identify many pivotal facts, treating them with the understanding they deserve seems damn near impossible as a nation of people*. Maybe some discomfort will help more of us see and understand what must be seen and understood for people to survive and prosper which is how society survives and prospers.

"With all my will and intention, I will now commit a 'hate speech' crime. I hate stupidity. I hate hysteria. I hate mob violence. I hate corruption. I hate the forces that obscure truth. I hate self-righteousness.

There's a lot of good in hating bad things. There's a lot of bad in loving bad things that are called good. All throughout history, people have gotten confused about good and bad.

"Without *free thought* and *free speech*, confusion will prevail, bringing perpetual darkness. The necessity of *freedom of thought* and *freedom of speech* rests on two principles. First, the value of individual integrity as the source for meaning and the incentive for survival. And second, the contribution to the reservoir of *thought wealth* available to the community – our collective consciousness – for meaning and survival."

As Harry is speaking, his head and eyes slowly pan the representatives before him, oscillating left to right, right to left. He notices the representative third from the right disapprovingly shaking her head. Harry addresses her, "I see you shaking your head Representative. I take that to mean you disagree with something I said."

The Chair interrupts. "Please confine your statements to what you have prepared, Mr. Archer!"

"I have, Chairman. I anticipated there'd be expressed disagreement with my remarks, as I am now seeing. I have prepared a response. If the distinguished representative or any on the committee disagrees with the perspective I am laying out, such disagreement deserves a response showing the rationale for my remarks. To respond to the representative is an act of respect for her challenge and an acknowledgment she cares about what matters. But if I'm wrong, that is, if the representative's challenge deserves no respect, and if she doesn't care about what matters, that means she has no business being on this committee unless this committee's purpose is a corrupt power play."

A mix of mild laughter and a murmur from the audience fills the chamber. The Chair strikes his gavel twice, "Order." The audible disruption subsides, the room now silent.

Again, another chess move. Harry knows there is no need to argue. So, his intention and strategy are not to do so, although he is game to throw down biting commentary that exposes the committee's fraud. Whatever anyone on the committee says or does Harry will respond by "framing" it in an "acknowledging comment" that conveys he trusts the public can well judge for itself what is happening. He thinks this can be effective, but risky. He is allowing "the game" to play out.

The Chair clears his throat and says, "Please continue, Mr. Archer."

Harry responds, "Thank you, Chairman. That was revealing."

Harry waits a moment before continuing, "Throughout history, humans have failed to strike the practical and moral balance of perhaps the most significant competing forces in the human psyche – the individual for and against the community, and the community for and against the individual.

"This failure plays out to extreme degrees, pushing and pulling on all manner of factions in society – our society. This failure is exploited by the *Party Regime*. Despite the takeover of governmental power by the *Party Regime*, no, rather *because* of their takeover, we are still confronted with this great question of reconciling the individual and the community.

"To tackle this great question, we need to bring both individual wisdom and collective wisdom to bare on what troubles us. We need to understand the dynamics of the individual and the dynamics of the collective. We need to understand the gains as well as the drawbacks of both collectivism without the individual and individualism without the collective.

"Collectively, we can never know what's real. This is because a *collective* perspective is a distortion of *individual* integrity and relevance. The effect of all things is a potential experience only an individual can apprehend. For better or worse, a collective can accomplish things that an individual cannot do alone. But the effects of what is done are only experienced individually, by each person in the collective. The individual's experiences may be the same, similar, dissimilar, different. The individual's experiences may be good, inconsequential, bad.

"This means eliminating the perspective and voice of the individual, as the *Regime* does, takes the most relevant factor – revealing what is real and what matters – out of the equation. If a person is standing with one barefoot in a bucket of ice and their other barefoot in a bucket of burning hot coals, it would be a fatally flawed perspective to view the effects through the prism that a foot's individual significance is unimportant and just a part of a collective. This collective view prevents knowing and appreciating what's real and what matters. Averaging out polar extremes does not give you an acceptable middle.

"Moreover, and ironically, when a regime is totalitarian like this *Regime*, the collective never experiences an 'acceptable middle.' The collective only experiences the worst of extremes in our institutions, customs, and governance. In just the last century totalitarian collectives from various regions have killed – murdered – through starvation, bullets, and other dehumanizing methods over a hundred million individual human beings. If you call these murdered souls 'PODs,' maybe for some people like those of the *Party Regime*, it takes the 'sting' out of the atrocity."

The audience in the chamber let out a murmuring wave of voices that conveyed approval and support for Harry's last sentence. Notably the Chair does not gavel or say "order" to quiet the spectators.

At the central broadcasting headquarters under control of the *Party Regime*, the broadcast manager is sitting at the console watching the live feed of the Congressional hearing on multiple monitors. She swivels her chair 180 degrees to face Winston Smith who is sitting in a large leather chair on a slightly raised platform behind her. The control booth is occupied by five other broadcast technicians. Winston is smoking a cigar which is now down half-length from its original size. Smoking is not allowed in the booth… except for Winston Smith.

Karen, the broadcast manager is alarmed, "This isn't going the way we expected, Mr. Smith. We gotta' stop this! Should I cut the feed and switch to backup programming?"

Winston draws on his cigar, raises his chin as he turns his head slightly to the right, and through pursed lips blows a stream of smoke into the air. "No, Ms. Karen, it's all right. Keep the feed going."

"Are you *sure*, Mr. Smith? What he's saying is prohibited by the *Party*!"

"It's okay, I take full responsibility. Keep the feed going." With a deep sense of fulfillment, Winston flicks his cigar ashes into the ashtray on the side table adjacent to his chair. The broadcast continues.

As the murmuring subsides Harry picks up where he left off: "We are now in the grips of a societal distortion constructed and maintained by the *Party Regime* to keep individuals subjugated to the will of the *Party Regime*. It's all about power. But in the end, even the *Party Regime* will fall under its own weight of hate, bigotry, and corruption. It will cannibalize itself until nothing is left… à la the French Revolution's *Reign of Terror*, where in the end, however righteous they proclaimed the cause to be, the revolutionaries became a mob. The mob employed the guillotine against the oppressive ruling class. And then turned the guillotine against itself. *Mobs murder reason*.

"In a truly apocalyptic way, our society is now poised for that kind of destruction. Using the word 'apocalypse' is not hyperbole. It is a serious purposeful use of the word. An apocalypse is not only complete destruction, it is *prophesized* destruction. Or, if you prefer to avoid religious, theological overtones, we can call it *predictable* destruction. Either way, we can see it coming in real time. Moreover, the destruction we are talking about is completely self-inflicted and therefore it doesn't have to happen. Religious or not, this destruction does nobody any good.

"How did this happen? We need to answer this question even though the answer is obvious and simple to anyone who values goodness and freedom. That's the answer right there – *you value goodness and freedom*. This *Regime* happened because too many of us didn't and don't value *goodness and freedom*. We allowed unworthy leaders to take over society, culture, religion, education, communication, commerce, transportation, and thoughts. And too many of those who positioned themselves as leaders shilled for *the Big Tech Three*, who used these demagogic leaders as useful idiots.

"We threw aside where the power of what used to be this Republic comes from – the people… *the people* – sovereign individuals that make up our society. As the imperfect founders of this Republic canonized in the *Constitution*, the power comes from *We the People*."

Harry cups the back of his right hand in his left hand.

"… And the rights of each individual come from no person or group of people but from *nature*. The document justifying the independence of this nation, declaring the principles linked to this nation's founding specifies such rights come from *the laws of nature and of nature's God*. The document of rights that was adopted as a requirement for this nation to become a nation stipulates that it's up to the individual to understand the meaning of God in their own way, including whether or not there is a God. The point is *unalienable rights exist* and we as individuals and a community of people will either honor those rights or violate them. The *Party Regime* exists to violate these rights.

"In this regard, if this Republic is to stand as a republic for the principles upon which it was founded its leaders must serve the public and preserve *unalienable rights*. Leaders are not here to be served by the public. A violation of one's individual rights in the name of the collective as the *Party Regime* perpetuates is a betrayal of the people and of what leadership should be.

"The *Party Regime* uses many weapons against us, the people – the nation. The most abominable sinful weapon is *racism*. The *racism* Rosa Parks *stood* against by *sitting* – taking an open seat on a public bus – is not what the *Party Regime* is fighting against. All decent people stand with Parks. Instead of fighting against *racism* the *Party Regime* aggresses against a phantom *racism* to exploit groups it pretends to help, but instead insultingly harms. The real racists are the members of the *Party Regime* as the party commits *racism* in its messaging rhetoric. It is a nonstop filtered reduction of all issues beginning and ending with *racism*. We are deprived of seeing anything for what it is because *racism* is always identified as the cause and effect. It is a predetermined intractable presence with no remedy or relief. Which is the intention of the *Party Regime* in this dystopian era called the *Great Awakening* and its adherents known as the *Awaken*. The intention of these warriors for dystopia is that there should never be an end to racial animus – no relief from *racism*.

"It is a requirement to 'bend the knee,' gaining you no absolution or forgiveness for your acquiescence. Rather, this act of repentance allows you to reside in the purgatory of the eternal sinner, which has become much coveted by the self-loathing *Awaken*. But there is a 'sleight of hand' performed by the self-righteous part of *Awakenness* that relieves them from suffering the ill effects of the self-loathing part. For an *Awaken* person it is simply – *You are bad, and I am good*. This is the airtight position of the *Awaken* and is exploited by the *Party Regime*. It is pathological. You've heard the word "pathological." But I want to make sure you know what it means. It means diseased. It is anything unhealthy, unwell, contaminated. Nothing good comes from it.

"*Racism* is a scourge, so is calling someone who is not racist a racist. At that point, *racism* ceases to have meaning. By its fraudulent use, the word '*racism*' – a word that should have profound meaning – is robbed of the serious impact it needs to have. The real racists are the members of the *Party Regime*.

"When I first heard the phrase '*content of their character*' I knew the person who spoke those words – not far from here – said something that day to affirm the respect for humanity that decency demands. The *Party Regime* is an enemy to such respect and decency as it maliciously and falsely vilifies good people as racist. Supporters of the previous administration – those who are good people whom the *Party Regime* wrongly and maliciously call racist – stand for the value Nelson Mandela expressed '*… live in a way that respects and enhances the freedom of others.*' *Racism* is incompatible with this value.

"This brings us to another evil of the *Party Regime* – the butchering of language. An ability setting us apart from all other species is the natural remarkable gift of verbal language. We can perpetually craft human verbal language for better interpersonal/community understanding and productivity. But too often we turn language against one another to inflict unjustifiable harm. The abuse of language and the acceptance of this abuse are among the highest shames of our misdeeds.

"A word comes into existence based on what it means at its birth. But dishonesty motivates corruption in all things, including words. We think in words. We think in language. If words are corrupted – if language is corrupted – then thought and thinking are confused and corrupted.

"Look at the motto and credo of the *Party Regime:*

DEATH IS LIFE, OPPRESSION IS LIBERTY, WEAKNESS IS STRENGTH

"Let me say it again slowly so there won't be any reason to disagree with me about the perversion of thought the *Party Regime* wants imposed onto every person.

DEATH IS LIFE … OPPRESSION IS LIBERTY … WEAKNESS IS STRENGTH

"Each phrase of the credo has the meaning of a word be the opposite of what it really means. The overexposure to only *Party Regime* and *Awaken* doctrine eventually renders the incapacity of having free ideas. This incapacity is the objective of the *Party Regime.*

"In its insatiable hunger for power, not the welfare of people, the *Party Regime* lapses into insensibility without being aware of it. Earlier this year, the *Party Regime* banned the word 'strong.' Yet in its credo – which I just twice recited – the word 'strength' is affirmed – perversely affirmed – but affirmed, nonetheless. If this is the vision of the party, it can only be expected that sensible people will rightly have nothing to do with it.

"The perversion of language is also seen in the *Party Regime* calling this time in history the *Great Awakening.* That term uses positive words to describe what is hardly a 'great awakening' but is rather another 'dark age' in history. Stupidity trumping intelligence marks this 'dark age.'

"If we lose language, we lose everything. And we will not recover."

Harry is interrupted by the representative seated next to the Chair to his left, "Mr. Archer, do you really believe that?"

With an air of Socratic methodology Harry calmly "turns the table" by responding, "The question, Sir, is do you really *not* believe that?"

There is an audible reaction including chuckles from the audience in the chamber collectively expressing a favorable slant toward Harry's response. Two strikes of the Chairman's gavel ring through the chamber.

Maintaining control of his oratory and his theater, Harry continues as he returns his right hand to rest on the top of the lectern, "Because of what I have said here, there are those who will be moved to think along the lines I have laid out. But there will be those, such as the 'distinguished' representative who just questioned me, who disagree with what I have said so far, and that breaks my heart, because it's those people to whom I want to appeal in the spirit of opening their hearts and minds to a way of thinking that values freedom and decency. Despite my failure to convince those people and my heartbreak because of it, I'd rather endure their disagreement, their disapproval, and even their contempt for me and what I say here, than to have their access to my words obstructed. Nor would I want their words obstructed or their voices silenced by their detractors, myself being one.

"But I will say more in an effort to reach those who are not yet convinced of my case for the sanctity of common freedom. I hope you and all who are listening will listen with great interest. I am *nearly* certain you will find value in what I have to share. I am *certain* you should find value in it.

"So far in the history of the world, this nation has done more than any other nation state to realize the highest quality of life for more people at any one time. The cause and effect of this is *the great expansion of suburbia*. Suburbia is the expression of accessible individualism. Suburbia is currently built through the energy derived from fossil fuels. And if individualism is unimpeded, there will be continuous advancements in the development of cleaner, reusable, and efficient sources of energy. If individualism is unimpeded, these newer energies and refinements will be brought to market to compete for value.

"Cities of all sizes have been a necessary and important part of the human story. As a civil engineer I can speak as an expert to the challenges and effects of public works. My career has been devoted to building things to advance the quality of life... for everyone.

"While cities solve very important problems, they also create serious problems. Communal resources can be well-accessed with high population density. This is both a solution and problem. High population density competes with individualism bringing about ever-diminishing returns on quality living and mental well-being. Suburbia lessens population density, allowing individualism more room to breathe. But individualism is an enemy of the *Party Regime*, making the *Party Regime* an enemy of life.

"Caught in the crosshairs of suburban expansion/ individualism and the 'religion' of the *Great Awakening* extinguishing individualism is *energy consumption ideology*. *Energy consumption ideology* prominently plays out in the theater of *global-climate-change politics*.

"Global-climate-change politics is not the *science* of *global-climate-change* which has a legitimate role in understanding how best to survive on this planet as long as possible with superior quality of life. When science is exploited for political advantage, it creates an increased danger that will turn science against our best interests. The politics of *global-climate-change* has interfered with the science of *global-climate-change*.

"Our best response to *global-climate-change*, and for that matter, to all challenges we face as a species, rests in another natural remarkable gift we have – our insatiable drive to innovate. But our application of what we innovate is a 'wild card.' Every innovation we humans discover, develop, and continuously refine has been a development for better and easier living, advancing the depth and quality of life. All these discoveries and developments have also been weaponized to cause destruction – sticks, stones, fire, water, gas, energy, organic chemicals, inorganic chemicals, gunpowder, nuclear fusion, the internet, religion, and everything else.

"In this fashion humans have done the same with societal governance. The struggle for influence and power is an unavoidable reality in organized society. From this reality *politics* organically emerge. For whatever good, politics can do, it can and does easily descend into a corrupt, malignant, destructive cancer on our well-being and very existence. *Politics* is easily made into a weapon conceived and operated to destroy everything. *Politics* used this way has no regard for truth, decency, or fairness. Such *politics* is a ravenous drive for acquisition of power superiority in the name of rightfulness despite how wrong it is. Such *politics* is wholly collective and unconcerned with individualism – the person. Such *politics* has little to do with a faithful representation of the will of the people. Such *politics* is against *freedom of thought* and *freedom of speech*. Such *politics* is an unnecessary evil.

"So, if what I say here about the depravities of *politics* is true, we have a conundrum, because our society moves everything through a political system. The remedy for this conundrum and for the problem with *politics* is simple – *freedom of thought* and *freedom of speech*. With *Freedom of thought* and *freedom of speech* there is a possibility to realize the parts in *politics* supported by integrity that would otherwise not be possible in the absence of *free thought and speech*. Individuals having access to all speech strengthens the better parts of *politics*. An informed, knowledgeable, critically thinking citizenry is key to good societal governance which can only come from *free thought and speech*.

"I'm defining *politics* the way it needs to be defined. Destructive *politics* happens when you hear only part of what there is to be heard… as destructive *politics* feeds on narrow twisted narratives and dies on information and context. Destructive *politics* can be defeated when you hear *all* of what there is to be heard.

"If we hold that *unalienable rights* are the core of our founding principles, we should understand *freedom of thought* and *freedom of speech* are inextricably linked to those rights. We have those rights by virtue of our existence. If we rise above political tribalism to harness the full brain trust available to us by way of *free thought* and *free speech*, our visionary spectrum widens for the benefit of both the individual and the *world community of individuals*.

"The possibilities of this brain trust and visionary spectrum are infinite, and highlight the human species as singularly different and singularly consequential from all other species on this planet. Rather than use the term *superior* to all other species, the human species has *a responsibility* no other species has. *This responsibility* makes us unique.

"The human species has a consciousness and self-awareness as a collective and as individuals existing in the cosmos. Additionally, this consciousness and self-awareness include a need and capacity for transcendence. The human species has a fixation with mystery and incorporates it for better and worse into the ethos of human existence and comprehension. This is astoundingly remarkable and essential to being human as opposed to being anything else."

Harry pauses looking down. Holding his chin between the thumb and forefinger of his right hand he conveys the seriousness of his conviction for what he is about to say. He moves his hand from his chin to his side. He looks up and quickly pans the committee left to right. He delivers the heart of his message. *"This responsibility* is conceived and fueled by something that exists only in the human species – *a flickering interest in morality*." He pauses then proceeds. "For some reason, every so often some humans pay attention to the idea of what is right or wrong, what is good or bad. This attention – this interest – is a distinctly human construct. Without humans in the universe there is no such thing as right and wrong – good and bad. Again, this is astoundingly remarkable!

"Despite the capacity for moral consciousness, humans across the world throughout the ages do not inherently know what is good… that is, what is *moral*. Despite reliance on goodness as a definitive force, humans are woefully ill-developed about it – which reveals *morality* as a vital force, subject to massively destructive corruption.

"Our confusion and struggle with *morality* are not just intellectual thought exercises occupying the discipline of philosophy. Our grasp of and orientation to what is good or bad has consequences to our well-being and our very survival. We will perish sooner or later if we fail to understand the role of goodness in our well-being and survival both as a species and as individuals.

"Goodness for its own sake is worthy and powerful. Goodness is the ultimate objective to advance the cause of survival because a good life for as many people as possible strengthens the incentive/reward for wise living.

"The human species as a singularly different species from all other species equally includes all genders in however they may be described and all races and all creeds. The corruption of our understanding of what is good or bad has wrought great devastation throughout history by eliminating equal regard for groups within the human species.

"Our failure to allow natural decency to prevail without being exploited by the political forces of *toxic groupism* will perpetuate a great moral void. Our well-being let alone our survival is incompatible with such a void. Our destruction would be assured without wise moral sensibilities – our grasp of what is good and what is bad.

"On the grandest level of contemplation are two extremes providing vastly different perspectives that arrive at the same conclusion. 1) That our human species is the only one in the universe with self-awareness and moral capacity. Or 2) the universe is teeming with life that includes species with such self-awareness and capacities as ours, if not more. In between these two extremes is that such life exists here and there in the universe in some quantity ranging from often to rare.

"In any of these cases, the meaning of *goodness* is profound as long as there is a species with at least two individuals engaged with one another perpetuating the capacity for *goodness*. When there is no longer such a species, nothing will matter. In such a universe, no one would be around to care. *Goodness* would have no meaning in that universe. There would only be survival and procreation."

"Mr. Archer," the representative four seats to the left of the Chair leans into his microphone, "as fascinating as your comments are about the universe, can you please come *down to earth*?"

Most of the representatives on the panel smile or chuckle. The loudest full laugh comes from the Chair. The only sound from the spectators in the chamber is a barely audible collective groan.

Harry responds. "Sir, I appreciate your need to limit the size of an idea. The mystery of the cosmos is certainly a big thing to comprehend – the biggest. My intention is to offer a big picture for your consideration so as to have a full perspective and not be trapped in a *small minded* view of things. But there are those who can't help being *small minded*."

The audience fills the chamber with laughter. The Chair gavels three strikes and calls for order.

The laughter fades, the chamber is quiet, Harry continues. "In accordance with the distinguished representative's request, getting back to earth which we never really left, the myriad of tribes, cultures, and civilizations inhabiting all prehistory and history reveals an awesome mix of great triumphs in human achievement as well as shameful atrocities. And so it goes with us. The achievements are astounding, and the atrocities overshadow our existence.

"Atrocities are cruelties meted out by humans onto other humans. Atrocities are unnecessary acts. The elements of cruel and unnecessary perpetuate each other, continuing to build monstrous effects. The internment of citizens of Japanese descent during World War II is an example of such. The cruelty of that governmental mandate went hand-in-hand with its lack of necessity. Such injustices are adopted through the dehumanization of people. This invents and nurtures the false justifications for atrocities. It happens all the time. And if we don't say and do anything against it, we are at fault.

"Nothing stops or prevents atrocities except two things – *goodness* and *courage*. Persecution, elitism, humiliation, torture, slavery, unjustified imprisonment, murder, genocide, and any cruelty inflicted on anyone by anyone cannot exist if the love of decency – otherwise called *goodness* – and the will to act – otherwise called *courage* – are present.

"Throughout history, particularly in the era of information technology, the bad things that have happened and continue to happen are far more the result of complacent people than bad people. A wise person told me that. And she is right. For a bad thing to take hold in society, complacent people must go along with the bad things bad people do."

Harry pauses on that point. His mouth is dry. But he waits before he reaches behind the lectern to retrieve the plastic bottle of water resting on the interior shelf. He placed it there before the hearing was gaveled into session. He wants what he just said to sink in… not be distracted by his actions to alleviate his dry mouth. When he senses the right moment Harry retrieves the bottle of water and slowly drinks without a noticeable gulpy swallow. He is very conscious of the spectacle of this event with the eyes of the masses on him; and the need to convey a confidence of sensibility and to look in control. This is yet another chess move he must execute flawlessly. As he puts the bottle of water back behind the lectern, he accidentally misses the shelf and the bottle falls, making a thud sound everyone in the chamber can hear as it hits the floor. There are some chuckles from the audience. The Chair strikes his gavel and says, "Order."

Harry bends to pick up the bottle. He puts it on the lectern shelf in the back. Oddly he feels calm, as if the bottle drop will work in his favor. He proceeds as if it didn't happen.

"Good people and bad people. There are those who challenge this premise of 'good' people and 'bad' people by saying, 'Good and bad are subjective.' To which I respond – yes, good and bad *are* subjective. Subjectivity defines good and bad. A wise moral code challenges our subjectivity to have transcendent values beneficial to both the individual and the collective.

"My appeal is to good people – people who value goodness – people who want to be good. My appeal is to not avoid identifying goodness – it is to be wise. Goodness and wisdom are the same. My appeal is for people to have the will and the courage to be good.

"A person's first act of life is to take a breath. It's also the last thing a person does. Breathing is life. Thinking is breathing. Therefore, thinking is life.

"Before this *Party Regime* came into power this nation's only reason for existing was to ensure its citizens *life, liberty, and the pursuit of happiness.* The *Party Regime* put a stop to the existence of that nation and replaced it with *fear, ignorance, and the corruption of power.*

"I have every intention to convince those amongst us to be wise and seek to re-establish the Republic that was lost when the *Party Regime* took it away – stole it. I want to show the *Party Regime's* case for power is a loss for everybody. I also have every intention that the *Party Regime* not ever be obstructed from making their case to be a ruling government. But I repeat: I will fight against the *Party Regime* with the things it fears most – *freedom of thought and speech.*

"The right to make a case for a position is the essence of the founding principles of this nation; of which I just stated I believe and support. But the *Party Regime* sees it differently. It should be obvious, allowing an argument against the *Party Regime* is not possible under its rule as the *Party Regime* prohibits such expression under the pain of extinction – or to be *vanished* – which I face in this hearing – this 'trial.'"

Harry looks down, shaking, then nodding his head. "Hmm, this *trial?*" He looks up and pans the representatives before him from left to right. "This travesty. The prohibition of thought and speech is the center of my case against this anti-breathe, anti-think, anti-life *Party Regime.* Despite this travesty of corrupt power and the risk to myself and my family who I love dearly, I am grateful to use this occasion to make the case for common freedom.

"The verdict in this case brought against me is already determined by what matters. It is only left to this committee – 'this jury'– whether you stand with what matters. Whether you stand with what is moral. Whether you stand with what is right.

"I'm not the only one being judged here. You – members of this committee – are being judged as well! You on this committee, sitting in judgment of me, is the same as sitting in judgment of 'the people.'" Harry pauses, "Well, have at it. *'Judge, and be prepared to be judged'* as Ayn Rand put it.

"I stand before you guilty of thinking and speaking. I choose to be guilty of thinking and speaking. If I did not think, then I would not breathe. If *anyone* did not think, then they would not breathe. And without breathing, there is no life. I choose to be guilty of the charges brought against me by the *Party Regime.* I choose to breathe… I choose to think… I choose to live."

Harry takes one last look at each official the way he did before he began his address. He then turns and steps toward the testifying table and sits where he sat when the hearing was called to order. There is a short silence in the chamber before the Chair clears his voice and says, "Thank you, Mr. Archer. The committee will adjourn to deliberate our recommendations." The sound of a single gavel strike ends the hearing. Then there is a long silence followed by a slow building sound of a low rumble of combined muttering voices filling the room.

Harry sits, staring down at the tabletop surface. He is spent. He is shaking inside and wonders if it's noticeable. Reporters and photographers flock around him. There is a flurry of questions and comments Harry cannot discern beyond hearing disconnected words like "you," "how," "what," "is," "will," "prison," "freedom," "angry." Eventually, he hears some phrases like "run for office," "write a book," "kill yourself," One complete question does stand out – "Harry, what's your favorite color?"

The congressional representatives and their staffers clear out of the hearing chamber. The audience in the spectator area behind Harry remains seated for some time. Eventually, Harry gets up and walks into the hallway, where the buzz of activity buzzes louder. As he walks outside to the plaza in front of the Capitol Building, Harry sees a huge assemblage of people. He figures people must have been watching the hearing on all manner of devices.

Part of Harry's "chess move" calculation was the *Party Regime* has him where they want him. The calculation was the *Party Regime* would use the hearing to broadcast to the masses across all platforms to humiliate Harry in front of everybody – PODs, regents, the *Party Regime*, everybody.

There is a low roar from the crowd. But Harry isn't sure if he hears disapproval or approval. Eventually, he realizes he is hearing both. There are loud cries of "traitor," "racist," "degenerate." But far louder and much greater in number are cheers of "thank you," "freedom," "let's be great today," "*every guy*," "Harry." Harry takes in the view and the moment of what is happening, then whispers to himself: "*Checkmate!*... For now."

VII

Public opinion, at least enough of it for now, views the congressional committee as disreputable – a joke. Because of the public reaction, the recommendations of the committee are rendered irrelevant. Harry was correct in his address to the committee. He and the committee were being judged. Opinion against the committee is so negative, the committee never completes its conclusion. Nor does it make any recommendations regarding Harry. Of course, political propaganda from the *Party Regime* continues with a vengeance. To counter this propaganda Harry promotes a caveat people should add to their respective psyches: *Whatever you are told, whatever you think, there may be other things to hear and think. Have an open mind. Be open to the world.*

Harry sees life as a *for now* thing. He manages his expectations, disappointments, and desires with this general view of life, people, and himself. No matter how good things are or how bad things are, everything is *for now*. Harry wrote in an article: *You cannot take for granted that anything cannot change for the better or for the worse.* As a "wink" to the reader he parenthetically added: *I know that's a double negative, but I like saying it this way.*

Almost on a moment-by-moment basis, Harry hears his own voice in his head reminding him, *"This too shall pass."* It's an old phrase from many origins with many variations in wording with an ageless universal appeal to wisdom. Throughout the ages, it holds the status of a timeless proverb.

The use of this saying – this perspective – has been life-saving to Harry. Whether suffering a flat tire or triumphing in the successful completion of a civil works project and all the highs and lows encountered every day, the reminder that good and bad oscillate keeps Harry grounded from the ill effects of emotional extremes.

A little more than a year before being elected to the presidency, on September 30, 1859, Abraham Lincoln gave an address to the Wisconsin State Agricultural Society. The speech was remarkable for the "Lincolnesque" insight and oratory. It was also uncharacteristically long for a Lincoln speech.

The speech has significance to Harry both as a civil engineer and as a person who craves wise insights. The final paragraph of the speech speaks to the tenet – *This too shall pass.* Harry thinks it's a good tenet for managing desires and expectations – ups and downs. But he also thinks it's an incomplete tenet. Harry thinks Lincoln acknowledges such in the closing remarks of his speech:

> "It is said an Eastern monarch once charged his wise men to invent him a sentence, to be ever in view, and which should be true and appropriate in all times and situations. They presented him the words: *'And this, too, shall pass away.'* How much it expresses! How chastening in the hour of pride! – how consoling in the depths of affliction! 'And this, too, shall pass away.' And yet let us hope it is not *quite* true. Let us hope, rather, that by the best cultivation of the physical world, beneath and around us; and the intellectual and moral world within us, we shall secure an individual, social, and political prosperity and happiness, whose course shall be onward and upward, and which, while the earth endures, shall not pass away."

Harry knows the future is uncertain. It always is. No matter what. But a person – a group of persons – a world of persons can have the will to act. Harry wrote in an article – *If we don't use our initiative, and if we don't use it well, it won't ever matter we ever existed. To the human species, the stakes are as high as it gets, to the universe it matters not.*

* * *

Harry and Penelope are walking along the path of the wooded greenbelt close to their apartment. Today they don't feel the need to go to their "secret place." Harry has a sense of relief he hasn't felt for a long time. He's smiling! It's just before sundown – the usual time they take this walk, when they have time or make time to do it. Like any couple taking walks together, these times are special and cherished. Harry thinks it's ironic they take these walks to get away from the troubles of the world, then wind up discussing the troubles of the world on their walks. To both of them this evening does feel different in a good way.

"Thanks for taking care of the business, Pen… while I was marauding as a pop/political outlaw/enemy of the state." There is one beat of a moment before they both reflexively break into a laugh.

They walk, holding hands.

"You ever think about the meaning of life, Pen?"

"Ooookay… you want to go there again, do you? Like we haven't talked about it before."

"I know. But to me it never gets old trying to 'squint' to see if you can see something you didn't see before. It's like a sneeze. A sneeze is very common and relatable. Unless I'm holding a cup of coffee or standing at the toilet taking a leak, I love a good sneeze – I love a good life. But I don't like it when other people sneeze. Hypocritical and selfish of me, right?"

"I thought you were talking about the *meaning* of life."

"I am! Life is a sneeze. It doesn't last long. It feels good to the sneezer. But not to anyone around the sneezer. Well, what I mean is somehow living the way you want – living freely – always bothers someone else."

"Hmm."

"If a community institution, like a nation, acknowledges the unalienable existence of natural status and rights – among them *life, liberty, and the pursuit of happiness* – that pretty much means that nation stipulates there is a meaning to life by canonizing life's meaning in its founding documents. *Life, liberty, and the pursuit of happiness* is not only itself a statement of life's meaning in a concise breakdown, but it's also a pathway to any more meaning a person may discover in their own life. The individual – a person – is not designed to be part of society that is *only* a collective. A collective is programmed and dependent entirely on the cooperation and talents of the individual. In the collective there is no thinking. But there are those in charge of the collective who think only about staying in charge. They see people as ants. Ants are nothing more than a collective. People are not ants. A person is not an ant."

Penelope squeezes Harry's hand, indicating she is listening.

They are quietly reflective as the sun begins to disappear. Then Harry says, "I've been thinking about a man's best day… I mean a person's best day… I mean anybody's best day. A person's best day should be their *last* day."

"A person's best day should be their *last* day?

"Yeah. Think about it. I know it sounds absurd. It's your last day and if you're conscious and know your time is coming to an end, that's pretty much a downer. Hard to see that as your best day. But if somehow you were resourceful to make a good life, and resourceful in crafting a good attitude, and appreciate the luck you've had, and don't despair too much the things that went against you, you can have a good shot at making your last day your best day.

"… And that's what you want! You want your last day to be your best day. Not that you're looking forward to it. But if you adapt your thinking about your last day as your best day… if you adapt that kind of thinking long before the day comes, not only might the depression of mortality be assuaged, your attention to enjoyment, fulfillment, and gratitude might be fully experienced in greater amounts throughout your life no matter its length."

"Harry… what you said is a good 'meaning of life' perspective. Very interesting insight. I like it. It takes a normally depressing thing and challenges any person to see it in a way that gives positive meaning to your life… each day of it… even your last."

Harry squeezes Penelope's hand as a way to say thanks for listening.

"By the way, Hare, don't tell anybody that thing about 'life's a sneeze.' And don't use it in your writings or broadcasts. It's the stupidest thing I ever heard. Although you did warn me when we first met you are 'the smartest stupid a person could be.' Let's just keep that to ourselves. You don't need to sound like an idiot outside of you and me."

Harry squeezes Penelope's hand again, this time to say thanks for looking out for me… *I love you, too.*

* * *

Harry knows he's a lucky person. He's grateful for the things he has. And he's driven to think, to try and unravel the mysteries of life, to be a better person.

However dark a society and culture can become, Harry looks to the light of wisdom as always having a chance to prevail. *Free thought* and *free speech* are where you find the light of wisdom. When Harry exercises his optimism, he thinks of the movie *Field of Dreams*. He has a variation on the signature line/credo from the movie. Harry's variation:

Think it well and say it well and they will come.

If you think it and say it well enough, it will be clear to anyone who looks and listens.

* * *

Since the Congressional hearing, public recognition of Harry increased on a huge scale. To the public at large he became known – branded – as the *Free Thought & Free Talk Guy*. Harry's radio broadcast is now a top nationally syndicated program. True to his *Field of Dreams-esque* credo – *Think it well and say it well and they will come* – they did come.

Harry is on air in the last part of today's broadcast:

"So, I was thinking about the meaning of life."

Harry feels a sneeze coming on and hits the 'sneeze/cough' button that mutes the noise, so it doesn't go out over the broadcast airwaves.

"Well, I swear to you, just this very moment the meaning of life came to me in a sneeze. You didn't hear me sneeze 'cause I muted it."

Penelope is at the office listening to the broadcast and saying out loud to herself, "Oh jeez, Harry, don't do it!"

Harry says, "The meaning of life is what you make the meaning of life to be for yourself. And if you're working at being good and living well the meaning of life is continuously evolving for you."

Smiling softly Penelope breathes a sigh of relief. Ahh, he didn't say "life's a sneeze." And she liked Harry's message to his listening audience about the meaning of life. She repeated in her head what Harry said:

The meaning of life is what you make the meaning of life to be for yourself.

Penelope continues listening to the broadcast:

"Your 'walk' through your immediate world and the way everyone's 'walk' through their immediate world intersects with the world at large is the product of all history. It's a 'walk' of enormous significance… for everyone. Aldous Huxley wrote: *We live together, we act on, and react to, one another; but always and in all circumstances we are by ourselves. The martyrs go hand in hand into the arena; they are crucified alone…. From family to nation, every human group is a society of island universes.* It's like what my good friend Bob recently said to me at a particularly challenging time, 'Harry… *we each spring back to being an 'island' – we're on our own.*'

"Our solitude as individuals makes me wonder if *freedom* or *dystopia* is simply a state of mind. Can a person who is free in their mind still be free under the oppression of totalitarianism?

Well, I can say this much, without freedom as a state of mind dystopian totalitarianism takes root and grows. Or better said metastasizes like a cancer. Or said yet another way like the frog in a pot of water slowly coming to a boil. Freedom of the mind staves off oppression and the extinction of humanity. But for freedom to be a state of mind it has to be valued. Freedom has to be valued over wanting to be taken care of by the state. Freedom vs. being taken care of – that's the *values war* in which we are engaged.

"To live life well it's worth developing a healthy perspective on *irony*. Irony is the unexpected that should have been expected if you simply paid attention. You have to pay attention in life. It's not hard to do. But too many of us don't do it… don't pay attention. Too many are distracted by nonsense. And if your life is oriented toward nonsense, you and those who care about you suffer unnecessarily. On a larger scale our society suffers unnecessarily due to its orientation toward nonsense. So, don't wait for society to completely align with what matters. In your lifetime it's not going to happen. You need to be the 'point person' on what matters. But you have to get it right. To do that you need to be wise.

"In your life as an individual, you are the decider for you. For this Republic as a collective, elections are the deciders for society. As it has been said elections have consequences. From the issues and candidates to the campaigns to the media to the vote count to whether the determined election results actually reflect what people want are consequences for all of us together. With every election cycle we will move closer to what matters or farther away from it.

"*A more perfect Union* is not a *perfect* Union. It's a work in progress. The strength of our union is us. And we are also the weakness of our union. You see what I mean about irony? Irony is ever-present. Irony forces us… wait, that's not right. Irony doesn't force anything. Irony taps us on the shoulder so to speak and asks us, 'are you sure? Is that your final answer?'

"In an effort to be reasonably right and reasonably sure there is an insidious force we need to repel – *the politics of destruction*. The politics of destruction is an indiscriminate lethal weapon. It will kill the bad things in our society and culture; it will also kill the good things. With the politics of destruction, if too many "worshippers" anoint the emergence of high-profile political figures that are treated like gods, a cult takes hold. These created demagogic demigods come to believe their own press; they act as the captains of the hysteria cult fueling the dystopic "killing fields."

"It's one good thing to appreciate and acknowledge the good deeds of imperfect people. It's yet another bad thing to worship anyone as a perfect god who holds themself as all virtuous over all others. The serious deification of anyone is a calamitous misappropriation of admiration and worship.

"Since your 'walk' in life is a product of history it's best you know history… its twists and turns. If you go along for the ride as a passenger, you'll wind up somewhere you don't want to be. If you want to be a driver of your own life, learn how to 'drive' by learning what history teaches. History showcases the good actors and bad actors. It's important to know them both. It's important to know which are good and which are bad, and how the good ones are called bad and the bad ones are called good.

"Something history tells us… no, 'shouts' at us… is another great irony. Great societies crumble not from outside but from within. Destruction of great societies is always self-destruction. Suppressing free thought and free speech is self-destruction. A society without 'free thought and free talk' is a weak society no matter how it 'flexes' its other 'muscles.'

"So, what's it going to be, good listeners? Each and every one of you as individuals, what do *you* choose? *Life, liberty, and the pursuit of happiness*. Or *fear, ignorance, and the corruption of power*. It's up to you.

"*Okay, that's enough for now*. Think about what I've said here. Behave yourselves… and as always, *best to you in all good things*."

Sounds of guitar intro to *Here Comes the Sun*: ♪ ♫ ♩…

It's a bright new day…

Finis

For now...

List of Characters

In

2024

In order of appearance

Harry Archer . . . . Penelope's husband, father, civil engineer, "thought adventurer"

Penelope Archer . . . . Harry's wife, mother, Harry's business partner

Daisy Archer . . . . Harry and Penelope's daughter, second year college student

Billy Archer . . . . Harry and Penelope's son, first year high school student

Jeff Miller . . . . Harry's high School friend

Miss. Garcia . . . . High school guidance counselor

Mr. Garcia . . . . Miss Garcia's husband

Mr. Clark . . . . High school English Literature teacher

Unnamed student	Student worker in high school guidance counselor office
Unnamed female voice	Student worker in high school guidance counselor office
Unnamed clients on Zoom	Unnamed clients on Zoom
Unnamed compliance officer	Unnamed compliance officer
Bennet Oberton	Former president
Skylar High	Traveler, journalist, and author
The Forbidden Laptop	Harry's secret laptop, it's illegal
Computer guy	Trusted/hacker computer guy
Receptionist	*Ministry of Correctness* office
Jim Biddle	Current president – *"The Big Guy"*
Unnamed woman	Worker at the *Ministry of Correctness*
Bob Burke	Officer in the *Ministry of Correctness*
Danny Tripp	Former president
Eric Blair	Podcast host
Tom Bright	Harry's friend
Rick Morrow	Harry's friend, works for the *Ministry of Movement*

Chuck Stephens . . . . Harry's friend, history professor
Winking gesture . . . . Like the author, a few of the characters display an impulse to wink
Harry the h-pawn . . . . A pawn (chess piece – specifically in the h-file position on a chessboard)
Winky the Makeshift Emoji . . . Always there when you need a wink (in footnote [5] & Appendix)
Unnamed woman . . . . Dressed in black suit wearing sunglasses
Unnamed man . . . . Dressed in black suit wearing sunglasses
Steve Reed. . . . . Harry's friend, contractor for Harry and Penelope's firm
Carol Reed . . . . Steve Reed's wife
David Jacob. . . . . Publisher
Allen . . . . Publishing Executive
Unnamed officers . . . . *Party Regime*
Winston Smith . . . . Secretary of Communication for the *Party Regime*
Harry's undrunk cup of coffee . . Starbucks *House Blend* with cream, until he drinks it
Detective Tennison . . . . Police detective
Detective Berry . . . . Police detective

Linda Graham.	Producer for Derrick Lime show – *It's Time for Lime*
Derrick Lime.	Host of a *YCN* cable news talk show
Unnamed older man	Make-up artist on Derrick Lime show
Unnamed crew technician.	Derrick Lime show
Unnamed Chairperson	Congressional committee member
Unnamed representative	Congressional committee member
Unnamed female representative.	Congressional committee member
Karen	Broadcast manager at central broadcasting headquarters
Unnamed male representative . .	Congressional committee member
Unnamed male representative . .	Congressional committee member

* * *

APPENDIX

THE PRINCIPLES OF THOUGHT

HOW WE THINK REFLECTS HOW WE SPEAK; AND HOW we speak reflects how we think. It's a *chicken and egg* thing. The effects beyond this self-perpetuating mental echo chamber are the trials and errors of human existence.

APPENDIX

CONTENTS

THE STORY BEHIND THE STORY

Tensions reach a breaking point. That's why *2024* was written. It's a story with a mission beyond its art. The breaking point we have reached requires us to reset our sensibilities – once again as has been necessary throughout history – to get us out of our current dark age. This story is an allegory, culturally aligning with another iconic allegory – George Orwell's novel *1984*.

In this current cultural/political turbulent era you hear the term "Orwellian" multiple times every day. There's a reason for that. It's processing. I'm a psychotherapist, so let me explain *processing* from a psychological perspective. Think about it like this: It's 120 degrees Fahrenheit in the shade. You are with another person and you say, "Boy it's hot!" Fifteen seconds pass, and then you say, "Boy it's *really* hot!" That's processing.

We have a need to process by saying and repeating the obvious. Particularly when we are experiencing extremes. It helps us cope. But we need to-do more than process. We have to attempt some agency – some action. Otherwise, we deteriorate into a state of *learned helplessness* – that's another psychological term.

We are way past the point where we need to do some serious processing and agency, or we will lose the culture and the Republic with it. This story is a vehicle for processing on multiple levels. It's provocative and hopefully for you, inspirational. Despite the dystopian theme you should be able to detect the optimism in it. But the optimism is only justified if we employ wisdom and courage. That's a big "if."

As a collective way to process, we hear "Orwellian" because it anchors us to dystopia as a reality, not a science fiction. Yet we use science fiction because it allows us to grasp the hard parts to understand about reality. Humans have to be coaxed into getting reality.

Reality is too disruptive for the faint of heart. So allegorical stories have a great purpose in helping us see what we need to see if we want to "keep it real."

This story *2024* is many things. One of those things is a straight-out homage to Orwell and his novel *1984*. I first read it in 1984 on a plane to Ixtapa Mexico. Orwell did much to sound an alarm on the gravitational pull toward depraved corrupted social systems to which humans subject themselves.

There are works of literature that are universally well known for their significance and cultural memes despite being widely unread in their original writing. In graduate school I read more about Freud from other writers before I directly read his translated works. So, it's possible to be familiar with the essence of some notable literature by way of cultural saturation, without reading it firsthand.

Most everyone who hasn't read *1984* knows what "Big Brother" means. That's a testament to the author, publisher, and pop cultural forces for hitting the "right notes" in such a way the essence of the work is so well known it doesn't have to be read firsthand to be appreciated.

So, even if you haven't read *1984*, this story – *2024* – stands alone as a read unto itself. There are numerous references/connections to Orwell's *1984* that hopefully the reader can appreciate with just cursory knowledge of Orwell's work. But reading this story may inspire readers who haven't read Orwell to put it on their "to do" list and read it… or if you have read it to reread it.

* * *

The next thing to understand about this story – *2024* – are the story elements that run parallel to real-life events, cultural/political dynamics, and public personalities. The allegory is tightly wrapped with Orwellian memes, identifiable real-life events, and impressionistic story content.

The supercharged world of power politics combines with the culture wars to render the ethos of our times. The election of Donald Trump triggered an ethos that unleashed the exploitation of passions and irrationality in too many people. The result was a downward spiral into "cultural dysfunction" if not full-on dystopia. Our society may have the patina of middle-class bourgeoisie, but the combination of ignorance, apathy, and corruption gave way to power grabs by a relatively small number of fringe activists. Their magnified influence and power erode the values that allowed a middle class to emerge and grow as a group of people who enjoy the most prosperity by the largest number of people in all history. Although we may still "look" prosperous, we are infected with too much *ideological power corruption* and willful blindness which is causing the pinnacle of our prosperity to turn downward rapidly.

The world experienced a seismic disruption the moment Trump was elected president. It wasn't so much because of Trump as it was because of the reaction to him. Throughout the world there are always totalitarian forces either fully in power or pent-up ready to explode on the scene to take power. Trump's election ignited the culture war that moved totalitarians to "weapon up" and fight to kill freedom at all costs.

The cliché – *freedom isn't free* – is both a statement of profound truth and a challenge to all of us about what we value. A person needs to be free. But to be free, a person needs to be responsible and keenly aware of enemies to freedom.

The era of the Trump presidency triggered a seismic upheaval in power politics, culture wars, and our psyche. The upheaval is the context and catalyst for the present era's use of Orwellian terminology in our society. Presidential administrations can be faithfully researched to understand their respective achievements and failures. The farewell speech of an outgoing president from one party compared to the inaugural speech of an incoming president from the other party presents an opportunity to see the rhetorical contrast in vision and values. The integrity of a speech is left for the public to decide, whether or not the public decides well.

This juncture in transfer of power is a story element in *2024*. It draws on the real speeches delivered respectively by

Donald Trump and Joe Biden. The transcripts of both speeches are presented in this Appendix:

A Tale of Two Speeches, Nonfiction

But first presented are the respective speeches of Danny Tripp and Jim Biddle. As allegorical characters in the story their speeches are an allegorical background story element. The speech by the Tripp character is the exact Trump farewell speech with changes in name references and other details for story continuity without changing the message content. Likewise, the speech by the Biddle character is the exact Biden inaugural speech with the same kind of changes for story continuity without changing the message content.

There are many literary applications and layers at work in this story. The references, cross-references, allusions, brand identifications, and such are a good exercise for intellectual muscles. The connections and references are like a wink to the reader. Which is another good muscle to use.

(^_‘)

DANNY TRIPP'S FAREWELL SPEECH

"My fellow countrymen: Four years ago, we launched a great national effort to rebuild our country, to renew its spirit, and to restore the allegiance of this government to its citizens. In short, we embarked on a mission to *let's be great today* – for all of us. As I conclude my term as President, I stand before you truly proud of what we have achieved together. We did what we came here to do–and so much more.

"This week, we inaugurate a new administration and pray for its success in keeping our nation safe and prosperous. We extend our best wishes, and we also want them to have luck – a very important word.

"I'd like to begin by thanking just a few of the amazing people who made our remarkable journey possible.

"First, let me express my overwhelming gratitude for the love and support of my wife, Maria, who was a spectacular First Lady. She stood with me and you – the people. Let me also share my deepest appreciation to my family. You fill my world with light and with joy.

"I also want to thank the man who served as Vice President in this administration, Max Pierce. I thank his wonderful wife, Kathrine, and his entire family.

"Thank you as well to my Chief of Staff; the dedicated members of the White House Staff and the Cabinet; and all the incredible people across our administration who poured out their heart and soul to fight for this nation.

"I also want to take a moment to thank a truly exceptional group of people: The Secret Service. My family and I will forever be in your debt. My profound gratitude as well to everyone in the White House Military Office, the teams of Marine One and Air Force One, every member of the Armed Forces, and state and local law enforcement all across our country.

"Most of all, I want to thank the people of this nation. To serve as your President has been an honor beyond description. Thank you for this extraordinary privilege. And that's what it is – a great privilege and a great honor.

"We must never forget that while we will always have our disagreements, we are a nation of incredible, decent, faithful, and peace-loving citizens who all want our country to thrive and flourish and be very, very successful and good. We are a truly magnificent nation.

"All of us were horrified by the assault on our Capitol. Political violence is an attack on everything we cherish. It can never be tolerated.

"Now more than ever, we must unify around our shared values and rise above the partisan rancor and forge our common destiny.

"Four years ago, I came to this office at the nation's capital as the only true outsider ever to win the presidency. I had not spent my career as a politician, but as a builder looking at open skylines and imagining infinite possibilities. I ran for President because I knew there were towering new summits for our nation just waiting to be scaled. I knew the potential for our nation was boundless as long as we put our nation first.

"So, I left behind my former life and stepped into a very difficult arena, but an arena nevertheless, with all sorts of potential if properly done. This nation had given me so much, and I wanted to give something back.

"Together with millions of hardworking patriots across this land, we built the greatest political movement in the history of our country. We also built the greatest economy in the history of the world. It was about 'Our Nation First' because we all wanted to *be great today*. We restored the principle that a nation exists to serve its citizens. Our agenda was not about right or left, it wasn't about Republican or Democrat, but about the good of a nation, and that means the whole nation.

"With the support and prayers of the people, we achieved more than anyone thought possible. Nobody thought we could even come close.

"We passed the largest package of tax cuts and reforms in this nation's history. We slashed more job-killing regulations than any administration had ever done before. We fixed our broken trade deals, withdrew from the horrible Trans-Pacific Partnership and the impossible Paris Climate Accord, renegotiated the one-sided South Korea deal, and we replaced

NAFTA with the groundbreaking USMCA – that's Mexico and Canada – a deal that's worked out very, very well.

"Also, and very importantly, we imposed historic and monumental tariffs on China; made a great new deal with China. But before the ink was even dry, we and the whole world got hit with the China virus. Our trade relationship was rapidly changing, billions and billions of dollars were pouring into the U.S., but the virus forced us to go in a different direction.

"The whole world suffered, but this nation outperformed other countries economically because of our incredible economy and the economy that we built. Without the foundations and footings, it wouldn't have worked out this way. We wouldn't have some of the best numbers we've ever had.

"We also unlocked our energy resources and became the world's number-one producer of oil and natural gas by far. Powered by these policies, we built the greatest economy in the history of the world. We reignited job creation and achieved record-low unemployment for all races as well as women – almost everyone.

"Incomes soared, wages boomed, this nation's dream was restored, and millions were lifted from poverty in just a few short years. It was a miracle. The stock market set one record after another, with 148 stock market highs during this short period of time and boosted the retirements and pensions of hardworking citizens all across our nation. 401(k)s are at a level they've never been at before. We've never seen numbers like we've seen, and that's before the pandemic and after the pandemic.

"We rebuilt the nation's manufacturing base, opened up thousands of new factories, and brought back the beautiful phrase: 'Made in this Nation.'

"To make life better for working families, we doubled the child tax credit and signed the largest-ever expansion of funding for childcare and development. We joined with the private sector to secure commitments to train more than 16 million workers for the jobs of tomorrow.

"When our nation was hit with the terrible pandemic, we produced not one, but two vaccines with record-breaking speed, and more will quickly follow. They said it couldn't be done but we did it. They call it a 'medical miracle,' and that's what they're calling it right now: a 'medical miracle.'

"Another administration would have taken three, four, five, maybe even up to ten years to develop a vaccine. We did in nine months.

"We grieve for every life lost, and we pledge in their memory to wipe out this horrible pandemic once and for all.

"When the virus took its brutal toll on the world's economy, we launched the fastest economic recovery our country has ever seen. We passed nearly $4 trillion in economic relief, saved or supported over 50 million jobs, and slashed the unemployment rate in half. These are numbers that our country has never seen before.

"We created choice and transparency in healthcare, stood up to big pharma in so many ways, but especially in our effort to get favored-nations clauses added, which will give us the lowest prescription drug prices anywhere in the world.

"We passed VA Choice, VA Accountability, Right to Try, and landmark criminal justice reform.

"We confirmed three new justices of the Supreme Court. We appointed nearly 300 federal judges to interpret our Constitution as written.

"For years, the people pleaded with our government to finally secure the nation's borders. I am pleased to say we answered that plea and achieved the most secure border in U.S. history. We have given our brave border agents and heroic ICE officers the tools they need to do their jobs better than they have ever done before, and to enforce our laws and keep this nation safe.

"We proudly leave the next administration with the strongest and most robust border security measures ever put into place. This includes historic agreements with Mexico, Guatemala, Honduras, and El Salvador, along with more than 450 miles of powerful new wall.

"We restored this nation's strength at home and our leadership abroad. The world respects us again. Please don't lose that respect.

"We reclaimed our sovereignty by standing up for our nation at the United Nations and withdrawing from the one-sided global deals that never served our interests. And

NATO countries are now paying hundreds of billions of dollars more than when I arrived just a few years ago. It was very unfair. We were paying the cost for the world. Now the world is helping us.

"And perhaps most importantly of all, with nearly $3 trillion, we fully rebuilt our nation's military – all made in this nation. We launched the first new branch of the Armed Forces in 75 years: The Space Force. And last spring, I stood at Kennedy Space Center and watched as astronauts of this nation returned to space on our nation's rockets for the first time in many, many years.

"We revitalized our alliances and rallied the nations of the world to stand up to China like never before.

"We obliterated the ISIS caliphate and ended the wretched life of its founder and leader, al Baghdadi. We stood up to the oppressive Iranian regime and killed the world's top terrorist, Iranian butcher Qasem Soleimani.

"We recognized Jerusalem as the capital of Israel and recognized Israeli sovereignty over the Golan Heights.

"As a result of our bold diplomacy and principled realism, we achieved a series of historic peace deals in the Middle East. Nobody believed it could happen. The Abraham Accords opened the doors to a future of peace and harmony, not violence and bloodshed. It is the dawn of a new Middle East, and we are bringing our soldiers home.

"I am especially proud to be the first President in decades who has started no new wars.

"Above all, we have reasserted the sacred idea that, in this nation, the government answers to the people. Our guiding light, our North Star, our unwavering conviction has been that we are here to serve the noble everyday citizens of this nation. Our allegiance is not to the special interests, corporations, or global entities; it's to our children, our citizens, and to our nation itself.

"As President, my top priority, my constant concern, has always been the best interests of our nation's workers and our nation's families. I did not seek the easiest course; by far, it was actually the most difficult. I did not seek the path that would get the least criticism. I took on the tough battles, the hardest fights, the most difficult choices because that's what you elected me to do. Your needs were my first and last unyielding focus.

"This, I hope, will be our greatest legacy: Together, we put our nation's people back in charge of our country. We restored self-government. We restored the idea that in this nation no one is forgotten, because everyone matters, and everyone has a voice. We fought for the principle that every citizen is entitled to equal dignity, equal treatment, and equal rights because we are all made equal by God. Everyone is entitled to be treated with respect, to have their voice heard, and to have their government listen. You are loyal to your country, and my administration was always loyal to you.

"We worked to build a country in which every citizen could find a great job and support their wonderful families. We fought for the communities where everyone could be safe and schools where every child could learn. We promoted a culture where our laws would be upheld, our heroes honored, our history preserved, and law-abiding citizens are never taken for granted. We should take tremendous satisfaction in all that we have achieved together. It's incredible.

"Now, as I leave the White House, I have been reflecting on the dangers that threaten the priceless inheritance we all share. As the world's most powerful nation, we face constant threats and challenges from abroad. But the greatest danger we face is a loss of confidence in ourselves, a loss of confidence in our national greatness. A nation is only as strong as its spirit. We are only as dynamic as our pride. We are only as vibrant as the faith that beats in the hearts of our people.

"No nation can long thrive that loses faith in its own values, history, and heroes, for these are the very sources of our unity and our vitality.

"What has always allowed us to prevail and triumph over the great challenges of the past has been an unyielding and unashamed conviction in the nobility of our country and its unique purpose in history. We must never lose this conviction. We must never forsake our belief in our nation.

"The key to national greatness lies in sustaining and instilling our shared national identity. That means focusing on what we have in common: the heritage that we all share.

"At the center of this heritage is also a robust belief in free expression, free speech, and open debate. Only if we forget who we are, and how we got here, could we ever allow political censorship and blacklisting to take place in this nation. It's not even thinkable. Shutting down free and open debate violates our core values and most enduring traditions. In this nation, we don't insist on absolute conformity or enforce rigid orthodoxies and punitive speech codes. We just don't do that. We are not a timid nation of tame souls who need to be sheltered and protected from those with whom we disagree. That's not who we are. It will never be who we are.

"For nearly 250 years, in the face of every challenge, we have always summoned our unmatched courage, confidence, and fierce independence. These are the miraculous traits that once led millions of everyday citizens to set out across a wild continent and carve out a new life in the great West. It was the same profound love of our God-given freedom that willed our soldiers into battle and our astronauts into space.

"As I think back on the past four years, one image rises in my mind above all others. Whenever I traveled all along the motorcade route, there were thousands and thousands of people. They came out with their families so that they could stand as we passed, and proudly wave our great national flag. It never failed to deeply move me. I knew that they did not just come out to show their support of me; they came out to show me their support and love for our country.

"This is a republic of proud citizens who are united by our common conviction that this nation is the greatest nation in all of history. We are, and must always be, a land of hope, of light, and of glory to all the world. This is the precious inheritance that we must safeguard at every single turn.

"For the past four years, I have worked to do just that. From a great hall of Muslim leaders in Riyadh to a great square of Polish people in Warsaw; from the floor of the Korean Assembly to the podium at the United Nations General Assembly; and from the Forbidden City in Beijing to the shadow of Mount Rushmore, I fought for you, I fought for your family, I fought for our country. Above all, I fought for this nation and all it stands for – and that is safe, strong, proud, and free.

"Now, as I prepare to hand power over to a new administration at noon on Wednesday, I want you to know that the movement we started is only just beginning. There's never been anything like it. The belief that a nation must serve its citizens will not dwindle but instead only grow stronger by the day.

"As long as the people hold in their hearts deep and devoted love of country, then there is nothing that this nation cannot achieve. Our communities will flourish. Our people will be prosperous. Our traditions will be cherished. Our faith will be strong. And our future will be brighter than ever before.

"I go from this majestic place with a loyal and joyful heart, an optimistic spirit, and a supreme confidence that for our country and for our children, the best is yet to come.

"Thank you, and farewell. God bless you. God bless our nation."

END

JIM BIDDLE'S PRESIDENTIAL INAUGURAL ADDRESS

"Chief Justice Richards, Vice-President Harold, Speaker Perogy, Leader Schlummer, Leader MacDonald, Vice-President Pierce. My distinguished guests, my fellow country people.

"This is our nation's day. This is democracy's day. A day of history and hope, of renewal and resolve. Through a crucible for the ages, this nation has been tested anew and this nation has risen to the challenge. Today we celebrate the triumph not of a candidate but of a cause, a cause of democracy. The people – the will of the people – has been heard, and the will of the people has been heeded.

"We've learned again that democracy is precious, democracy is fragile and, at this hour my friends, democracy has prevailed. So now on this hallowed ground where just a few days ago violence sought to shake the Capitol's very foundations, we come together as one nation under God–indivisible–to carry out the peaceful transfer of power as we have for more than two centuries.

"As we look ahead in our unique way, restless, bold, optimistic, and set our sights on a nation we know we can be and must be, I thank my predecessors of both parties. I thank them from the bottom of my heart. And I know the resilience of our Constitution and the strength, the strength of our nation, as does President Carter, who I spoke with last night who cannot be with us today, but who we salute for his lifetime of service.

"I've just taken a sacred oath each of those patriots have taken. The oath first sworn by George Washington. But the nation's story depends not on any one of us, not on some of us, but on all of us. On we the people who seek a more perfect union. This is a great nation; we are good people. And over the centuries through storm and strife in peace and in war we've come so far. But we still have far to go.

"We'll press forward with speed and urgency for we have much to do in this winter of peril and significant possibility. Much to do, much to heal, much to restore, much to build, and much to gain. Few people in our nation's history have been more challenged or found a time more challenging or difficult than the time we're in now. A once in a century virus that silently stalks the country has taken as many lives in one year as in all of World War II.

"Millions of jobs have been lost. Hundreds of thousands of businesses closed. A cry for racial justice, some 400 years in the making, moves us. The dream of justice for all will be deferred no longer. A cry for survival comes from the planet itself, a cry that can't be any more desperate or any more clear now. The rise of political extremism, white supremacy, domestic terrorism, that we must confront, and we will defeat.

"To overcome these challenges, to restore the soul and secure the future of this nation, requires so much more than words. It requires the most elusive of all things in a democracy – unity. Unity. In another January on New Year's Day in 1863 Abraham Lincoln signed the Emancipation Proclamation.

When he put pen to paper the president said, and I quote, 'If my name ever goes down in history, it'll be for this act, and my whole soul is in it.'

"My whole soul is in it today, on this January day. My whole soul is in this. Bringing this nation together, uniting our people, uniting our nation. And I ask everyone to join me in this cause. Uniting to fight the foes we face – anger, resentment, and hatred. Extremism, lawlessness, violence, disease, joblessness, and hopelessness.

"With unity we can do great things, important things. We can right wrongs, we can put people to work in good jobs, we can teach our children in safe schools. We can overcome the deadly virus, we can rebuild work, we can rebuild the middle class and make work secure, we can secure racial justice and we can make this nation once again the leading force for good in the world.

"I know speaking of unity can sound to some like a foolish fantasy these days. I know the forces that divide us are deep and they are real. But I also know they are not new. Our history has been a constant struggle between our ideal, that we are all created equal, and the harsh ugly reality that racism, nativism, and fear have torn us apart. The battle is perennial, and victory is never secure.

"Through civil war, the Great Depression, World War, 9/11, through struggle, sacrifice, and setback, our better angels have always prevailed. In each of our moments enough of us have come together to carry all of us forward and we can do that now. History, faith, and reason show the way. The way of unity.

"We can see each other not as adversaries but as neighbors. We can treat each other with dignity and respect. We can join forces, stop the shouting, and lower the temperature. For without unity there is no peace, only bitterness and fury, no progress, only exhausting outrage. No nation, only a state of chaos. This is our historic moment of crisis and challenge. And unity is the path forward. And we must meet this moment as a nation.

"If we do that, I guarantee we will not fail. We have never, ever, ever, ever failed when we've acted together. And so today at this time in this place, let's start afresh, all of us. Let's begin to listen to one another again, hear one another, see one another. Show respect to one another. Politics doesn't have to be a raging fire destroying everything in its path. Every disagreement doesn't have to be a cause for total war, and we must reject the culture in which facts themselves are manipulated and even manufactured.

"My fellow country people, we have to be different than this. We have to be better than this and I believe we are so much better than this. Just look around. Here we stand in the shadow of the Capitol dome. As mentioned earlier, completed in the shadow of the Civil War. When the union itself was literally hanging in the balance. We endure, we prevail. Here we stand, looking out on the great Mall, where Dr. King spoke of his dream.

"Here we stand, where 108 years ago at another inaugural, thousands of protesters tried to block brave women marching for the right to vote. And today we mark the swearing in of the first woman elected to national office, Vice President Harold. Don't tell me things can't change. Here we stand where heroes who gave the last full measure of devotion rest in eternal peace.

"And here we stand just days after a riotous mob thought they could use violence to silence the will of the people, to stop the work of our democracy, to drive us from this sacred ground. It did not happen, it will never happen, not today, not tomorrow, not ever. Not ever. To all those who supported our campaign, I'm humbled by the faith you placed in us. To all those who did not support us, let me say this. Hear us out as we move forward. Take a measure of me and my heart.

"If you still disagree, so be it. That's democracy. That's our nation. The right to dissent peacefully. And the guardrail of our democracy is perhaps our nation's greatest strength. If you hear me clearly, disagreement must not lead to disunion. And I pledge this to you. I will be a President for all of you, all of you. And I promise you I will fight for those who did not support me as for those who did.

"Many centuries ago, Saint Augustine – the saint of my church – wrote that a people was a multitude defined by the common objects of their love. Defined by the common objects of their love. What are the common objects we love, that define us? I think we know. Opportunity, security, liberty, dignity, respect, honor, and yes, the truth.

"Recent weeks and months have taught us a painful lesson. There is truth and there are lies. Lies told for power and for profit. And each of us has a duty and a responsibility as people of this nation and especially as leaders. Leaders who are pledged to honor our Constitution to protect our nation. To defend the truth and defeat the lies.

"Look, I understand that many view the future with fear and trepidation. I understand they worry about their jobs. I understand like their dad they lay in bed at night staring at the ceiling thinking: 'Can I keep my healthcare? Can I pay my mortgage?' Thinking about their families, about what comes next. I promise you; I get it. But the answer's not to turn inward. To retreat into competing factions. Distrusting those who don't look like you, or worship the way you do, who don't get their news from the same source as you do.

"We must end this uncivil war that pits red against blue, rural versus urban, conservative versus liberal. We can do this if we open our souls instead of hardening our hearts, if we show a little tolerance and humility, and if we're willing to stand in the other person's shoes, as my mom would say. Just for a moment, stand in their shoes.

"Because here's the thing about life. There's no accounting for what fate will deal you. Some days you need a hand. There are other days when we're called to lend a hand. That's how it has to be, that's what we do for one another. And if we are that way our country will be stronger, more prosperous, more ready for the future. And we can still disagree.

"My fellow country people, in the work ahead of us we're going to need each other. We need all our strength to persevere through this dark winter. We're entering what may be the darkest and deadliest period of the virus. We must set aside politics and finally face this pandemic as one nation, one nation. And I promise this, as the Bible says, 'Weeping may endure for a night, joy cometh in the morning'. We will get through this together. Together.

"Look folks, all my colleagues I serve with in the House and the Senate up here, we all understand the world is watching. Watching all of us today. So, here's my message to those beyond our borders. This nation has been tested and we've come out stronger for it. We will repair our alliances and engage with the world once again. Not to meet yesterday's challenges but today's and tomorrow's challenges. And we'll lead not merely by the example of our power but the power of our example.

"Fellow country people, everyone, friends, neighbors, and co-workers. We will honor them by becoming the people and the nation we can and should be. So, I ask you let's say a silent prayer for those who lost their lives, those left behind, and for our country. Amen.

"Folks, it's a time of testing. We face an attack on our democracy, and on truth, a raging virus, a stinging inequity, systemic racism, a climate in crisis, this nation's role in the world. Any one of these would be enough to challenge us in profound ways. But the fact is we face them all at once, presenting this nation with one of the greatest responsibilities we've had. Now we're going to be tested. Are we going to step up?

"It's time for boldness for there is so much to do. And this is certain, I promise you. We will be judged, you and I, by how we resolve these cascading crises of our era. We will rise to the occasion. Will we master this rare and difficult hour? Will we meet our obligations and pass along a new and better world to our children? I believe we must and I'm sure you do as well. I believe we will, and when we do, we'll write the next great chapter in the history of this nation. This nation's story.

"A story that might sound like a song that means a lot to me; it's called Our Anthem. And there's one verse that stands out at least for me and it goes like this:

'The struggles and hopes of centuries have brought us to this day, what shall be our legacy, what will our descendants say?

Let me know in my soul when my time is through, this nation, oh this national, I gave my all to you.'

"Let us add our own work and prayers to the unfolding story of our great nation. If we do this, then when our days are through, our children and our children's children will say of us: 'They gave their best, they did their duty, they healed a broken land.'

"My fellow country people I close the day where I began, with a sacred oath. Before God and all of you, I give you my word. I will always level with you. I will defend the Constitution; I'll defend our democracy.

"I'll defend this nation and I will give all – all of you – keep everything I do in your service. Thinking not of power but of possibilities. Not of personal interest but of public good.

"And together we will write a national story of hope, not fear. Of unity not division, of light not darkness. A story of decency and dignity, love and healing, greatness and goodness. May this be the story that guides us. The story that inspires us. And the story that tells ages yet to come that we answered the call of history, we met the moment. Democracy and hope, truth and justice, did not die on our watch but thrive.

"That this nation secured liberty at home and stood once again as a beacon to the world. That is what we owe our forbearers, one another, and generations to follow.

"So, with purpose and resolve, we turn to those tasks of our time. Sustained by faith, driven by conviction, and devoted to one another and the country we love with all our hearts. May God bless this nation and God protect our troops."

END

A TALE OF TWO SPEECHES

By Harry Archer

(Originally published as authored by Staff Writer.)

ELECTED LEADERS, THOSE SEEKING ELECTED OFFICE, and those gaining prominence in the culture establish bona fides – whether false or authentic – by way of their spoken and/or written public commentary. Speeches such as commencements, eulogies, church sermons, State of the Union addresses, farewell addresses, and inaugurations are opportunities for the speech giver to do something rare and profound – to connect the abstraction of living in society to living a private life. A speech should seek to close the gap on the alienation we all have with ourselves and others.

Public speeches on the occasions of a grand platform should be aspirational and inspirational. The trick is to inspire aspiration by word and delivery that resonates with the audience. Danny Tripp's farewell speech and Jim Biddle's inaugural speech resonated with their respective supporters – inspiring aspirations.

The wisdom and sincerity of a speech giver are left to the judgment of the public – individually. But the noise and pressure of the collective can contaminate and confuse an individual's thinking causing them to misinterpret the speech. That's why there needs to be integrity in your thinking.

Let's look at the two speeches back-to-back: The Farewell speech of Danny Tripp – the outgoing president who ran for re-election against Jim Biddle, and the Inauguration address of Jim Biddle – the incoming president. The two speeches are opportunely juxtaposed not only to see the differences in rhetorical messaging but demark the full-scale change of political culture defined by power and control. Another name for power and control is tyranny. It can be understood that although "just" governments do not want to be seen as a tyranny it is inescapable that in some way all governments are tyrannical. So, no matter how democratic the system of government, the electorate is essentially deciding which tyranny to go with.

Let's first break down the Danny Tripp Farewell speech:

Danny Tripp's farewell speech is well-messaged and delivered. It is precisely what the nation needs to hear from an outgoing president during a time of tremendous political/governmental/cultural upheaval. The speech is mature, sensible, and gracious.

But half the electorate don't think Danny Tripp is in any way *mature, sensible,* or *gracious.* They think he is a narcissistic self-absorbed monster. From this perspective cognitive dissonance prevents Tripp-haters from hearing and/or believing what Tripp says in his speech, let alone being able to reflect on Tripp's term as president and what he accomplished, if anything.

Despite what Tripp-haters think in context to the culture, collective psychology, and the political climate, the Tripp speech stands out for being relevant and simple. The first thing about it unsurprisingly to Tripp supporters is he graciously acknowledges the forthcoming transition of power from his administration to the administration of his opponent. "This week, we inaugurate a new administration and pray for its success in keeping our nation safe and prosperous. We extend our best wishes, and we also want them to have luck – a very important word." There is no refusal to leave, no tantrum, no crying, no drama. To many hysterical Tripp-haters this must be impossible to reconcile. It doesn't fit with how they perceive with certainty who Tripp is. But Tripp-haters don't have to reconcile anything because it doesn't matter what Tripp says. For them Tripp only tells lies and says bad things.

The end of that sentence – "… luck – a very important word." – sounds typical of Tripp. I'm not sure "… a very important word" is in the script as Tripp often goes off-script to extemporaneously add something for emphasis. However, with Biddle coming into office, it would surely be Tripp's opinion the nation will need *luck*. Tripp would naturally think *luck* is an important word because he would think the nation and people are headed for disaster under the Biddle administration. If we go fully cynical, Tripp saying *luck* and adding extemporaneously "a very important word" is a restrained and veiled dig at Biddle and a "you'll be sorry" dig at Biddle voters.

Tripp never concedes losing the election. Although he doesn't say it in this speech, to the contrary Tripp asserts he won, and further asserts that due to fraud the election is certified as a win for Biddle. Nonetheless, having exhausted his rightful options, without success, to prevent the certification of Biddle's ascension to the presidency, Tripp cooperatively and peacefully vacates the office at the end of his term.

In his farewell speech Tripp acknowledges with gratitude the love and support of his family. He thanks some people by name and those unnamed who contributed to the successes of his administration. Tripp thanks the people of this nation and sensibly, realistically, respectfully acknowledges our disagreements. Tripp offers that our differences don't detract from our goodness as a nation.

Tripp appropriately addresses the recent riot at the Capitol building, "All of us were horrified by the assault on our Capitol. Political violence is an attack on everything we cherish. It can never be tolerated."

Tripp expresses in a personal way his reason to have sought the office he was now leaving. He conveys being motivated by his desire to give back to the nation what he has been so grateful to have gotten from this country.

Tripp credits the nation's people for a great political movement that brought about the many unprecedented achievements during his term in office. He lists the achievements and provides context to their importance.

Tripp points to the strength of our nation meeting the challenges and instabilities presented in the world. This includes the pandemic that brought suffering on a historic scale at a time of peace and prosperity for this nation. He acknowledges the tragic loss of life and the economic hardship related to the pandemic. Tripp also speaks of the aggressive pandemic recovery effort led by this nation – which includes vaccine development and delivery in astonishingly record time.

On the heels of mentioning the Middle East peace treaties his administration brokered, Tripp says, "I am especially proud to be the first President in decades who has started no new wars."

The last parts of the speech are a good wrap-up. It's not bitter or hateful. The speech ends with gratitude and a confidently positive outlook. This from a man his opponents call a "baby," "pathological," a "monster."

Now let's look at the Jim Biddle Inaugural speech:

Jim Biddle's Inaugural speech is well crafted. It is delivered warmly and personably. But the speech doesn't escape the gravitational pull of being pedestrian. Out of the "chute" Biddle says, "This is democracy's day." It sounds good, but with the backdrop of half the electorate not trusting election results calling this "democracy's day" insults those questioning election credibility. Like it or not, too many people have no confidence in our elections. Ignoring this will not make that go away.

Moreover, from the time the media called the election for Biddle, he called for *unity* for this deeply divided country. Biddle's call for unity is as if he believes he can wave a magic wand to make *unity* happen. The central theme of Biddle's speech is his call for unity.

Biddle's central message collides with his proclamation of "This is democracy's day." Given the deep political divisions in public sentiment that cut the nation in half, calls for *unity* wrapped in the word "democracy" – a word half the public think is falsely and insincerely used – has the effect of telling half the nation they don't matter. That they are defeated and should shut up and go along with the ruling regime.

A healthy democracy respects the differences in free thought. But the *Party Regime* established totalitarian rule where free thought is not allowed, calling it democracy. Without knowing or caring, Biddle is fronting for the *Party Regime*. Biddle goes on about democracy as if his audience, like schoolchildren, needs a lesson. But the lesson is not instructive. It is a lofty narrative of ideals, historical predecessors, a sacred oath, and platitudes. It all sounds good but means nothing.

With the *Party Regime* pulling the Biddle "puppet strings," totalitarianism is being passed as democracy. Totalitarian political messaging needs to be condensed as a pinpoint axiom of undisputed truth whether or not truthful. We can call this messaging a "virtue cause." The message needs to ignite passion and bestow virtue on the holder/adopter/advocate of the message. On top of that, the message needs to denigrate any alternate view of the message, rendering any slight opposition as abhorrent to decency and humanity. Such messaging ensnares people who value decency and/or simplicity to side with political movements that promote the patina of a "virtue cause" while it hides the political movement's real purpose – which is to gain and maintain power and control. When publicly pressed on where they stand on a "virtue cause," such ensnared people recite/chant/regurgitate the adopted slogans signaling their alignment with an approved "virtuous position." This messaging and ensnarement are the "glue" of totalitarianism causing decent people to have a reflex of allegiance to the totalitarian power.

The *Party Regime* commandeered two messages – "virtue causes" – for this purpose: *Racism* and *Climate Change*. To the extent and effect *racism* and *climate change* should be addressed, these matters are worthy and relevant. But the *Party Regime* disingenuously appropriates these serious issues for their "virtue appeal" – not their merits – to demagogically exploit people's insecurities of failing to be virtuous. The irony is the *Party Regime* makes these issues worse, serving the purpose of perpetuating issues the *Party Regime* has no intention to resolve. As such, resolution of these issues would threaten the need for and existence of the *Party Regime*. The real reason for and of the *Party Regime* is power.

In line with this totalitarian messaging is the part in Biddle's speech obligatory in all *Party Regime* rhetoric. Out of nowhere and connected to nothing relevant are the rally cries the *Party Regime* hides behind to take and keep power. Biddle says the phrases "A cry for racial justice… A cry for survival comes from the planet itself… white supremacy…" *Racism* and *Climate Change*.

Biddle comes to the part of his speech where he first says *unity*. The first thing Biddle says about *unity* is insightful and correct, "… the most elusive of all things in a democracy – unity." From there, however, Biddle meanders loftily, pairing *unity* to anything with which he can try to make stick – "great things", "important things", "right wrongs", "good jobs", "safe schools", "secure racial justice."

Biddle continues talking about *unity*, ideas of coming together, and such. And then Biddle says, "Every disagreement doesn't have to be a cause for total war, and we must reject the culture in which facts themselves are manipulated and even manufactured." This is particularly ironic in terms of its truth and Biddle's (and the *Party Regime's*) absence of self-awareness. *Hypocrisy is the poison upon which corrupt societies feed. Freedom of speech allows lies. And not having freedom of speech allows lies to live and thrive.*

Biddle yields, "If you still disagree, so be it." But in the imagined "unified" world of which he speaks, Biddle offers nothing for dissension to be heard and respected.

Biddle says, "We must end this uncivil war that pits red against blue, rural versus urban, conservative versus liberal." The term "uncivil war" is clever if it implies differences will always exist… even divide us; but differences and divides should be civil.

Biddle makes a reference to standing in another person's shoes. This old cliché analogy for wisdom in understanding others should not be minimized. Despite or because the lack of adherence to this wisdom by too many people too much of the time, it needs to be said and understood. It's good Biddle says it… whether or not Biddle himself understands its importance.

The rest of Biddle's speech is filled with a lot of nice ideas and generic challenges that could fit in any era. He repeats his themes, "We face an attack on our democracy, and on truth, a raging virus, a stinging inequity, systemic racism, a climate in crisis…."

As Biddle reaches the end of the speech his words and tone are force crafted to have a crescendo effect built on platitudes. One can risk being too cynical for criticizing this part of the speech. So, it's best not to nitpick. The rest of the speech is fine.

Biddle closes with high-minded sounding rhetoric typical of speeches in want of sounding high-minded. *Unity* is mentioned again.

Party Regime officials declare the Biddle speech to be the best inaugural speech ever.

* * *

There you have it. Two speeches, two views, two visions. It's up to you how rhetorical presentations fit with your world-view. Don't squander the opportunity to size up what can be seen and heard in the *packaging of ideas. Be wise.*

END

A TALE OF TWO SPEECHES

Nonfiction

To tell the story here within there are citations that must be acknowledged upon which the two speeches discussed in the story and presented in the appendix were based in nonfiction. The speeches are Donald Trump's January 19, 2021, farewell speech and Joe Biden's January 20, 2021, presidential inauguration speech. As these speeches are rendered faithful to their respective messages, they were modified for story continuity. For source integrity the speeches are presented here in their original text:

Donald Trump's
Farewell Speech
January 19, 2021

My fellow Americans: Four years ago, we launched a great national effort to rebuild our country, to renew its spirit, and to restore the allegiance of this government to its citizens. In short, we embarked on a mission to make America great again – for all Americans. As I conclude my term as the 45th President of the United States, I stand before you truly proud of what we have achieved together. We did what we came here to do – and so much more.

This week, we inaugurate a new administration and pray for its success in keeping America safe and prosperous. We extend our best wishes, and we also want them to have luck – a very important word.

I'd like to begin by thanking just a few of the amazing people who made our remarkable journey possible.

First, let me express my overwhelming gratitude for the love and support of our spectacular First Lady, Melania. Let me also share my deepest appreciation to my daughter Ivanka, my son-in-law Jared, and to Barron, Don, Eric, Tiffany, and Lara. You fill my world with light and with joy.

I also want to thank Vice President Mike Pence, his wonderful wife Karen, and the entire Pence family.

Thank you as well to my Chief of Staff, Mark Meadows; the dedicated members of the White House Staff and the Cabinet; and all the incredible people across our administration who poured out their heart and soul to fight for America.

I also want to take a moment to thank a truly exceptional group of people: The United States Secret Service. My family and I will forever be in your debt. My profound gratitude as well to everyone in the White House Military Office, the teams of Marine One and Air Force One, every member of the Armed Forces, and state and local law enforcement all across our country.

Most of all, I want to thank the American people. To serve as your President has been an honor beyond description. Thank you for this extraordinary privilege. And that's what it is–a great privilege and a great honor.

We must never forget that while Americans will always have our disagreements, we are a nation of incredible, decent, faithful, and peace-loving citizens who all want our country to thrive and flourish and be very, very successful and good. We are a truly magnificent nation.

All Americans were horrified by the assault on our Capitol. Political violence is an attack on everything we cherish as Americans. It can never be tolerated.

Now more than ever, we must unify around our shared values and rise above the partisan rancor, and forge our common destiny.

Four years ago, I came to Washington as the only true outsider ever to win the presidency. I had not spent my career as a politician, but as a builder looking at open skylines and imagining infinite possibilities. I ran for President because I knew there were towering new summits for America just waiting to be scaled. I knew the potential for our nation was boundless as long as we put America first.

So, I left behind my former life and stepped into a very difficult arena, but an arena nevertheless, with all sorts of potential if properly done. America had given me so much, and I wanted to give something back.

Together with millions of hardworking patriots across this land, we built the greatest political movement in the history of our country. We also built the greatest economy in the history of the world. It was about "America First" because we all wanted to make America great again. We restored the principle that a nation exists to serve its citizens. Our agenda was not about right or left, it wasn't about Republican or Democrat, but about the good of a nation, and that means the whole nation.

With the support and prayers of the American people, we achieved more than anyone thought possible. Nobody thought we could even come close.

We passed the largest package of tax cuts and reforms in American history. We slashed more job-killing regulations than any administration had ever done before. We fixed our broken trade deals, withdrew from the horrible Trans-Pacific Partnership and the impossible Paris Climate Accord, renegotiated the one-sided South Korea deal, and we replaced NAFTA with the groundbreaking USMCA – that's Mexico and Canada – a deal that's worked out very, very well.

Also, and very importantly, we imposed historic and monumental tariffs on China; made a great new deal with China. But before the ink was even dry, we and the whole world got hit with the China virus. Our trade relationship was rapidly changing, billions and billions of dollars were pouring into the U.S., but the virus forced us to go in a different direction.

The whole world suffered, but America outperformed other countries economically because of our incredible economy and the economy that we built. Without the foundations and footings, it wouldn't have worked out this way. We wouldn't have some of the best numbers we've ever had.

We also unlocked our energy resources and became the world's number-one producer of oil and natural gas by far. Powered by these policies, we built the greatest economy in the history of the world. We reignited America's job creation and achieved record-low unemployment for African Americans, Hispanic Americans, Asian Americans, women – almost everyone.

Incomes soared, wages boomed, the American Dream was restored, and millions were lifted from poverty in just a few short years. It was a miracle. The stock market set one record after another, with 148 stock market highs during this short period of time, and boosted the retirements and pensions of hardworking citizens all across our nation. 401(k)s are at a level they've never been at before. We've never seen numbers like we've seen, and that's before the pandemic and after the pandemic.

We rebuilt the American manufacturing base, opened up thousands of new factories, and brought back the beautiful phrase: "Made in the USA."

To make life better for working families, we doubled the child tax credit and signed the largest-ever expansion of funding for childcare and development. We joined with the private sector to secure commitments to train more than 16 million American workers for the jobs of tomorrow.

When our nation was hit with the terrible pandemic, we produced not one, but two vaccines with record-breaking speed, and more will quickly follow. They said it couldn't be done but we did it. They call it a "medical miracle," and that's what they're calling it right now: a "medical miracle."

Another administration would have taken three, four, five, maybe even up to ten years to develop a vaccine. We did in nine months.

We grieve for every life lost, and we pledge in their memory to wipe out this horrible pandemic once and for all.

When the virus took its brutal toll on the world's economy, we launched the fastest economic recovery our country has ever seen. We passed nearly $4 trillion in economic relief, saved or supported over 50 million jobs, and slashed the unemployment rate in half. These are numbers that our country has never seen before.

We created choice and transparency in healthcare, stood up to big pharma in so many ways, but especially in our effort to get favored-nations clauses added, which will give us the lowest prescription drug prices anywhere in the world.

We passed VA Choice, VA Accountability, Right to Try, and landmark criminal justice reform.

We confirmed three new justices of the United States Supreme Court. We appointed nearly 300 federal judges to interpret our Constitution as written.

For years, the American people pleaded with Washington to finally secure the nation's borders. I am pleased to say we answered that plea and achieved the most secure border in U.S. history. We have given our brave border agents and heroic ICE officers the tools they need to do their jobs better than they have ever done before, and to enforce our laws and keep America safe.

We proudly leave the next administration with the strongest and most robust border security measures ever put into place. This includes historic agreements with Mexico,

Guatemala, Honduras, and El Salvador, along with more than 450 miles of powerful new wall.

We restored American strength at home and American leadership abroad. The world respects us again. Please don't lose that respect.

We reclaimed our sovereignty by standing up for America at the United Nations and withdrawing from the one-sided global deals that never served our interests. And NATO countries are now paying hundreds of billions of dollars more than when I arrived just a few years ago. It was very unfair. We were paying the cost for the world. Now the world is helping us.

And perhaps most importantly of all, with nearly $3 trillion, we fully rebuilt the American military – all made in the USA. We launched the first new branch of the United States Armed Forces in 75 years: The Space Force. And last spring, I stood at Kennedy Space Center in Florida and watched as American astronauts returned to space on American rockets for the first time in many, many years.

We revitalized our alliances and rallied the nations of the world to stand up to China like never before.

We obliterated the ISIS caliphate and ended the wretched life of its founder and leader, al Baghdadi. We stood up to the oppressive Iranian regime and killed the world's top terrorist, Iranian butcher Qasem Soleimani.

We recognized Jerusalem as the capital of Israel and recognized Israeli sovereignty over the Golan Heights.

As a result of our bold diplomacy and principled realism, we achieved a series of historic peace deals in the Middle East. Nobody believed it could happen. The Abraham Accords opened the doors to a future of peace and harmony, not violence and bloodshed. It is the dawn of a new Middle East, and we are bringing our soldiers home.

I am especially proud to be the first President in decades who has started no new wars.

Above all, we have reasserted the sacred idea that, in America, the government answers to the people. Our guiding light, our North Star, our unwavering conviction has been that we are here to serve the noble everyday citizens of America. Our allegiance is not to the special interests, corporations, or global entities; it's to our children, our citizens, and to our nation itself.

As President, my top priority, my constant concern, has always been the best interests of American workers and American families. I did not seek the easiest course; by far, it was actually the most difficult. I did not seek the path that would get the least criticism. I took on the tough battles, the hardest fights, the most difficult choices because that's what you elected me to do. Your needs were my first and last unyielding focus.

This, I hope, will be our greatest legacy: Together, we put the American people back in charge of our country. We restored self-government. We restored the idea that in America no one is forgotten, because everyone matters, and everyone has a voice. We fought for the principle that every citizen is entitled to equal dignity, equal treatment, and equal rights because we are all made equal by God. Everyone is entitled to be treated with respect, to have their voice heard, and to have their government listen. You are loyal to your country, and my administration was always loyal to you.

We worked to build a country in which every citizen could find a great job and support their wonderful families. We fought for the communities where every American could be safe and schools where every child could learn. We promoted a culture where our laws would be upheld, our heroes honored, our history preserved, and law-abiding citizens are never taken for granted. Americans should take tremendous satisfaction in all that we have achieved together. It's incredible.

Now, as I leave the White House, I have been reflecting on the dangers that threaten the priceless inheritance we all share. As the world's most powerful nation, America faces constant threats and challenges from abroad. But the greatest danger we face is a loss of confidence in ourselves, a loss of confidence in our national greatness. A nation is only as strong as its spirit. We are only as dynamic as our pride. We are only as vibrant as the faith that beats in the hearts of our people.

No nation can long thrive that loses faith in its own values, history, and heroes, for these are the very sources of our unity and our vitality.

What has always allowed America to prevail and triumph over the great challenges of the past has been an unyielding and unashamed conviction in the nobility of our country and its unique purpose in history. We must never lose this conviction. We must never forsake our belief in America.

The key to national greatness lies in sustaining and instilling our shared national identity. That means focusing on what we have in common: the heritage that we all share.

At the center of this heritage is also a robust belief in free expression, free speech, and open debate. Only if we forget who we are, and how we got here, could we ever allow political censorship and blacklisting to take place in America. It's not even thinkable. Shutting down free and open debate violates our core values and most enduring traditions. In America, we don't insist on absolute conformity or enforce rigid orthodoxies and punitive speech codes. We just don't do that. America is not a timid nation of tame souls who need to be sheltered and protected from those with whom we disagree. That's not who we are. It will never be who we are.

For nearly 250 years, in the face of every challenge, Americans have always summoned our unmatched courage, confidence, and fierce independence. These are the miraculous traits that once led millions of everyday citizens to set out across a wild continent and carve out a new life in the great West. It was the same profound love of our God-given freedom that willed our soldiers into battle and our astronauts into space.

As I think back on the past four years, one image rises in my mind above all others. Whenever I traveled all along the motorcade route, there were thousands and thousands of people. They came out with their families so that they could stand as we passed, and proudly wave our great American flag. It never failed to deeply move me. I knew that they did not just come out to show their support of me; they came out to show me their support and love for our country.

This is a republic of proud citizens who are united by our common conviction that America is the greatest nation in all of history. We are, and must always be, a land of hope, of light, and of glory to all the world. This is the precious inheritance that we must safeguard at every single turn.

For the past four years, I have worked to do just that. From a great hall of Muslim leaders in Riyadh to a great square of Polish people in Warsaw; from the floor of the Korean Assembly to the podium at the United Nations General Assembly; and from the Forbidden City in Beijing to the shadow of Mount Rushmore, I fought for you, I fought for your family, I fought for our country. Above all, I fought for America and all it stands for–and that is safe, strong, proud, and free.

Now, as I prepare to hand power over to a new administration at noon on Wednesday, I want you to know that the movement we started is only just beginning. There's never been anything like it. The belief that a nation must serve its citizens will not dwindle but instead only grow stronger by the day.

As long as the American people hold in their hearts deep and devoted love of country, then there is nothing that this nation cannot achieve. Our communities will flourish. Our people will be prosperous. Our traditions will be cherished. Our faith will be strong. And our future will be brighter than ever before.

I go from this majestic place with a loyal and joyful heart, an optimistic spirit, and a supreme confidence that for our country and for our children, the best is yet to come.

Thank you, and farewell. God bless you. God bless the United States of America.

END

Joe Biden's
Presidential Inauguration Address
January 20, 2021

Chief Justice Roberts, Vice-President Harris, Speaker Pelosi, Leader Schumer, Leader McConnell, Vice-President Pence. My distinguished guests, my fellow Americans.

This is America's day. This is democracy's day. A day of history and hope, of renewal and resolve. Through a crucible for the ages, America has been tested anew and America has risen to the challenge. Today we celebrate the triumph not of a candidate but of a cause, a cause of democracy. The people – the will of the people – has been heard, and the will of the people has been heeded.

We've learned again that democracy is precious, democracy is fragile and, at this hour my friends, democracy has prevailed. So now on this hallowed ground where just a few days ago violence sought to shake the Capitol's very foundations, we come together as one nation under God – indivisible – to carry out the peaceful transfer of power as we have for more than two centuries.

As we look ahead in our uniquely American way, restless, bold, optimistic, and set our sights on a nation we know we can be and must be, I thank my predecessors of both parties. I thank them from the bottom of my heart. And I know the resilience of our Constitution and the strength, the strength of our nation, as does President Carter, who I spoke with last night who cannot be with us today, but who we salute for his lifetime of service.

I've just taken a sacred oath each of those patriots have taken. The oath first sworn by George Washington. But the American story depends not on any one of us, not on some of us, but on all of us. On we the people who seek a more perfect union. This is a great nation; we are good people. And over the centuries through storm and strife in peace and in war we've come so far. But we still have far to go.

We'll press forward with speed and urgency for we have much to do in this winter of peril and significant possibility. Much to do, much to heal, much to restore, much to build, and much to gain. Few people in our nation's history have been more challenged or found a time more challenging or difficult than the time we're in now. A once in a century virus that silently stalks the country has taken as many lives in one year as in all of World War II.

Millions of jobs have been lost. Hundreds of thousands of businesses closed. A cry for racial justice, some 400 years in the making, moves us. The dream of justice for all will be deferred no longer. A cry for survival comes from the planet itself, a cry that can't be any more desperate or any more clear now. The rise of political extremism, white supremacy, domestic terrorism, that we must confront, and we will defeat.

To overcome these challenges, to restore the soul and secure the future of America, requires so much more than words. It requires the most elusive of all things in a democracy – unity. Unity. In another January on New Year's Day in 1863 Abraham Lincoln signed the Emancipation Proclamation. When he put pen to paper the president said, and I quote, 'If my name ever goes down in history, it'll be for this act, and my whole soul is in it.'

My whole soul is in it today, on this January day. My whole soul is in this. Bringing America together, uniting our people, uniting our nation. And I ask every American to join me in this cause. Uniting to fight the foes we face – anger, resentment, and hatred. Extremism, lawlessness, violence, disease, joblessness, and hopelessness.

With unity we can do great things, important things. We can right wrongs, we can put people to work in good jobs, we can teach our children in safe schools. We can overcome the deadly virus, we can rebuild work, we can rebuild the middle class and make work secure, we can secure racial justice and we can make America once again the leading force for good in the world.

I know speaking of unity can sound to some like a foolish fantasy these days. I know the forces that divide us are deep and they are real. But I also know they are not new. Our history has been a constant struggle between the American ideal, that we are all created equal, and the harsh ugly reality that racism, nativism, and fear have torn us apart. The battle is perennial, and victory is never secure.

Through civil war, the Great Depression, World War, 9/11, through struggle, sacrifice, and setback, our better angels have always prevailed. In each of our moments enough of us have come together to carry all of us forward and we can do that now. History, faith, and reason show the way. The way of unity.

We can see each other not as adversaries but as neighbors. We can treat each other with dignity and respect. We can join forces, stop the shouting, and lower the temperature. For without unity there is no peace, only bitterness and fury, no progress, only exhausting outrage. No nation, only a state of chaos. This is our historic moment of crisis and challenge. And unity is the path forward. And we must meet this moment as the United States of America.

If we do that, I guarantee we will not fail. We have never, ever, ever, ever failed in America when we've acted together. And so today at this time in this place, let's start afresh, all of us. Let's begin to listen to one another again, hear one another, see one another. Show respect to one another. Politics doesn't have to be a raging fire destroying everything in its path. Every disagreement doesn't have to be a cause for total war, and we must reject the culture in which facts themselves are manipulated and even manufactured.

My fellow Americans, we have to be different than this. We have to be better than this and I believe America is so much better than this. Just look around. Here we stand in the shadow of the Capitol dome. As mentioned earlier, completed in the shadow of the Civil War. When the union itself was literally hanging in the balance. We endure, we prevail. Here we stand, looking out on the great Mall, where Dr. King spoke of his dream.

Here we stand, where 108 years ago at another inaugural, thousands of protesters tried to block brave women marching for the right to vote. And today we mark the swearing in of the first woman elected to national office, Vice President Kamala Harris. Don't tell me things can't change. Here we stand where heroes who gave the last full measure of devotion rest in eternal peace.

And here we stand just days after a riotous mob thought they could use violence to silence the will of the people, to stop the work of our democracy, to drive us from this sacred ground. It did not happen, it will never happen, not today, not tomorrow, not ever. Not ever. To all those who supported our campaign, I'm humbled by the faith you placed in us. To all those who did not support us, let me say this. Hear us out as we move forward. Take a measure of me and my heart.

If you still disagree, so be it. That's democracy. That's America. The right to dissent peacefully. And the guardrail of our democracy is perhaps our nation's greatest strength. If you hear me clearly, disagreement must not lead to disunion. And I pledge this to you. I will be a President for all Americans, all Americans. And I promise you I will fight for those who did not support me as for those who did.

Many centuries ago, Saint Augustine – the saint of my church – wrote that a people was a multitude defined by the common objects of their love. Defined by the common objects of their love. What are the common objects we as Americans love, that define us as Americans? I think we know. Opportunity, security, liberty, dignity, respect, honor, and yes, the truth.

Recent weeks and months have taught us a painful lesson. There is truth and there are lies. Lies told for power and for profit. And each of us has a duty and a responsibility as citizens as Americans and especially as leaders. Leaders who are pledged to honor our Constitution to protect our nation. To defend the truth and defeat the lies.

Look, I understand that many of my fellow Americans view the future with fear and trepidation. I understand they worry about their jobs. I understand like their dad they lay in bed at night staring at the ceiling thinking: 'Can I keep my healthcare? Can I pay my mortgage?' Thinking about their families, about what comes next. I promise you; I get it. But the answer's not to turn inward. To retreat into competing factions. Distrusting those who don't look like you, or worship the way you do, who don't get their news from the same source as you do.

We must end this uncivil war that pits red against blue, rural versus urban, conservative versus liberal. We can do this if we open our souls instead of hardening our hearts, if we show a little tolerance and humility, and if we're willing to stand in the other person's shoes, as my mom would say. Just for a moment, stand in their shoes.

Because here's the thing about life. There's no accounting for what fate will deal you. Some days you need a hand. There are other days when we're called to lend a hand. That's how it has to be, that's what we do for one another. And if we are that way our country will be stronger, more prosperous, more ready for the future. And we can still disagree.

My fellow Americans, in the work ahead of us we're going to need each other. We need all our strength to persevere through this dark winter. We're entering what may be the darkest and deadliest period of the virus. We must set aside politics and finally face this pandemic as one nation, one nation. And I promise this, as the Bible says, 'Weeping may endure for a night, joy cometh in the morning'. We will get through this together. Together.

Look folks, all my colleagues I serve with in the House and the Senate up here, we all understand the world is watching. Watching all of us today. So, here's my message to those beyond our borders. America has been tested and we've come out stronger for it. We will repair our alliances and engage with the world once again. Not to meet yesterday's challenges but today's and tomorrow's challenges. And we'll lead not merely by the example of our power but the power of our example.

Fellow Americans, moms, dads, sons, daughters, friends, neighbors, and co-workers. We will honor them by becoming the people and the nation we can and should be. So, I ask you let's say a silent prayer for those who lost their lives, those left behind, and for our country. Amen.

Folks, it's a time of testing. We face an attack on our democracy, and on truth, a raging virus, a stinging inequity, systemic racism, a climate in crisis, America's role in the world. Any one of these would be enough to challenge us in profound ways. But the fact is we face them all at once, presenting this nation with one of the greatest responsibilities we've had. Now we're going to be tested. Are we going to step up?

It's time for boldness for there is so much to do. And this is certain, I promise you. We will be judged, you and I, by how we resolve these cascading crises of our era. We will rise to the occasion. Will we master this rare and difficult hour? Will we meet our obligations and pass along a new and better world to our children? I believe we must and I'm sure you do as well. I believe we will, and when we do, we'll write the next great chapter in the history of the United States of America. The American story.

A story that might sound like a song that means a lot to me; it's called American Anthem. And there's one verse that stands out at least for me and it goes like this:

"The work and prayers of centuries have brought us to this day, which shall be our legacy, what will our children say?

Let me know in my heart when my days are through, America, America, I gave my best to you."

Let us add our own work and prayers to the unfolding story of our great nation. If we do this, then when our days are through, our children and our children's children will say of us: "They gave their best, they did their duty, they healed a broken land."

My fellow Americans I close the day where I began, with a sacred oath. Before God and all of you, I give you my word. I will always level with you. I will defend the Constitution; I'll defend our democracy.

I'll defend America and I will give all – all of you – keep everything I do in your service. Thinking not of power but of possibilities. Not of personal interest but of public good.

And together we will write an American story of hope, not fear. Of unity not division, of light not darkness. A story of decency and dignity, love and healing, greatness and goodness. May this be the story that guides us. The story that inspires us. And the story that tells ages yet to come that we answered the call of history, we met the moment. Democracy and hope, truth and justice, did not die on our watch but thrive.

That America secured liberty at home and stood once again as a beacon to the world. That is what we owe our forbearers, one another, and generations to follow.

So, with purpose and resolve, we turn to those tasks of our time. Sustained by faith, driven by conviction, and devoted to one another and the country we love with all our hearts. May God bless America and God protect our troops.

END

WHAT A TRIPP

By Harry Archer

OKAY, I'M HAVING FUN WITH DANNY TRIPP'S NAME. But it's too easy because the sound and verbal meaning of his name fit with the wild ride he took us on. "Tripp's wild ride" was wilder than "Mr. Toad's wild ride."

Where did this guy come from? Well, the answer will be hard to swallow for Tripp-haters, but he came from all of us – you and me. Let me explain: None of us are really satisfied with who's running our government. And there is no reason a sensible person should be satisfied. The "ground" was and remains fertile for government "cleansing." Or as Tripp put it when he ran for president and throughout his presidency – "take out the trash." That message hit the right note and appealed to enough of us to put Tripp in the Executive Mansion as his supporters wanted a different kind of president that would "take out the trash." Of course, Tripp-haters thought *he* was the trash, showing one person's "trash" is another person's "gold." Particularly in the "Divided" States of this Nation.

Indeed, Danny Tripp was a different kind of president. He was an unlikely guy to assume office. Even those supportive of his candidacy thought it improbable he would be president. But things happen for a reason even if you don't like the reason.

Danny Tripp was an anomaly in politics and governance. His election to the presidency was not only improbable but it was impossible. When the impossible happens, people are forced to rethink their assumptions to account for what they thought impossible to be understood as actually possible. But the Tripp-hating half of the electorate does not entertain such rethinking. They hold firm – Danny Tripp is impossible. They strengthen their mental fortress with extreme projecting, creating an alternative reality that conflicts with the half of the electorate that likes, even loves Danny Tripp. Alas, we all live in one or the other parallel universes.

Which universe you live in will determine what you conclude about this article. It's okay; it can't be helped. Although if you're adventurous, "wormholes" from one universe to the other are available by way of open-minded sensibility or a collapse of sensibility, depending on the universe you "wormhole" into if inclined to leave the universe you currently occupy. Perhaps this article will be the open-minded "wormhole" for you. Let's see where you wind up after reading this.

* * *

Danny Tripp doesn't fit any of the conventions public leaders are expected to follow. Tripp is without adherence to any party or political philosophy. This makes him a blasphemer of the highest order regarding the orthodoxy of conventional political science. If you think Tripp was a successful president you may likely attribute his nonadherence to any party or political philosophy as partly or entirely the reason he was successful.

When Tripp speaks, the media, which is emphatically anti-Tripp, report negative meanings Tripp doesn't convey. Tripp counterattacks by calling the media "the phony media." The two sides – Tripp and the media – are at war. The electorate polarizes around the political and culture wars playing out in broadcast and social media.

This war *is* a civil war. The Tripp-hating side gave no quarter to their enemy – Tripp and his supporters or anyone who doesn't hate Tripp the way Tripp-haters hate Tripp. This set the stage for the influencers of the *Tripp-hating Party* to move to empower the *Party Regime*.

To win the presidency, Tripp ran on the simple message of "*Let's Be Great Today*." The message resonated with enough voters to get him elected. Tripp-haters and the *Tripp-hating Party* were horrified and angered by the election results. Tripp proceeded to govern by the *Let's Be Great Toady* message, which became his doctrine. The Tripp-haters' anger, horror, and hatred continued to mount, reaching hysteria. The more hysterical Tripp-haters became, the more Tripp-supporters' conviction for the *Let's Be Great Today* doctrine strengthened. The differences between the two groups – the two universes – are now unbridgeable.

In his one term as president, the Tripp administration accomplished a staggering number of things previous administrations had not done. The economy came out of a slow recovery into a robust prosperity benefiting most everyone. Unemployment went down and groups of people including African Americans, Hispanics, and women saw a historic rise in their incomes. The stock market reached record highs which benefited pension funds and small private investors as well as large financial institutions. The nation became energy independent – this hadn't been done in generations. This created a financial boon as there was a lowering of operational costs for businesses across the board, as well as an increase in production of goods and services, leading to greater profits and more jobs. The media hardly reported it.

Trade agreements were redrawn, correcting imbalances that were unfair to the nation for decades. Meaningless alliances creating the illusion that serious climate and environmental issues were being addressed were broken off. The nation was now in a stronger position to deal with climate and environmental issues as opposed to giving "lip service" and adorning "window dressing" to the issues by maintaining ineffective alliances… not to mention the waste of money – tribute – to stay in such alliances. The media reported this as policy failures.

The same kind of alliance agreement but related to nuclear armaments were broken off by the Tripp administration because the agreements actually guaranteed nuclear armament of rogue regimes hostile to this nation. Tribute was also to be paid to the hostile regimes, which the Tripp administration stopped. Again, the agreements were no more than "lip service" and "window dressing" to cover up dangerous situations. The media reported this as policy failures.

For years Veterans Administration and veteran affairs had been mismanaged and not held to account. Veterans who served and sacrificed for the nation in need of lifesaving medical treatment – including psychiatric and substance dependency treatment – were kept on waiting lists for treatment they never received. Thousands of veterans died for failure to receive treatment. This was a shameful problem that previous administrations not only failed to address, they institutionally and bureaucratically made the problem worse. That was remedied by the Tripp administration. Under the Tripp administration veterans could receive treatment within two weeks, authorizing treatment for any veteran outside of the Veterans Administration if necessary. Additionally, Veteran Administration officers and managers could now be fired for corruption or incompetence. The media hardly reported it.

In the Middle East regional and religious intractable conflicts are an ever-present way of life for everyone. The ill-effects of Middle East conflicts reach the world at large. The Middle East is a powder keg that explodes periodically and is always loaded to explode again. This constant state of conflict has existed for generations throughout the modern era. The general feeling on all sides is hopelessness. The Tripp administration took a different path than previous administrations to address the ever-present Middle East problem.

In the short time of the Tripp term, the Tripp administration took the lead to coordinate monumental historic peace agreements, including state recognition, the establishment of diplomatic relations, and signed trade agreements between and among countries that had been mortal enemies. For this Tripp was nominated for the Nobel Peace Prize. The media hardly reported it.

Early into the Tripp administration, the ruling regime in one Middle Eastern country committed atrocities against its people, including dispersing lethal gas. The Tripp administration took swift action to protect innocent people from further harm at the hands of the dictatorial ruling regime. The Tripp administration launched a surgical airstrike that destroyed runways at a military facility servicing the regime's air delivery of lethal gas and other weaponry. The airstrike was successful in both retaliating against the atrocities and protecting innocent people. The media hardly reported it.

The Tripp administration ordered similar airstrikes to surgically take-out military leaders of terrorist regimes who had committed terrorist activities for years, murdering thousands of people. These missions ordered by the Tripp administration were successful in their purpose. They introduced a remarkable shift in how the military can be used when it is decided military intervention is justified without committing the military to war, let alone a protracted war at great cost including human treasure without good results. The media reported this as policy failures.

The Tripp administration showed the effective use of military action as a decisive and definitive response to threats to the nation as well as being a deterrent to overt military actions against the nation. In line with this shift in military use was the doctrine Tripp enacted bringing an end to the nation's part in other countries' "forever wars," as Tripp called them. It's possible the Tripp administration demonstrated that although there can be instances that a military strike may be an option, military wars are wholly unnecessary. Never in history had that loomed as a possibility until the Tripp administration. The media were silent.

Tripp's leadership, compassion, and his knowing what matters was demonstrated when as Commander in Chief he made a particular call. A sophisticated surveillance drone deployed by our nation flying in legal airspace was unlawfully shot down by a terrorist regime. Our nation's retaliation was expected. A retaliation airstrike was in preparation and poised to strike awaiting Tripp's order. Tripp asked many questions of his military experts detailing the strike. He asked more than a few times how many of the enemy's military personnel would be killed by the strike. That estimate kept changing as the time to launch the strike closed in. At the last moment, Tripp asked again what the casualty estimation was. Based on the number given to him, he calmly said, "That's too many real people affecting too many real families. Abort the strike." The media hardly reported it.

Under the Tripp administration, military troops were brought home from foreign deployment, particularly from hostile zones, leaving the fewest number of troops stationed outside of the nation in many decades. Under the Tripp administration, protracted military engagements were ended. Under the Tripp administration, no military wars were begun. The media was silent.

The moment Tripp was elected, impeachment was the goal of the opposition party. But what had Tripp done for which they could impeach him? Well, he got elected. That sounds good enough for those in opposition to Tripp. But could they come up with something more? That shouldn't be a problem. After all, they think – Tripp was a monster who left "neon-flashing" signs as evidence of his crimes. The opposition party – later to become the *Party Regime* – launched an aggressive special investigation against Tripp the moment he was sworn into office. A proctology exam couldn't have been more probing than the $40,000,000 three-year investigation.

In the concluding report of the investigation, many indiscretions and "horrific" acts on Tripp's part were described. Despite or because of the report's findings, the opposition party did not bring articles of impeachment against Tripp. Even to Tripp-haters, the findings of the report didn't reveal anything for which Tripp could be impeached. But that didn't deter those who still lusted for Tripp's end. So, only days after the report was delivered showing no cause for impeachment, the opposition party obtained a recording of a phone conversation Tripp had with a leader of an allied country. With this recording the opposition party thought they had finally struck "impeachment paydirt." But as with all evidence the evidence may say more about the "eye of the beholder" than it does about the evidence.

Articles of Impeachment citing the "crime" of what Tripp said in the recorded conversation with the head of the allied country were brought to the Senate. The opposition party prosecuted their case with a vengeance. Tripp was acquitted.

Then, with no pause, the beginning casualties of a pandemic visited the nation from outside her borders. In a short time, the nation was embroiled in a world health crisis. To mitigate casualties – deaths – and keep hospitals from being overwhelmed, Tripp decisively shut down a booming economy.

Fresh off the failed impeachment, the opposition party prosecuted through the media Tripp's incompetence and complicity in all things pandemic. The pace and fluidity with which the opposition party beat a steady drum of "Tripp Bad" – like a "bad trip"– was astounding. In the context of political propagandistic "flame-throwing" the media went against Tripp to hyper magnify the "flame-throwing" at him over his response to the pandemic. The media's reporting on Tripp was a marvel and a horror to Tripp supporters. They could ponder the question – *Is there no decency? Is there no truth?* The answer for Tripp supporters – *Not in the bizarro universe.*

The pandemic was managed and mismanaged through layers of social, governmental, and private industry structures, as well as individual initiatives for successes, failures, and everything in between. Amidst the spectrum of pandemic causes and effects and effects and causes was the remarkable strength of the economy. There were plunges in employment and many business sectors, yet some kind of consumer confidence existed, contributing to record highs in the stock market. The economy tanked with the initial shut down but a second recovery – like the recovery Tripp presided over when he initiated policies after taking office – took hold with steady momentum. The comeback and recovery from the pandemic were in full swing.

Multiple effective vaccines were developed and began to be administered with the objective to vaccinate anyone who wanted it, at no cost. This development was a historic achievement in innovation, industriousness, and private/governmental coordination. It usually takes five to ten years for a vaccine to come to market, if it comes at all. The vaccines developed to meet the challenge of this pandemic were available in ten months after the illness first appeared in the nation.

But to the opposition party, the pandemic brought more. The pandemic brought a weak reason to make adjustments to election procedures for the upcoming election in which Tripp was running for a second term. Indications were that Tripp would be easily reelected based on enough of the electorate thinking his first term was decidedly successful according to all historical metrics reflecting voter approval. But in the name of public safety during the pandemic, in-person voting was made optional and mail-in voting – to be distinguished from absentee voting – was made available. Ballots were mailed out en masse to addresses where anyone other than the intended person on the registered voter roll could be residing.

If your sarcastic cynicism went into overdrive it might sound like this: *Not that anyone let alone a political party would ever commit voter fraud; but with mail-in voting someone might get the idea to see a big opportunity to get away with fraud since with mail-in it's so easy, it's so scalable, and no one can prove it.*

As predicted, the election was certified as going to Jim Biddle. If you're still having some sarcastic cynical overflow you might think: *Of course, Biddle won. He ran a brilliant campaign.*

Half the electorate smelled a rat. True to form, Tripp did not concede losing to Biddle. He pointed to many things, including the mail-in voting that corrupted the process to work against the will of the people.

This ignited a new chapter in the *Tripp Presidency saga.* An important part of the narrative for the opposition party and Tripp-haters was the fantasy of Tripp being dragged out of the Executive Mansion in some kind of restraint harness as he cries to his mommy, "I don't want to go!" It's an important image, if not alone for the nullification of cognitive dissonance Tripp-haters crave. They don't want to give up their view of Tripp as humiliated, even though his farewell speech is gracious and positive. The thing is, as satisfying as the image of Tripp being dragged out in a restraint is for Tripp-haters, it's a high cartoonish bar to reach to get validation for their worldview. And that's the problem. The vitriol of Tripp-hatred has gotten to be ridiculous beyond any legitimate dislike of him.

The undeniable reality of the other *universe* from the Tripp-hating *universe* challenges us to be wiser about power politics controlled by the media. Tripp is very popular with his supporters – half the electorate – immensely popular with most. Throughout his term Tripp held many rallies in support of his administration and its accomplishments. More rallies than any President before him. The rallies were attended by overflowing crowds. Tripp was the most accessible president to the public, press, and media in history.

So, it was inevitable when the election of Biddle was certified there would be an outcry from half the electorate. A Tripp rally was held for Tripp to address the matter to his supporters. The rally was attended by throngs of people. Juxtaposed to the rally in time and space, rioters – likely most of them Tripp supporters – stormed their way into the Capitol Building. The rioters caused directly or indirectly loss of life, and directly caused damage to hallowed property.

Not yet satiated with their impression of Tripp humiliation, the opposition party, the media, and *the Big Tech Three* swooped in to hold Tripp accountable for the riot. Within days an article of impeachment was brought to the Senate – the second time Tripp was impeached. No president had ever been impeached twice. Tripp was breaking all kinds of records. To Tripp supporters, because of the enormous achievements of his administration, his enemies' relentless persecution of Tripp was a "badge of honor" rather than a humiliation. If the opposition party was trying to humiliate Tripp and cancel his influence, their impeachment actions had the opposite effect. They were martyring a popular figure.

The events of the four years making up the Tripp Presidency set the groundwork for what came with a vengeance. The opposition party with *The Big Guy* Jim Biddle as its figurehead now in the Executive Office of the Presidency launched the *Party Regime*.

What a wild ride! What a Tripp!

END

THE RIDDLE OF BIDDLE

By Harry Archer

RIDDLE ME THIS. WHAT DO YOU GET WHEN YOU LOSE sight of what matters? You get what you deserve.

Life is filled with riddles and mysteries. Humans can be artful, clumsy, ingenious, and dumb about intellectual challenges. The phenomenon of Jim Biddle presents like a riddle: He did not capture the imagination of the electorate. Yet he ascended to the presidency. The reason that happened is because politics is less about ideology and more about *perception*. And it doesn't matter if the *perception* is false… it actually helps. His party needed an empty suit they could fill with anything they thought could be called anti-Tripp. Biddle was the best empty suit for the job. That and the election "clown car/funhouse," mixed in with mass willful blindness and blinding Tripp-hate got Biddle into the Executive Mansion.

Jim Biddle – *The Big Guy* – is an old established political figure from a bygone era. He is a nostalgic relic right out of central casting as a retail politician at a wholesale price. He can never do anything wrong even though he does everything wrong because after all it's just politics. Biddle's ascension to the presidency is the most unlikely likely thing to happen. For his party, Biddle's placement into the presidency has to happen even though it never should have happened. He fits perfectly in this role.

Biddle has always been charmingly goofy. At least throughout his political career – his only career – many people publicly say he is a pleasant and likable guy. But with politics being a show people, particularly politicians, don't say what they really think and feel. And despite being called likable, Biddle often comes off as a jerk.

Biddle is the oldest person sworn into the office of the Presidency. His advancing cognitive impairments are mixing with his "goofy charm" to render him incapable for the executive position. No matter though. The *Party Regime* doesn't need a leader. They just need a "place holder." And if Biddle is shown the "place" by his handlers he can "hold" it… and/or be propped up if he slips.

Over recent years, an extreme radical fringe emerged on the edge of Biddle's political party. This radical fringe is based on changing the culture and center of power by declaring virtue superiority. Its sole weapon is fear. With public demonstrations gaining media attention and support, this radical fringe presents false choices for institutions and people to side with virtue couched in anti-racism and climate-change rhetoric. Institutions and people afraid to appear against virtue, side with this radical fringe and its rhetoric. This causes this radical fringe to have exaggerated disproportionate power in the direction of absolute influence.

Institutions and people are now measured by virtue purity

standards which are inevitably violated by everyone, most particularly the party elite who set the standards, while society and the culture are embroiled in a "cannibalistic feeding frenzy" to be "king of the hill" for virtue. Any institution or person not approved by the virtue elite/police/judge/intelligentsia/mob is held to public ridicule, stripped of citizen standing, and robbed of their ability to make a living. From this level of fear the "*Awaken*" movement emerged. In the culture it's not only fashionable to be *Awaken*, it's mandatory. From this pressurized movement, *awakenness* gains leadership seats in the halls of government at all levels.

The odd thing though is the vast majority of the public don't agree with *Awaken* orthodoxy. The political movement mounted by the opposition party to defeat Tripp's bid for re-election faced a surge to nominate an *Awaken* candidate *too* radical to defeat Tripp. Facing the likely outcome of Tripp's re-election, the opposition party maneuvered its political machine to get the primary votes necessary to nominate Jim Biddle. He can be marketed as a stable, moderate candidate and the antidote to the "bad" character of Danny Tripp. In office, Biddle's perceived moderation, stability, and decency is used by his party to mask the enactment of the *Awaken* agenda. Once in office Biddle's party became the *Party Regime*. Biddle was their "Trojan Horse."

We are all bound by *perception*. As William Blake wrote in his book *The Marriage of Heaven and Hell "If the **doors of perception** were cleansed every thing would appear to man as it* *is, Infinite. For man has closed himself up, till he sees all things thro' narrow chinks of his cavern."*

If our *perception* remains narrow, we will live in the narrow confines of that *perception. Free thought* and *free speech* will widen our *perception.*

END

WHAT'S GOING ON?

By Harry Archer

Preamble

As a civil engineer I have a duty to build with integrity on a foundation of integrity. Civil engineering is the ever-present awareness that what you build will affect everybody. The harm done to all of us in the false name of virtue is a rot on integrity and our individual souls. 2+2=4 no matter who you are or what group you declare you belong to. For the bridge to hold, for the engineer who builds it, and for the public who uses it, 2+2=4.

The light of wisdom is our only way out of this rot. This article is written to be that kind of light. I hope you will read it. I hope it will speak to what matters to you.

* * *

I WILL TELL YOU WHAT HAPPENED. YOU WILL EITHER understand what I am telling you and it will change everything or you will not understand, and it will change nothing.

From the beginning, the human species was challenged with survival. Quality of life beyond survival was not only irrelevant it wasn't even a conceptual thing… it wasn't a thing at all.

The species lived in families and groups. They needed to live in families and groups in order to survive. Being in families and groups afforded the advantage to work as teams – increasing survival odds. The better and stronger the teams, the better the chance to survive.

Forming teams is a process of organization. The level of organization runs along an infinite spectrum from organically pre-rudimentary to high degrees of sophistication and algorithmic refinement. It starts with people self-selecting jobs and tasks according to their respective proximities, talents, strengths, inclinations, interests, instincts, and imaginations. Personalities interact and leaders and followers emerge with or without conflict, playing out in a dynamic complex of relationships.

The organizational structure and character are a function of all the elements of human nature – selfishness, selflessness, generosity, greed, compassion, indifference, practicality, impracticality, patience, impulsiveness, confidence, fear, trust, mistrust, kindness, cruelty, sensitivity, insensitivity, courage, cowardice, knowledge, ignorance, wisdom, stupidity, virtuousness, immorality, and all that identifies human nature. The expression and restraint of human nature determine the state of all humankind whether an individual, a couple, a family, a group, a tribe, a community, a village, a city, a city-state, a confederation, a nation, an empire, a global entity.

The great riddle consuming all human existence is – How does an individual live with everyone else? The riddle is extrapolated – How do all group entities from the smallest (couple) to the largest (global entity) live among one another? (Should extraterrestrials of a like developmental level be encountered the riddle would include them. But for now, let's keep it real.)

Organizing includes the utilization of tools and weapons. The initial tools and weapons of humankind are things found in nature in their natural state and purposed and repurposed for their use. That would be things like sticks and stones.

The initial use of sticks and stones starts the technology revolution. Sticks and stones are the prehistoric precursors to all technology – the bowl, plow, boat, windmill, gun powder, telescope, car, television, Saturn Rocket, personal computer, and "pet rock" – funny how we go full circle with everything. Modification of sticks and stones introduces the next level of technology. The ends of sticks are sharpened into spears and such. Stones are chiseled to make chisels, knives, spear tips, and such.

A small group from within coalesces into some kind of organization. As different small groups organize, some groups are successful, others struggle to exist, and some go extinct. Different groups encountering one another may pick and choose to leave one another alone, cooperate on specific matters, war with them for whatever reason.

The increased refinement in organization of a given group leads to the creation of a society and with it, a culture. Governance and a system of governance becomes an ever-increasing need until it becomes essential.

Governance means decisions are made to affect the society. This requires the recognition of persons to have the authority to do the deciding. The way people in any given society establish the deciders – the leaders – has been lopsided for most all history toward aggressive power acquisition, which more often includes violence and brutality. Lineage claims were usually attached to the ruling/deciding/leading class creating a mechanism for succession to leadership.

The emergence of warlords in society is a frequent way leaders become leaders throughout history. (Warlord-type leaders existed in pre-historic times so warlords are not new when societies come into the world of recorded history.) Class stratification of the group/society population also emerges interrelated to the establishment of leadership authority.

Class stratification is the defining foundation of an orderly society. But if the stratification is permanently fixed with no upward or downward mobility based on individual personal action and merit, an intractable unearned privileged class stratification will give way to the ultimate destructive conflict affecting all humans. With *fixed* class stratification you get a lot… and you lose everything.

That's basically what happened. But stick with me and I'll tell you more… because you need to know more.

One's Prospects

The governance of a society is somewhere on the vertical continuum from pure capitalism to pure communism. It is also a function on the horizontal continuum from a pure democracy to pure totalitarian.

A simple yet profoundly succinct way it has been popularly put is there are two classes of people – *the haves and the have-nots.* Another way to put it with additional critical meaning is – *the sayers and the sayers-not.* Or those with a voice and influence and those with no voice and no influence.

However you put it, the nature of this distinction is a primitively basic self-identifier. A person from childhood identifies and accepts being one or the other – a *have/sayer* or a *have-not/sayer-not.* Moreover, throughout history this distinction – being one or the other – is determined with few exceptions by your birth and not your actions. The circumstances you are born into of which you have no control fixed your station in life for all your life. Additionally, immutable traits such as gender and race, which are also out of your control, fixed your station forever as well.

Throughout history, throughout the world, this has had two bad socio/psychological effects. 1) People accept their lot in life and fail to develop ambition, suppressing personal aspirations and dreams, hence creating destitution of mind and body. Ironically, even the privileged class is badly affected by the fixed (static) class system because they don't develop a sense of appreciation or a sense of merit. And 2) Over time, pent-up dissatisfaction and destitution combined with a nothing-to-loose prospect explode into an insurrection against the oppressor – the privileged. A class war ensues a' la the French Revolution of 1789.

Consequently, a society based on an intractable class system is destined to implode. But an implosion on a catastrophic scale does not necessarily lead to a new society that offers anything better than the previous one. Often it is worse.

Whatever improvements made to society, *what must be present is a common understanding and acceptance of the possibility through personal initiative, one can improve their self and their station in life no matter the circumstances they were born into or their immutable traits. This is key to a successful society.*

The Great Civilizations of History

Before the middle part of the Holocene Epoch (a period of about 10,000 years ago to the present day) but still over a long period of time in human terms, out of the primordial muck of the prehistoric primitive drive of the human species for survival, eventually evolves eras where mass civilizations emerge. The Sumerians of Mesopotamia may have been the first such civilization. China, Egypt, and the Indus are other early civilizations.

Societal classification of rank and privilege defining the stratification of the population is a firmly established critical functioning characteristic of human group/nation-state existence – It's the way we are. As such, enactment and maintenance of societal structures play out like a cosmic, eternal *Game of Thrones*.

The ambitions, strengths, intrigues, fortunes, conspiracies, forces between and among individuals and groups vie for position and power. Such groups include counsels of civil affairs, counsels of mystical transcendency (religion and religious institution), and counsels of militia forces. All of this combines into an orderly society ethos that embeds into the individual and collective psyche.

There is always a challenge to any established order. The way an order is challenged and successfully changed or overthrown completely is by attacking the order's weakness – there are always weaknesses.

Ancient Eastern civilizations lay down the principle of respect for elders. Western civilization introduced the idea of the republic. Yet whether Eastern or Western, all the great civilizations despite their advancements benefiting humanity, have brought horrific cruelty and atrocity to humanity on a massive scale. Slavery exists in all the great societies. There were the Aztec and Incan abominations of mass sacrifice. There were religious persecutions in Europe throughout history that oppressed all people and included witch hunts, witch trials, and witch burnings. There were the genocidal policies against Native Americans in both North and South America. There were genocidal starvations in the Soviet Union and China. There were the killing fields of Cambodia under the Khmer Rouge regime. There was the final solution wrought by the Third Reich.

Cruelty and atrocity are a well-developed, well-honored enterprise in human existence. Of course, cruelty and atrocity are abhorred and condemned as well. But they could not exist without being evilly honored or evilly ignored.

Ignorance and complacency are a part of the *evilly honoring/evilly ignoring* dynamic. Ignorance and complacency are the most destructive parts of evil. Because without ignorance and complacency evil would have no place to implant itself, nourish itself – and grow.

This underscores the responsibility of how a civilization moves are ultimately determined by the people, not the leaders. No matter how oppressed a people are at any given time the people at large must use their initiative to achieve and maintain justice in society. Their initiative is their voice and their unalienable right to use it.

The best way to secure your right to speak freely is to stand up and secure the rights of others to speak freely, particularly those with whom you disagree or find offensive. All the cruelty and atrocity – for which humans have a penchant – can only be combated to eliminate through the power of *free thought* and *free speech.*

It's a simple and most profound equation:

Free Thought and Free Speech =
Less Cruelty and Less Atrocity

A Call to Arms: Our Voices

It's time to speak. It's been time for too long. The greatest weapon against ignorance and self-destruction is *free thought* and *free speech.*

If we fail to keep the channels of communication open to *free thought* and *free speech*, we lose all basic freedoms. We lose the on-going war against cruelty and atrocity.

The *Awaken* movement is dedicated to obliterating *free thought* and *free speech*. The *Awaken* movement uses the appeal to virtue superiority to attract good people to support the regime they want to establish. Their appeal to virtue superiority hides their goal to extinguish *free thought* and *free speech*... and the platforms to exercise such.

You are a part of the struggle the human species has been engaged in from the beginning of humankind. It is a struggle for survival. And because of our uniqueness as a self-reflective species, it is a struggle for our soul.

There is everything to lose if we don't speak. There is everything to gain if we do speak.

END

CULTURE DRIVES THE HERD WHY HONEY BEES AND STAND-UP COMEDIANS ARE ESSENTIAL

By Harry Archer

It may not be uplifting, but we are part of a herd. That's the rawest way to say culture. One person is a unique soul. Two people interrelated with one another are a society. Society is a grouping of individuals – people – or a herd.

Honey Bees & Stand-Up Comedians

There are two things necessary to maintain a good quality of life: Honey bees and stand-up comedians. Even if your current quality of life is poor, it would be much worse without honey bees and stand-up comedians. It would not only be bad without honey bees and stand-up comedians, it would be a catastrophic threat to the existence of the human species.

Given the range of consciousness we have, it's a hard-wired condition: There are infinite things we take for granted that are vital to life. The Sun is vital to life on Earth. We know that. But we take it for granted that the Sun will always be there. (Cosmically, it won't always be there. But on the time/space scale to which we can relate, the Sun is constant.)

Honey bees are no less vital than the Sun. And yes, surprise, stand-up comedians are no less vital to us than honey bees and the Sun.

If we give a different name respectively to honey bees and stand-up comedians the distinction of how these two are vital can be better seen: Let's name honey bees "pollinators for all edible plants." Let's name stand-up comedians "warning detectors for idiocy." Can you see now? Can you understand? If eithe *pollinators for all edible plants* or *warning detectors for idiocy* go extinct, we are all done for!

I don't know what the *Awaken* think about honey bees, although my cynical bias imagines the *Awaken* can easily take issue with the systematic unequal class structure of bee society including the non-unionized worker bees. I do know, however, the *Awaken* are waging war against stand-up comics. The *Awaken* don't like comedians doing their job – warning us about our idiocy. It exposes the *Awaken*. The silencing and *vanishing* of stand-up comedians – of stand-up comedy as a whole – is a battleground in the culture war the *Awaken* are currently winning.

The combatants in the culture war have a battle cry for their opponents to *wake up!* Everyone is saying it – *wake up* – at and about their political enemies. But the overall issue isn't so much *wake up* as it is *grow up!* The un-*Awaken* need to add *grow up* to their battle cry arsenal against the *Awaken*. If you look past the danger, lunacy, and destruction of *Awaken* doctrine you see the followers of *awakenness* have a world view that is immature, naïve, and childish. Yes. They need to *grow up!*

* * *

How any herd does its living is what culture is. Culture is everything we interact with that involves the existence of others beyond ourselves. Standing in line at a grocery store checkout counter is culture. Standing in line is cultural.

The conflicts we have in our society are culture wars. If we are in conflict with someone or a group, we are in a culture war.

The reason the *Party Regime* came to power is they won the culture battles for now. The un-*Awaken* are not good at fighting the culture battles, let alone the culture war. It is particularly disheartening to see the absurdity of the entire apparatus of the *Party Regime,* the *Awaken,* the media, and *the Big Tech Three* win battles with weak meaningless rhetoric against good ideas and measures. "This is not who we are" – a plaintive cry often made by *Awaken* advocates is not a serious answer to dealing with a problem such as out-of-control violent crime in our urban communities. Yet the *Awaken* plead with childish banality in addressing real world issues requiring adult sensibilities.

Politics is sexy. We are drawn to politics because the media is yelling at us, "Look over here! Look at this politician! Look at how bad they are! They're in control of your life!" We are told the action is where the politics is. It's not. The "action," or "frontline," is not in politics, it's in the culture. Your heart and mind – everybody's heart and mind – is oriented to culture. That's where you live. That's what you care about. That's what you respond to.

The *Awaken* are the ideological epicenter for the cultural revolution of this era. The *Great Awakening* is the pop/political/pop/cultural identifier of this era. The *Great Awakening* is the branded moniker that empowers the *Awaken* movement with self-anointed righteousness. The culture war is a holy war to the *Awaken*. The *Awaken* are "jihadists" against the un-*Awaken*. As a holy war, it starts with Western civilization as the great Satan.

In these culture/holy wartimes, the complexities of domestic and foreign policy decisions are not based on cost benefit analysis – which can lead to broad consensus across ideological differences. Let me say that in different words, because it's important to know more agreement exists if you are willing to acknowledge good results outweigh political ideology. No matter your political persuasion or ideology, there is a good chance that when issues are decided by weighing the pros and cons – the costs and benefits – bipartisan agreement is likely.

When good faith analysis of pros and cons puts bipartisan agreement in reach, it's a foolish failure to let power politics block such agreements being made. Yet the culture war has prevented these agreements. With our political enemies we are in a double headlock of assured mutual destruction of sensible decision-making. Issues are not processed on merits. The issues aren't the issue. The "evilness" of one's opponent is the issue.

That's not to say there isn't evil present. Stupidity and willful blindness feed evil, and therefore by extension serve the will of evil, so evil is done. The only antidote to such pernicious political targeting is critical thought and free speech – the banes of *Awaken* ideology.

I used to use the term "atheist" the way you use the term "atheist." You and I know what it means. But it occurred to me one day, I don't know why, that there is no such thing as atheism or atheists. I realized something I offer you to realize, if you have not already: Everybody has a religion. Everybody believes something. Everybody has a god.

Let's consider how religion, beliefs, and gods inevitably come into play, and play culturally in the ongoing story of the human species. It's remarkable. And it's critical to understand.

The greatest discovery the human species has made is *morality*. What's remarkable about this unique discovery is our species brought this into a universe void of consciousness and therefore void of care and void of cultivation and nourishment of *morality*. The universe has no use for *morality*. The universe has no use for our species. The universe has no use for "use."

So, with no cosmic energy to support it, humans eventually and quite inconsistently decided to have *morality* be essential in living. But there's a complication. The nature of the human species is to bring *contradiction* into the mix in all matters. We can call anything *good* or *bad*. From the beginning, humans have confused *good* and *bad*. With *morality*, humans undertook the challenge of *contradiction* and *confusion*. Realizing the human limitation of perspective and transcendence, a guiding principle emerged to help a "self-bound" person correctly distinguish between *good* and *bad* in any given matter – *The Golden Rule* – treat others the way you want to be treated. The brilliance of *the Golden Rule* is it uses the inescapable self-interest to understand the essence of *morality*. It's a simple accessible, profound, and existential, reusable revelation for *good* human interaction.

As *morality* is the greatest discovery, the worst discovery humans made is *politics,* particularly *cruel politics. Cruel politics* is a moral failing. Even if rationalized to serve a *good, cruel politics* quickly erodes reality and truth to the point where *good* is not the purpose. *Cruel politics* itself becomes the purpose and exists for itself. *Cruel politics* forms into a party. The party becomes a false god to worship. If *good* was ever the cause it is forgotten and supplanted by a "golden calf" – the party.

Whether it's a political party, Zeus, the God of Abraham, nature, a philosophical tenet, or something else it's the nature of the human psyche to have a belief in something transcendent. The reason we have religion, the reason we have science, the reason we have institutions of public order like government is our awareness of ourselves in the vastness of eternity in time and space. This awareness causes the drive to seek transcendence beyond who we are to be who we are transcendently.

This is a big lift. It's a big lift in every conceivable dimension and beyond. What this means is on our archetypical, collective, individual way to transcendence we have to make it up as we go. We have to make up, invent, and imagine what the world, the ocean, the sky, and the stars are. We, therefore, must create a lot of mythology. Despite most all of our grasp on life being mythological, it's through this path with free thought and free expression that we will ever have a chance to know what is real.

All the ridiculous things we wrote before and continue to write needed to be written, as we are a work-in-progress limited by the times and culture of our generation. We can still advance beyond our times. But we cannot advance to a better future if we erase the past. We must not throw away what we wrote (recorded) including petroglyphs (look it up), however bad it was. And of course, it wasn't all bad. Much of it was wonderful.

When Isaac Newton shared what he learned about gravity, his findings were not racial specific. It works for all races. Yet the *Awaken* tell us acceptance of Newtonian physics is racial supremacy. You can believe that if you want. But where will that lead you? Will you be better for it? Newton nailed it for complex cellular objects. His work is valuable to this day. But Newtonian physics doesn't explain quantum physics. Yet it's no less valuable. We must *add* to our knowledge and understanding, not *subtract* from it. Studying the ancient Greek gods will still benefit us. In doing so we will better understand intellectual, psychological, and transcendent drives in humans.

All of what I discussed here is culture. There are good directions to go and there are bad directions to go. And it matters. Bad culture will drive us to – you guessed it – bad places. Good culture will drive us to good places.

END

THE AGE OF INSANITY

The Age of Insanity is the working title of a book Harry is thinking about writing which evolved from the notes he keeps on his illegal laptop computer. Harry reached a point where he decided "insanity" was the one word that said the most about the current condition of society. Moreover, despite being a dire acknowledgment he noticed saying the word "insanity" in his head to describe the state of society gave him some kind of mental relief. In this Harry realizes acknowledgment of reality is the reason for his sense of relief. He reasons twisting yourself into nonreality perspectives to suit ridiculous narratives is what causes mental instability, destress, and insanity. This realization and understanding drive Harry to write this book.

Harry thinks "insanity" is not a word anyone likes to say in describing a situation, particularly when self-invested. Saying it out loud to explain something always comes with frustration because people have a "knee jerk" opposition reaction when it's said. More so when it's accurate. He notices it doesn't get better when people start to realize that insanity is a correct description because now you have to deal with the reality of insanity and its impact which is mostly not manageable. Harry is aware how bleak it is when insanity is present let alone running rampant. That's why he began thinking about writing the book. At least for him it's a way to process the insanity in "the age of insanity" and at most for others who read it to help enough people to recover society from insanity.

Notations for book project – *The Age of Insanity:*

- At the core of what we think is what we feel emotionally. It's not useful to good sensibility, but it's what we as humans have to work with. The challenge in understanding things in the best available "light" is to align our feelings with what matters. And what matters is defined by values. A person needs to adopt values and understand the consequences of those values.
- To understand the workings of tyranny and totalitarianism you need to understand the monopolization of power and information dissemination. Ironically, in a totalitarian tyranny – such as the *Party Regime* – power does not reside in the government. The government is a tool – a pawn – for the *Party Regime.*
- The top of the "food chain" is *the Big Tech Three.* That's where power resides. *The Big Tech Three control the largest financial resources and monetary distribution in the world. If money can buy it, the Big Tech Three own it and control it.*
- *For the Big Tech Three "monopoly" is the name of the game. To maintain a monopoly on money the Big Tech Three must maintain a monopoly on thought. To maintain a monopoly on thought, the Big Tech Three must maintain a monopoly on information. To maintain a monopoly on information, the Big Tech Three must maintain a monopoly on media.*
- *The Big Tech Three* must maintain a monopoly on everything and everybody. The monster of monopolization is all

consuming: education, government, banking, commerce, the military, culture, and media are the institutions consumed by the monopolistic appetite of *the Big Tech Three*.

There's yet another layer to the power structures affecting all of us all the time. "Corporatocracy" is an "ocracy" we should discuss. It's a simple idea – if I am the only person anyone could get toothpicks from – that is, everyone in the world including all countries and all companies and all entities in the world can only get toothpicks from me – that means by my exclusive control of all things to do with a small sliver of wood, I own everyone and everything. That's basically what a corporatocracy is.

The free market and a corporatocracy are not the same. Corporatocracy takes the "free" out of free market. A corporation – or just a small business – can start off in the free market as they usually do. But their ambitions and growth, which can be initially advantageous to the market, can lead to supreme dominance of the market, causing the downward spiral of diminishing returns to the end users. The availability, reliability, and quality of the simple toothpick go down as the cost goes up.

- There is another insidious factor infecting corporatocracy dynamics. It manifests like an autoimmune condition that can be fatal for business, commerce, employment across all sectors, and the general welfare of the public.

Corporatocracy is shortsighted. It snatches up a quick buck at the expense of future economic stability.

If a company puts its finger in the wind of the breeze today and decides to take a severe course based on the direction of that breeze, it won't be prepared to deal with the blizzard that blows in the opposite direction the next day. Moreover, if the course decisions of a company are made to satisfy the ideological demands of a political party and if that company has a monopolistic or quasi-monopolistic position in the market, a collapse of interconnected economic infrastructure "dominos" will start to fall.

This occurred when a state legislature passed laws to improve voting regulations. The *Awaken*, backed by the *Party Regime*, created a false outrage toward the new legislation charging voter suppression. Targeting that state for punishment for the new laws enacted, prominent, dominant corporations in the corporatocracy had a "knee jerk" response and blindly made business decisions negatively affecting the economy across many sectors. The corporations are not motivated by principle. Rather they are driven to align with *Awaken* doctrine and appear to be principled and virtuous, foolishly believing their share in the market would increase or be protected.

Bad call. Not true. Job layoffs, defaults on business contracts, cancelled business, and other negative market disruptions occurred. Crime, domestic violence, and suicides spiked. The new improved voting regulations went into effect despite the tantrums from the *Awaken*.

There's a moral to this story. Political "trade winds and currents" are always unreliable where real life is concerned. Business should focus on business, not on such "trade winds."

- But there are cracks in the power of the corporatocracy and monopolization. An example is traditional religion, which is a nemesis of *the Big Tech Three*. To combat religion *the Big Tech Three* offers itself and its *Awaken* doctrine as the "true" religion. *The Big Tech Three* evangelizes for its religion through the power it has to ration goods, services, and jobs to the public it monopolizes. *The Big Tech Three* is a formidable religion with innumerable devoted worshipers.
- Character, independence, risk-taking, and vision are examples of resistance to monopolization. Ironically, monopolies are born from such character – which is why for their own good and the good of the world around them, individuals need to develop a moral and ethical base.

End of notes

THE COMPLETE GLOSSARY

From Harry's Journaling

Because language and words are changeable, this document contains a glossary section. The section explains the meaning of words and terms. It emphasizes the fate of everything rests on language. Language and its distortion are the cause and result of human destruction.

But language can also be the salvation from corruption and ultimate destruction. Language got us into this mess. Language can get us out of this mess.

Thus, is offered this glossary. Be wise in its use.

Glossary
of
The Great Awakening

Apocalypse – The catastrophic end of times. Complete and utter annihilation of all things human. Apocalypse is a Greek word meaning revelation. It's notable such a final destruction not only destroys, but also reveals it's too late for those who are blind to the cause of the destruction to be redeemed.

Armageddon – The final battle between *good* and *evil.* It can refer to the battle itself and/or the place of the battle. The stakes are as high as it gets. It's do or die for eternity. As grave as it is with the odds stacked against life, Armageddon is at least a battle that can be fought to affirm goodness and prevail for life. In these times, this nation is the place of Armageddon.

Awaken – If there was a single term to identify the annihilation of sensibility in these times, "awaken" is the term. Its seminal roots originated from a precursor term – "political correctness." This earlier term referred to avoidance of all forms of expression, particularly language and speech perceived to exclude, marginalize, or insult groups of people. On the surface, the idea of political correctness may seem like a reasonable attempt to maintain decency and respect for all people. But the level of sensitivity and "correctness" required by those who care, or want to look like they care, can be extreme and absurd. Ultimately, political correctness chokes off and debilitates any serious and thoughtful discourse on important subjects. Political correctness hijacks all meaning and relevance. It gives over to nonsense and small-mindedness. The newer term – *Awaken* – adds more to the principles of political correctness. To be *Awaken* denotes being an adherent to not only politically correct principles, it asserts virtue superiority for adherents and contempt for those not *Awaken.* Depending on your perspective, the term "awaken" is either a "badge of honor" – whose adherents are proud to wear and be identified as – or "awakenness" is a joke, and the use of the term is to ridicule and insult. In this regard, thoughtful critical thinkers, as they always do, can decide for themselves how to think about the term "awaken." It should be noted "awakenness" has no limit on who will be found guilty of failing to be "properly *Awaken*." This includes all the *Awaken* themselves. "Awakenness is not only a cannibalistic condition, it's a self-cannibalistic autoimmune condition. Everybody and everything are doomed under *Awaken* doctrine.

Comrade – A fellow member of a group with no reference to gender or any difference or distinction. Although the meaning in its purest form is positive bonding between and among people with overtones of friendship and affection, comrade can also mean more specifically a member of the Soviet Communist Party or any communistic/socialistic offshoot practiced anywhere in the world. Depending on your values and perspective, the political connotation lends wanted or unwanted intrigue to its meaning.

Crazy Making – You know what the word "crazy" means. It's a good word. *Any word with a "Z" in it, or a sound like a "Z" in it, is a good word.* It's particularly a good word when mental health professionals like psychologists and psychiatrists use it. They sound more honest and accurate when they bypass clinical terminology and just say "crazy." If the "crazy shoe" fits, then the person or thing it fits is not grounded in reality. Whatever comes from such crazy persons or things is disastrous. The "making" part of the term refers to how to make a "not crazy" person or thing crazy. The way that's done is to say crazy things over and over again – to and say it like everybody thinks it's reality. The media engage at crazy making all the time. So does the *Party Regime*. They don't stop there though. They turn the tables on their political opponents and accuse them of doing the crazy making. It's essentially projecting – which means accusing someone of doing what the accuser is doing… It's crazy making!

Cross-Sectional Interest Buffet-Feeding – I made up the term. *Cross-sectional* is the spectrum of all the causes supporting a core narrative. *Interest* is the cause *du jour*… of interest. *Buffet-feeding* is a metaphor for the "pick and choose" way news, media, and activists cobble together a "Frankenstein monster" of an idea and call it a legitimate point upon which to hold a conviction.

Ego Strength – Ego is the essence of a person. An ego is unique to every person – their unique self. In short, the ego is a person's conscious sense of self. The "strength" part of the term refers to how well-developed in maturity the ego is to give a person a healthy amount of certainty about themself and the world. In this regard good ego strength means not being confused by things that are not confusing. In a world of ideological, philosophical, and political controversy and conflict, a person must have a base ego strength for stable functioning and general well- being. Good thought processing requires good ego strength.

Freedom Lecture(s) – Well, the *Freedom Lectures* are definitely lectures – more like unhinged rants – but have nothing to do with freedom – more like anti-freedom. The purpose of the *Freedom Lectures* is to keep PODs enslaved. The *Freedom Lectures* are broadcast every evening on all communication devices. Listening is mandatory for all PODs. This tells you all you need to know about the fraud times a million in the *Party Regime*. In the *Party Regime*, words mean the opposite of what they're supposed to mean. It works! "Freedom" in the *Party Regime* is slavery.

Great Awakening – The name of the era proclaimed by the *Party Regime* to brand the *Party Regime's* purpose and contribution to humanity. It's an exaltation of a noble inspiration and cause that in reality is a cruel fraud. Its fraudulence works the same as the previous term *Freedom Lecture*. The words mean the opposite of what they're supposed to mean. In this term *Great* is actually horrific and *Awakening* is actually willful blind ignorance. The term is another example of the cruel corruption of and by the *Party Regime*. (See Awaken in Glossary.)

Hope and Change Reich – "Hope and Change" was the campaign slogan of candidate for president and then President Bennet Oberton. He is a charismatic popular political leader. "Hope and Change" is the forerunner brand to the *Great Awakening* brand. "Reich" is German for realm. The *Regime* added the word "Reich" to canonize the founding principles of the new *Regime*, that like the German Nazi Party, was established to reign for a thousand years. Although not intending to be aligned with Nazism, the ironic reality is the *Party Regime* exacts a brutal totalitarian/fascism reminiscent of Nazism that is "Reich-like. Remarkable.

Killing Fields – The killing fields specifically refer to the oppression, brainwashing, torture, starvation, and genocide inflicted by the totalitarian regime under the Communist Party Kampuchea also known as the Khmer Rouge in Cambodia from 1975 to 1979. The term "killing fields" can be used generically to refer to any atrocity on a large scale. The breadth and depth of depravity have never had any limits to it in human history so far. It's mind numbing. *No matter when or where a "killing fields" happens, we all pay dearly for it forever.*

Ministry of Compliance – Ministries are established in governments to show the power, force, and commitment to enforced compliance to mandated rules. That's what ministries are to public perception. In their operation they are vast bureaucracies. Bureaucracies are the cruelest form of enforcement, as they dehumanize governance – the opposite of what good governance does, which is to respect the humanity of all persons. A ministry in the hands of the *Party Regime* is hell on earth. Add to that the ministry's target – in this case *compliance* – you get hell on hell. In the case of compliance, the *Party Regime* exacts its standards by way of totalitarian authority according to *Awaken* doctrine. What could possibly go wrong?

Ministry of Correctness – Just like the previous term *Ministry of Compliance*, the description and perspective on government ministries are the same for this term. The target of this ministry is *correctness.* In the case of correctness, who makes that decision? In the *Party Regime*, the question itself is a blasphemous crime. The *politically correct* movement preceded the *Party Regime* by demonizing normal speech. *Political correctness* impugned innocent speech, wrongly asserting hostile motives to innocent speech. This movement empowered the establishment and founding of the *Party Regime.*

Ministry of Diversity – Just like the previous term *Ministry of Compliance*, the description and perspective on government ministries are the same for this term. The target of this ministry is *diversity*. This ministry enforces quotas on race, gender, gender identification, sexual orientation, age, national origin, spoken language, disability, height, weight, hairstyle, tattoos, body piercings, mental stability, feelings, and stuff that's impossible to imagine. Under the *Party Regime* and the *Awaken* doctrine, the irony is there is no diversity for what matters – *diversity of thought.* Go figure.

Ministry of Movement – Just like the previous term *Ministry of Compliance*, the description and perspective on government ministries are the same for this term. The target of this ministry is *movement.* It used to be the Department of Transportation. But the *Party Regime* can't leave bad enough alone. With the name change also came increased regulations and oversite way beyond transportation matters. It got to a point any ministry could do anything any other ministry could do. It appears there may soon be established a *Ministry of Everything.*

Ministry of Resources – Just like the previous term *Ministry of Compliance,* the description and perspective on government ministries are the same for this term. The target of this ministry is *Resources.* That can mean anything the ministry wants it to mean.

Party Regime – "Regime" means the power and administration of governance – the sovereign government. Regime particularly means authoritarian. The forces of party politics and empowerment vie to establish authority and to establish a regime to exercise its authority. In these times and in this historical context, *Party Regime* is not being used as a generic term. It specifically means what used to be this nation. Until or unless we can be a free nation "again," *Party Regime* is the appropriate term.

POD or **PODs** – Stands for *Person of Destiny.* Its common use is to say it as a one-syllable word. "POD" is used to replace the word "citizen." The *Party Regime* considers citizen a higher station in society than "regular" people should be thought of. The term "POD" – or "PODs" for colloquial plural reference to the people – is intended to diminish a person and the people in general. The sound of the term "POD" is disrespectful and dehumanizing. Dehumanization of people is a continuous function of the *Party Regime*. The credo ***You are your group!*** is part of the propagandic indoctrination of the *Party Regime*. Along these lines, "pod people" is the colloquial term for a species of plantlike aliens in the 1955 novel and 1956 movie both titled *Invasion of the Body Snatchers*. The novel and movie reference is a cultural identifier reinforcing "pod person" as being undesirable. The novel and movie are also a look at dystopia via foreign invasion from either other earth nations or outer space.

POD Training Camps – This term refers to elementary and secondary education. It is commonly used in place of the word "school" – although "school" is still, for now, an acceptable word. The term reinforces the indoctrination philosophy of the *Party Regime* for preparing children from their earliest awareness for their mandated role in society as PODs.

Proclamation PR-1 – Proclamations made by the *Party Regime* are designated "PR" for *Party Regime*. It has a double meaning, as "PR" also stands for public relations. Proclamations from the *Party Regime* also have an important propaganda component, which is public relations serving the *Party Regime*. Proclamations are numbered in numerical order. The first – *Proclamation PR-1* – established the era of the *Great Awakening*. It defines the *Great Awakening* and the principles upon which the *Party Regime* is based and to which the *Party Regime* is committed. (See *Great Awakening* in Glossary.)

Regent – The term used to describe and address the elite privileged people in society. They are the "betters" in the *Party Regime*. In a classless society, as the *Party Regime* espouses to be, the designation of *regent(s)* is another fraud perpetrated by the *Party Regime*.

Reimagined Election Act – This is a legislative act the *Party Regime* pushed through, signed by President Biddle, federalizing all elections requiring states to adhere to ongoing adjustments exacted by the federal government. The act restructures election law, allowing fluid unrestricted adjustments to voting regulations at any time during an election cycle and voter count. This assures election results favored by the *Party Regime* and contradictory to the actual legitimate votes.

Reimagine Rallies – These are Rallies held by the *Party Regime*. They are mass public indoctrinations for enacted new state policies and doctrines. The rallies are power spectacles designed to whip PODs into a hysterical frenzy. If that weren't dark enough these rallies also occasion violence initiated by thugs planted by the *Party Regime* into the crowd. The media misreports these events. Their broadcasts are propaganda for the *Party Regime*. This creates a chaotic confusion as to who's responsible – individuals or groups – for the violent disruptions and disorder. Innocent people are targeted, harassed, and arrested. They are often not seen or heard from again.

The Big Tech Three – The dominance of *the Big Tech Three* over information control is absolute. *The Big Tech Three* has complete power over culture, society, economics, commerce, transportation, communication, media, education, science, medicine, psychology, religion, politics, philosophy, thought, and everything. *The Big Tech Three* are comprised of the smallest number – primarily three entities of conglomerates in charge of all technology – of oligarchs in control of the largest number of people in world history.

The Trinity – I made up this term as it relates to the political climate of these times. I did not make up the traditional use of the term – the Trinity – known for the Christian doctrine of God – the Father, Jesus Christ – the Son, and the Holy Spirit. According to Christian doctrine all are one and eternal. The term – trinity – is often used loosely across any variety of subject disciplines, such as cooking ingredients, sports, music, and more. The *Awaken,* the *Party Regime,* and *the Big Tech Three* are *the Trinity* of the *Great Awakening. The Trinity* of the *Great Awakening* is an encapsulation of its origins, doctrines, and functional structure.

The YALI Transition – This refers to the *Party Regime's* program to confiscate education – more specifically, the system of all post-secondary education. The *Party Regime* took control of all public and private colleges and universities. This included seminaries and trade schools. (See "YALI" in Glossary.)

Think Right Program – This is a public service campaign run by the *Party Regime*. It is an ongoing propaganda campaign to brainwash PODs on how and what to think according to the *Party Regime*. Its forerunner is *political correctness*.

Thought & Locator Chip – A computer chip implanted in the left arm on the inside between the wrist and elbow. The *Party Regime* initiated a program mandating PODs be implanted with the chip. It can be anticipated that *regents* would eventually be subject to mandated chip implantation. All totalitarian regimes cannibalize and turn on their own. The chip can read and record the thoughts of its host. Although not yet perfected, the chip will also be able to lodge thoughts into the host. The chip also tracks and locates the host 24/7. The *Department of Central Command* under the *Ministry of Movement* monitors the chips.

Vanished – Silencing voices is the first step and sometimes the only step to vanishing. For the *Awaken*, the *Party Regime*, *the Big Tech Three – the Trinity* – and much of the media, the existence of different or opposing ideas are not to be tolerated. Vanishing different and opposing ideas and the people and sources holding and expressing such ideas is the action against those people and sources to make them *vanished*. Once *vanished* you have no say, standing, recognition, or agency in your community, culture, and society at large. If you are *vanished*, you are erased from existence.

Vanish Culture – This term relates to the previous term as "vanished" or vanishment is the reason and process *the*

Trinity (see Glossary) uses to erase people's voices against *the Trinity* and the *Great Awakening*. The "culture" part of the term reflects the expansion of influence and acceptance by a culture, within society, of vanishment as a good and reasonable consequence for dissenting voices and the dissenters who own those voices. The influence of the *vanish culture* is an indicator of the state of the Republic, liberty, society, and the general culture.

YALI – Stands for *Young Adults' Learning Institution*. It's a change in name, philosophy, curriculum, and control of all public and private colleges and universities. Private institutions are now forbidden. All institutions are public – controlled by the *Party Regime*. (See *"The YALI Transition"* in Glossary.)

* * *

To repeat: Be wise.

* * *

QUOTES TO REMEMBER

THE PREFACE TO THIS STORY REFERENCES PERSONS throughout history who contributed ideas and philosophies to the catalog of human thought and values. Likewise, within this story are references to other such persons identified in classical education and history who impacted a part of the human narrative. A sample of quotes is presented here from each person referenced. Also presented are other quotes from the Preface and story. Page numbers denote the quote is in the Preface or story on the cited page. Be informed. Be enlightened. Be aware. Be Inspired. Enjoy… where enjoyment can be had.

Abraham

- *Here I am.*

Moses

- *I am not eloquent.*
- *BOLD Immersion was about exposing students to a talented and diverse community, learning about the technology industry from a non-technical point of view, and growing my skills.*

Homer

- *Hateful to me as the gates of Hades is that man who hides one thing in his heart and speaks another.*
- *By their own follies they perished, the fools.*

Confucius

- *Never do to others what you would not like them to do to you.*
- *They must often change, who would be constant in happiness or wisdom.*
- *Wisdom, compassion, and courage are the three universally recognized moral qualities of men.*

Buddha

- *We are what we think. All that we are arises with our thoughts. With our thoughts, we make the world.*
- *Three things cannot be long hidden: the sun, the moon, and the truth.*
- *You only lose what you cling to.*

Socrates

- *An unexamined life is not worth living.*
- *To find yourself, think for yourself.*
- *There is only one good, knowledge, and one evil, ignorance.*

Plato

- *Love is a serious mental disease.*
- *Only the dead have seen the end of war.*
- *Be kind, for everyone you meet is fighting a hard battle.*

Aristotle

- *Happiness depends upon ourselves.*
- *Man is by nature a political animal.*
- *Anybody can become angry – that is easy, but to be angry*

with the right person and to the right degree and at the right time and for the right purpose, and in the right way – that is not within everybody's power and is not easy.

- *You will never do anything in this world without courage. It is the greatest quality of the mind next to honor.*

Jesus Christ (Yeshua ben Yosef)

- *Let the day's own trouble be sufficient for the day.*

Hypatia

- *Reserve your right to think, for even to think wrongly is better than not to think at all.*

Muhammed

- *Kindness is a mark of faith, and whoever has not kindness has not faith.*
- *None of you truly believes until he wishes for his brother what he wishes for himself.*
- *Four things support the world: the learning of the wise, the justice of the great, the prayers of the good, and the valor of the brave.*

Thomas Aquinas

- *A man has free choice to the extent that he is rational.*
- *The highest manifestation of life consists in this: that a being governs its own actions. A thing which is always subject to the direction of another is somewhat of a dead thing.*

- *Perfection of moral virtue does not wholly take away the passions, but regulates them.*

Leonardo da Vinci

- *The noblest pleasure is the joy of understanding.*
- *Nothing strengthens authority so much as silence.*
- *Nothing can be loved or hated unless it is first understood.*

William Shakespeare

- *Hell is empty and all the devils are here.*

Galileo Galilei

- *All truths are easy to understand once they are discovered; the point is to discover them.*
- *In questions of science, the authority of a thousand is not worth the humble reasoning of a single individual.*

John Locke

- *What worries you, masters you.*
- *No man's knowledge here can go beyond his experience.*
- *I have always thought the actions of men the best interpreters of their thoughts.*

Jonathan Swift

- *When a true genius appears in this world, you may know him by this sign, that the dunces are all in confederacy against him.*

Johann Sabastian Bach

- *If I decide to be an idiot, then I'll be an idiot on my own accord.*

Wolfgang Amadeus Mozart

- *To talk well and eloquently is a very great art, but that an equally great one is to know the right moment to stop.*

William Blake

- *If the* ***doors of perception*** *were cleansed every thing would appear to man as it is, Infinite. For man has closed himself up, till he sees all things thro' narrow chinks of his cavern.* (Pages 279 & 280)

Ludwig van Beethoven

- *This is the mark of a really admirable man: steadfastness in the face of trouble.*

Abraham Lincoln

- *You can fool all the people some of the time, and some of the people all the time, but you cannot fool all the people all the time.*
- *If destruction be our lot, we must ourselves be its author and finisher. As a nation of freemen, we must live through all time, or die by suicide.*
- *The philosophy of the school room in one generation will be the philosophy of government in the next.*
- *… the better angels of our nature.* (Page 168)

Harriet Beecher Stowe

- *The past, the present, and the future are really one: they are today.*
- *The obstinacy of cleverness and reason is nothing to the obstinacy of folly and inanity.*

Sigmund Freud

- *Civilization began the first time an angry person cast a word instead of a rock.*

Madame Marie Curie

- *Nothing in life is to be feared, it is only to be understood. Now is the time to understand more, so that we may fear less.*

Joseph Stalin

- *It is enough that the people know there was an election. The people who cast the votes decide nothing. The people who count the votes decide everything.* (Page 96)
- *We don't let them have ideas. Why would we let them have guns?*

Albert Einstein

- *Two things are infinite: the universe and human stupidity; and I'm not sure about the universe.*
- *If you can't explain it simply, you don't understand it well enough.*

Aldous Huxley

- *We live together, we act on, and react to, one another; but always and in all circumstances we are by ourselves. The martyrs go hand in hand into the arena; they are crucified alone.... From family to nation, every human group is a society of island universes.* (Page 199)

George Orwell

- *Big Brother is watching you.* (Page 329)
- *All animals are equal, but some animals are more equal than others.*
- *War is peace. Freedom is slavery. Ignorance is strength.* (Page 329)
- *But if thought corrupts language, language can also corrupt thought.*
- *Who controls the past controls the future. Who controls the present controls the past.*
- *During times of universal deceit, telling the truth becomes a revolutionary act.*
- *Freedom is the freedom to say that two plus two make four. If that is granted, all else follows.*
- *There are some ideas so wrong that only a very intelligent person could believe in them.*
- *Political chaos is connected with the decay of language.*
- *Each generation imagines itself to be more intelligent than the one that went before it, and wiser than the one that comes after it.*

- *Good writing is like a windowpane.*

Ayn Rand

- *To say 'I love you' one must first be able to say the 'I.'*
- *The man who lets a leader prescribe his course is a wreck being towed to the scrap heap.*
- *Racism is a doctrine of, by and for brutes.*
- *Judge, and prepare to be judged.* (Page 190)

Viktor Frankl

- *It is well known that humor, more than anything else in the human make-up, can afford an aloofness and an ability to rise above any situation, even if only for a few seconds.*

Rosa Parks

- *All I was doing was trying to get home from work.*

Nelson Mandela

- *Real leaders must be ready to sacrifice all for the freedom of their people.*
- *A fundamental concern for others in our individual and community lives would go a long way in making the world the better place we so passionately dreamt of.*
- *Money won't create success, the freedom to make it will.*
- *I like friends who have independent minds because they tend to make you see problems from all angles.*

- *For to be free is not merely to cast off one's chains, but to live in a way that respects and enhances the freedom of others.* (Page 177)
- *Resentment is like drinking poison and then hoping it will kill your enemies.*

Ray Bradbury

- *You don't have to burn books to destroy a culture. Just get people to stop reading them.*
- *We are an impossibility in an impossible universe.*
- *I hate all politics. I don't like either political party. One should not belong to them - one should be an individual, standing in the middle. Anyone that belongs to a party stops thinking.*

Anne Frank

- *Whoever is happy will make others happy too.*

Maya Angelou

- *Prejudice is a burden that confuses the past, threatens the future and renders the present inaccessible.*
- *My mission in life is not merely to survive, but to thrive; and to do so with some passion, some compassion, some humor, and some style.*

Martin Luther King, Jr.

- *I look to a day when people will not be judged by the color of their skin, but by the content of their character.* (Page 177)

- *The ultimate measure of a man is not where he stands in moments of comfort and convenience, but where he stands at times of challenge and controversy.*
- *Nothing in all the world is more dangerous than sincere ignorance and conscientious stupidity.*
- *History will have to record that the greatest tragedy of this period of social transition was not the strident clamor of the bad people, but the appalling silence of the good people.*
- *Rarely do we find men who willingly engage in hard, solid thinking. There is an almost universal quest for easy answers and half-baked solutions. Nothing pains some people more than having to think.*
- *The limitation of riots, moral questions aside, is that they cannot win and their participants know it. Hence, rioting is not revolutionary but reactionary because it invites defeat. It involves an emotional catharsis, but it must be followed by a sense of futility.*

William Gibson

- *When the past is always with you, it may as well be present; and if it is present, it will be future as well.*
- *Cyberspace. A consensual hallucination experienced daily by billions of legitimate operators, in every nation.*
- *Cliches became cliches for a reason; that they usually hold at least a modicum of truth, and the following cliche is truer than most: You can't know where you're going if you don't know where you've been.*

Howard Asher

- *There's a dangerous tendency for humans to be too ridiculous and too stupid for their own good.* (Page vii)

The character **Harry Archer**

- *The more something is valued the more you should reach for it. Better to reach for what you want and have your heart broken for not getting it, than to not reach at all.* (Page 9)
- *It only takes one generation through corrupt education to wipe out the worthy achievements of humankind and throw our species into an intractable dark age.* (Page 18)
- *Homelessness is a humanitarian disaster reflecting a political and moral failure.* (Page 29)
- *Eliminating the past stagnates the present and dooms the future.* (Page 98)
- *We're screwed… forever.* (Pages 110 & 113)
- *Being up to the task isn't the issue. Being selected to do the task is what matters. So do it.* (Page 118)
- *Cognitive dissonance is inconvenient to fools.* (Page 140)
- *Okay, that's enough for now.* (Pages 141 & 202)
- *As easy as it can be to identify many pivotal facts, treating them with the understanding they deserve seems damn near impossible as a nation of people.* (Page 169)
- *Mobs murder reason.* (Page 174)
- *Whatever you are told, whatever you think, there may be other things to hear and think. Have an open mind. Be open to the world.* (Page 192)

- *You cannot take for granted that anything cannot change for the better or for the worse.* (Page 193)
- *If we don't use our initiative, and if we don't use it well, it won't ever matter we ever existed. To the human species, the stakes are as high as it gets, to the universe it matters not.* (Page 194)
- *Think it well and say it well and they will come.* (Page 198)
- *The meaning of life is what you make the meaning of life to be for yourself.* (Page 199)
- *Hypocrisy is the poison upon which corrupt societies feed. Freedom of speech allows lies. And not having freedom of speech allows lies to live and thrive.* (Page 241)
- *What must be present is a common understanding and acceptance of the possibility through personal initiative one can improve their self and their station in life no matter the circumstances they were born into or their immutable traits. This is key to a successful society.* (Page 286)
- *Free Thought and Free Speech = Less Cruelty and Less Atrocity* (Page 288)
- *Any word with a "Z" in it, or a sound like a "Z" in it, is a good word.* (Page 304)
- *No matter when or where a "killing fields" happens, we all pay dearly for it forever.* (Page 307)

The character **Penelope Archer**

- *The most insidious kind of destruction is assuming good things exist without caring for them.* (Page 52)

Harry's unnamed **High School History teacher**

- *... If you don't know history you won't get the jokes.* (Page 98)

The charter **David Jacob's** desk plaque

- *The pen can be sharper than the sword. But a dull pen is no match for a dull sword.* (Page 116)

The character **Bob Burke**

- *... we each spring back to being an "island" – we're on our own.* (Pages 151 & 199)

The character **Derrick Lime**

- *Knowing a person is different than knowing about a person.* (Page 160)

John F. Kennedy

- *Too often we enjoy the comfort of opinion without the discomfort of thought.* (Page 168)

John Adams

- *Facts are stubborn things; and whatever may be our wishes, our inclinations, or the dictates of our passion, they cannot alter the state of facts and evidence.* (Page 169)

Many Sources

- *This too shall pass.* (Pages 193)

DID YOU NOTICE?

Orwellian Acknowledgements and Tropes

- For no other reason than to beat the homage drum, *2024* is structured the same as Orwell's novel *1984*. There are three parts identified as ONE, TWO, and THREE. The chapters in each part are identified by Roman numerals in the following manner: ONE, II, III, IV, V, VII, VIII; TWO, II, III, IV, V, VI, VII, VIII, IX, X; THREE, II, III, IV, V, VI, VII. There are no worded titles for the parts or chapters. Also, like *1984*, this story has an APPENDIX. In Orwell's novel the appendix is titled *THE PRINCIPLES OF NEWSPEAK*. In this story the appendix is titled *THE PRINCIPLES OF THOUGHT*.
- The first sentence of each of the three parts in this story – *2024* – are the first words (in present tense) of each of the three parts respectively from Orwell's *1984*. They are as follows:

  IT'S A BRIGHT COLD DAY IN APRIL.
  IT'S THE MIDDLE OF THE MORNING.
  HE DOES NOT KNOW WHERE HE IS.

- In *1984* there is a story element about an ominous figure called *Big Brother*.

  In *2024* there is a character element referred to as *The Big Guy*.

- In *1984* there is the ominous warning: *BIG BROTHER IS WATCHING YOU.*

  In *2024* there is the ominous warning: *There is nothing you can do without us knowing about it!*
- In *1984* there is the three-slogan credo repeated throughout the story:

  WAR IS PEACE
  FREEDOM IS SLAVERY
  IGNORANCE IS STRENGTH

  In *2024* there is the three-slogan credo repeated throughout the story:

  DEATH IS LIFE
  OPPRESSION IS LIBERTY
  WEAKNESS IS STRENGTH

- In *2024* there is a character, Eric Blair. George Orwell is Eric Blair's pen name.
- In *1984* there is a story element about 2+2=5.

  In *2024* there is a story element about 2+2=5.

  In real world culture wars, there is controversy about 2+2=5.
- In *1984* there is a character – O'Brien – who says:

  "If you want a picture of the future, imagine a boot stamping on a human face… forever."

  In *2024* the characters Harry Archer and Steve Reed say and repeat:

"We're screwed… forever."

Moreover, in *2024* the word "forever" pops up several times:

- The edict to ware facemasks forever.
- The forever *Party Regime.*
- Racism is forever, and society is guilty and must pay forever.
- It is the goal of the *Party Regime* to use the *Awaken* doctrine to bury forever the country's history and culture.
- … forever branding the publishing firm as a source and demonstration of *freedom's reward to humanity.*
- … we can go around forever trying to make sense of the senseless.
- He's been in Congress forever.
- Forever wars.
- … immutable traits such as gender and race, which are also out of your control, fixed your station forever…
- … we all pay dearly for it forever.

The word and idea of *forever* has a profound impact on our psyche – individually and collectively. Ironically, it both terrifies and comforts us depending on who you are and what the *forever* is about. The counterbalancing idea that nothing is forever – *this too shall pass* – or the way Harry sees life as a "for now" thing, is a vital component to a healthy psyche that also terrifies and comforts us. Free thinking and will to act – agency – "smooths" our uneasy relationship with the intractable/moveable dynamics of life in the ecosystem, in the cosmos at large, and in our small petty banalities.

- In *1984* the central character is Winston Smith.

  In *2024* there is a character named Winston Smith.

- There is a line past the midpoint of this story – *2024* – that alludes to the last line in Orwell's *1984*.

  In *1984* it ends:

  He loved Big Brother.

  In *2024* the spoken line is:

  "I love *The Big Guy*."

- In *1984* it begins:

  It was a bright cold day in April…

  As previously noted, it ends:

  He loved Big Brother.

  In *2024* as previously noted it begins:

  It's a bright cold day in April.

  It ends:

  It's a bright new day…

Other non-Orwellian Acknowledgments and References

- The title of Harry Archer's book is *I Built It*, subtitled *The Personal Empowerment of Following Your Dream*. This is a reference to President Barak Obama's statement "… if you've got a business… you didn't build that. Somebody else made that happen." Obama essentially diminished, or discounted altogether, all entrepreneurs' industry, hard work, vision, personal risk, and value brought to the community at large. The literary element of Harry's book is a statement that stands in stark opposition to Obama's perspective on personal investment in business as related in his statement.

- Harry was born on January 15 – Martin Luther King Jr's Birthday.
- The term *crazy making* in the story is a reference to the term used currently in pop/political, propagandistic, rhetorical weaponry: *gaslighting*. The term *gaslighting* comes from the title and plot point of the 1944 film *Gaslight* with Ingrid Bergman and Charles Boyer. It's the story of a husband's cruelty toward his wife by making her think she's crazy by confusing her with the gaslight (the film is set in the late 19th century – most lighting is by gaslight) to their apartment being on or off. Okay, let's not get caught up on improbable details. The point is the colloquial term *gaslighting* means messing with someone's grasp on reality.

  As the terms are conceived, there certainly is *gaslighting* and *crazy making* going on in pop/political society and culture. The question is who is doing it to whom? Moreover, the term *gaslighting* is not only weaponized in politics; it's purposely misapplied in *fake news* rhetorical dynamics. *Gaslighting* also gets into Orwellian *doublespeak* territory. *2024* uses a literary element referring to a movie called *Crazy Making* to allude to the pop/culture/pop/political references of *gaslighting*. There's lots of referencing and cross referencing going on.

- There are many other acknowledgments and references throughout *2024*. While reading or rereading the story, keep your "radar detector" on.

NOTES

Parts ONE, TWO, & THREE

The opening words of Part ONE, Part TWO, and Part THREE in this story – *2024* – are the same opening words (in present tense) of Part ONE, Part TWO, and Part THREE (respectively) from *1984* written by George Orwell.

Part ONE, Chapter VI

Theme from *Mission: Impossible* written and composed by Lalo Schifrin. Cited in this story – *2024* – as the character Harry Archer "de des" it in his head.

Part TWO, Chapter V

Music and lyrics of *Harvest Moon* written by Neil Young. Recorded by Neil Young. Cited in this story – *2024* – as a played-recorded cover by The Brothers Comatose & AJ Lee. *If you haven't heard this version, you should.

Part THREE, Chapter II

Music and lyrics of *You Can't Always Get What You Want* written by Mick Jagger and Keith Richards. Recorded by the Rolling Stones. Cited in this story – *2024* – as a played recorded cover by an anonymous singer.

Part THREE, Chapter II & Chapter VII

Music and lyrics of *Here Comes the Sun* written by George Harrison. Recorded by the Beatles. Cited in this story – *2024* – as the recorded version by the Beatles.

Part THREE, Chapter VII

Abraham Lincoln's address before the Wisconsin State Agricultural Society. Milwaukee, Wisconsin, September 30, 1859. Partially recited in this story – *2024*.

* * *

THE AUTHOR

Howard Asher, Psy.D., is a licensed psychotherapist in California, with a clinical practice in the Los Angeles area. He is the author of *A Lose Grip* – a historical, cultural, political, and psychological analysis on our extraordinary times. It provides a perspective for the understanding required to achieve and maintain well-being in a challenging world.

An advocate for free speech, Dr. Asher sounds an alarm warning our strength as individuals and as a republic rest in the preservation of First Amendment rights foundational to America. He believes these rights are key to not only our well-being but our very existence.

With his "uncommon sense" perspective on people and the world, Dr. Asher expounds on the compelling topics of our times. He is also a consultant to many business sectors, including the arts, education, health care, and media. Dr. Asher has appeared on television, radio, podcasts, and internet live streams. To contact Dr. Asher, visit his website: dr-howard-asher.com.

You Can Do Something.

You can also check out the *2024* Free Thinking Society and join as a *Thought Adventurer.*

Website: dr-howard-asher.com.

www.ingramcontent.com/pod-product-compliance
Lightning Source LLC
Chambersburg PA
CBHW020555310726
48979CB00008B/1224/J

9781733002042